How far would you go
to keep a promise?

HOUSE
ON FIRE

D. Liebhart

For my mother and brother, who (in the real story) did all the heavy lifting. And for my father, how I wish I could have saved you.

*M*y mother asked me to kill my father on Christmas. I remember it was Christmas, because it isn't the kind of thing you forget. And if I have to pick a beginning for this tragedy that's as good a place as any. Aristotle was wrong, you know. Tragedies don't have structure. They don't line up neatly into three acts. Tragedy prefers the blindside. You're sitting at the intersection waiting for the light, when *Bam!* It comes out of nowhere.

I'd just checked on my teenage son, Jax. He'd sequestered himself in the guest room far from his cousins which, given the finger-breaking incident, was probably the safest choice. Then, I stopped to look in on my sister's kids in the living room. She'd asked me to keep an eye on the younger ones while she hunted the Valley for cranberry sauce.

Mom had forgotten this holiday staple and was frantically scolding herself in the kitchen because cranberry sauce, *whole* cranberry sauce, was my father's favorite part of Christmas dinner. For fifty years she'd been getting up at the crack of dawn to make turkey, stuffing, brussels sprouts and this weird marshmallow ambrosia, yet my father's favorite dish came out of a can.

I'd only meant to glance at Colleen's kids then go help Mom, but something about the scene transfixed me. The floor was littered with bows and wrapping paper, like Santa's workshop had exploded and these five kids were the only survivors. It was like looking back through a window in time.

Colleen, our older brother Adam, and I had celebrated every Christmas of our youth in that living room. Our parents always made it magical. You'd get something you'd forgotten you wanted or didn't even know you wanted. You went to sleep on Christmas Eve with this feeling, this luscious anticipation of magic, certain that something totally unexpected was not only possible, but was about to happen. When was the last time I felt like that? Like life could surprise you and it would be good.

A screech shattered the moment.

"Raaaannce!!" Luca howled.

Lance, Colleen's eight-year-old, had grabbed his little brother's Thomas the Train and was holding it high above his head, laughing while Luca stood on his tippy-toes desperately reaching for the toy, his bright orange-red hair bursting in all directions as if it were screaming too.

"Lance!" I snapped.

Lance ignored me and kept taunting his brother. Mostly my sister's kids are saints. She has nine, though only five are still young enough to be at home. They say *please* and *thank you* without being reminded, do dishes without being asked. But not Lance. He's a dick which, when I'm not actually dealing with him, is relatively satisfying. A chink, a lot too late, in Colleen's otherwise halcyon existence.

"Lance!" I repeated. He turned and stared, his green eyes burning. He wasn't scared of me. We both knew it. I could trek back downstairs to get his dad, but Liam was no match for this little nightmare either.

The only real leverage anyone had was how much trouble he'd be in with Colleen if she found out. He was sizing up how likely it was that I'd call on my sister to do the dirty work. He scowled, then handed the train back to his brother.

"And tidy up before your mom gets back," I added before heading out of the room.

The kitchen was sweltering, over-heated from the efforts of the ancient oven to produce yet another family feast. In classic Los Angeles fashion, it was eighty degrees outside, and the kitchen was at least ten degrees hotter than that. I wished I was the one off hunting cranberries. Colleen had volunteered the second Mom mentioned the cranberry sauce, before I even registered it as an opportunity to escape. The house felt more cramped and uneasy every year, maybe because all the kids were getting bigger, or maybe because of Dad and his dementia.

Mom grabbed the oven door and gave it a tug. Her short, grey hair fluttered in the gust of heat that escaped. She slid the turkey out and, with her fingertips, carefully flicked at the edge of the aluminum foil tent covering the bird. Steam rose up from the pan as she got it loose.

"I can't take this anymore," she said without looking at me. It was as though she was scolding the bird for its lack of appreciation. She retrieved a ladle from the counter and began basting the turkey with its juices. I glanced around. Every surface was cluttered with bowls and utensils. She'd probably been up since five, preparing this enormous Christmas meal for a bunch of people, including me, who really didn't recognize how much work it was.

"Maybe we should do a *potluck* next year," I said teasingly, knowing she'd never go for it. Her disdain for potlucks was legendary. Working yourself to death in the kitchen—particularly on holidays—fulfilled some recondite, motherly obligation handed down from previous generations.

"Bernadette Louise Rogers," she snapped, letting the oven door slam shut. "You have *Christmas* dinner and a *Christmas* tree on *Christmas*."

Her sharp tone surprised me. I only got my full name when in trouble, which was infinitely better than Bernie, the nickname I'd been trying to kill for more than forty years.

"I was just kidding," I said. My nonchalant attitude toward traditional holidays, even before Shayne, always irked her—I've never had a tree in my adult life—but her emotion seemed disproportionate to my attempt at humor. "Why do you think I come here every year? I love that everything is exactly the same as it was when I was a kid."

"I'm sorry," she said but she didn't sound any less upset. "It's just..." She stopped, then stood there, her cheeks flushed and shiny with sweat. She seemed to be focusing on something internal, gathering up all her emotions and stuffing them away in some sacred hiding spot like she had my whole life. She picked up a stack of plates from the counter and handed them to me. "Go set the table."

Confused, I went through the other door of the kitchen to the dining area. She was probably just tired, that heat could give anyone a crispy edge. I laid out the plates, the same everyday dishes we'd had as kids. When I came across the chipped one, I deliberately set it in my sister's spot, then felt guilty and went back and switched it to mine. Mom was working on the brussels sprouts when I returned, slicing an X into the bottom of each one then tossing it into the pot of boiling water on the stove.

"You have to do something," she said, still not looking at me.

"Do you want me to make the stuffing?"

She turned. Her face tightened, and the section of skin between her eyebrows gathered together in furrows of disappointment.

"That's not what I mean," she said.

I was failing her, not deciphering subtle expressions the way I was supposed to, the way I'd been able to when I was little and well-versed in this language of looks, where the slight shift of an eyebrow meant she'd seen through a fib and was about to deliver

4

a spanking. I replayed the holiday in my mind trying to find the Rosetta stone that would help me translate the conversation we were having into usable information. I couldn't.

"Mom, I give up. I don't know what we're talking about."

"If he knew this was going to happen to him, he would have gone out in the backyard and blown his brains out."

Aha! We were talking about Dad. I nodded. Whenever the subject of Alzheimer's or terminal cancer came up he'd say those exact words: "Don't let me get like that. I'd rather go out in the backyard and blow my brains out." It was stupid really. Something people say but don't think will ever happen. He didn't own a gun. I'm not even sure how well he could use one. He'd been a radio operator in the Navy in a time of peace. I'd never seen him touch a firearm.

"What can I do?" I asked. We'd tried having someone stay with him at the house, so Mom could get out once or twice a week. A home health agency sent a sweet, middle-aged Hispanic woman named Magda. Mom was only a few blocks away driving with Colleen's daughter Laura to the mall when a terrified Magda called. Dad had accused her of stealing and locked her outside. The next time they sent a tall, muscular guy named Walter. Dad punched him. The agency told us not to call again.

"Do you want to try an adult daycare place?" I said, when she didn't respond.

"They won't take him because he's aggressive." The word caught in her throat. My dad would never have been described as aggressive by anyone before the dementia.

"A nursing home?" I said, even though I knew better.

"No, no, no," she said, getting a little louder with each word.

"Then, what? What am I supposed to do?"

"You could help him go peacefully," she said, her voice a hopeful whisper. "You know how to do that."

I stood there waiting for her to say more, to explain, because she couldn't possibly be saying what I thought she was. But there was no more.

"Mom? What do you mean help him go peacefully? It sounds like you're asking me to *kill* Dad."

She stared, her expression hovering somewhere between blank and quizzical, like I'd come out of nowhere with this idea and she was trying to figure out what *I* meant instead of me trying to figure out what *she* meant. But then she gave an almost imperceptible nod, as if by not saying the words she was doing something less than committing, was somehow retaining plausible deniability.

"I thought things were okay," I said, even though things hadn't been okay in years. But I thought they were as okay as they could be under the circumstances. She turned back to her salad, opened a jar of disconcertingly bright red cherry halves and laid them in the shape of a flower on the white bed of marshmallows, something I'd seen her do so many times it was reassuring.

"You have to tell me what's going on," I said. "I can't do anything if I don't know what's going on."

"He's getting up in the middle of the night and going for walks. He keeps asking me to take him home. When I tell him this is home, he gets angry. When we were driving last week, he told me to take him home then grabbed the wheel. I had to scream at him to get him to let go. I thought we were going to have an accident."

"Grandma?" The voice came from the doorway behind me. I turned to see my nephew Logan who, although the same age as Jax, seemed more child-like, innocent. "I can't find Grandpa."

My mother took a deep breath, her shoulders and chest rising as her rib cage filled with air. Her small frame, thin limbs, and tiny hands had always made her seem delicate, bird-like, which only became more pronounced with her shrinking. When I was sixteen, she and I were the same height. Now at forty-seven and seventy-two, I was still five-three but she was barely five feet.

The big inhale made her seem like a diminutive creature puffing itself up to look bigger so as not to get consumed by a predator. She let the breath out in a huge sigh.

"We're not done, okay?" I said to my mother, then turned to Logan. "You check the TV room. I'll check the workshop."

He nodded and left. We all knew the drill.

J walked through the dining room and out to the back balcony. I made a quick survey of the empty yard below, then stepped back into the house.

"Is the workshop locked?" I shouted to my mom, who remained in the kitchen, apparently not intending to join the search for Dad.

"He has a million extra keys," Mom said, which only sort of answered the question but was completely clear to me. Colleen and I had suggested she change the lock, but she refused. Every time Mom took away Dad's keys, he managed to find them or come up with yet another spare set. It was like he had a collection stashed somewhere, as if he suspected people in the future were going to conspire against him and he'd planned ahead.

Mom said if she changed the lock, they'd be in a constant battle, which, since she was the one living with him, we had to respect. But a man with no short-term memory and access to power tools felt like a recipe for disaster. Logan was coming up the stairs from the TV room, as I was going down. Even without the head shake, I knew from his face that Dad wasn't in the TV room.

"Can you check out front?" I said.

Logan nodded.

I crossed through my parents' room to the back balcony. As I opened the sliding glass door, I kicked off my clogs. Bare feet were safer on the ladder-like, wooden steps down to the back-yard that Adam, with his penchant for naming things, had dubbed the "death stairs" when we were kids.

My parents' modest two-story house followed a common design of hillside homes in the San Fernando Valley. It was inverted. The top story, with the kitchen, living room, and garage, was at road level. The bedrooms were on the story below. You got to the backyard, which was relatively flat because the house was at the base of the hill, via the death stairs or by walking down around the side of the house.

As I went down the steps, I tried to will the future into existence. Dad would be in the workshop when I got down there. I'd walk in, promise him a cold beer, and we'd go back up into the house. It wasn't far-fetched. A lot of the time when you couldn't find Dad, he was fiddling with tools and shuffling boxes in the workshop, his body and hands remembering old skills and knowledge that his brain had long forgotten.

My hopes dwindled when I got to the bottom of the stairs, however. The workshop door was closed. He never closed it when he was in there. But you couldn't count on things that used to be certainties, so I treaded along the crunchy, dry grass to check.

The half-finished story under the house contained Adam's old bachelor pad on the side and Dad's workshop at the back. The workshop was this wedge shape where Dad had put in a floor and shelves. If you were facing the door, it seemed like you were in a square room. But if you turned around, you were looking into the ever-shrinking space where the dirt of the hill rose to meet the bottom of the house, an area Adam had christened the Bermuda Triangle.

I opened the door and turned on the light, glancing around as if Dad's presence wouldn't be obvious, as if he might be hidden amongst the muddle of worn boxes scattered across the shelves, a microcosm of his mind: things slowly drifting out of place until all that was left was a jumble.

My dad had crafted under-appreciated masterpieces here while us kids played in the yard—chicken coop for Colleen's 4-H project, jungle gym for Adam, playhouse for me—but at some point, the three of us always ended up in that strange, shadowy angle under the house, daring each other to go further and further into the Bermuda Triangle, searching for the invisible portal we imagined there. A spot where you could cross into another dimension.

"One day something's going to pull you in," Dad used to say, which always made me dart back out certain I felt something reaching for me.

Every time I came in here looking for him, I checked that dark space under the house, as if I might catch him returning from another plane. But, of course, there was no Dad. I turned off the lights and headed back toward the stairs.

Logan was standing in the center of the kitchen when I returned. He frowned and shook his head. Mom stayed unduly focused on the meal as if she were more concerned about the mashed potatoes than my dad, which was weird. Normally, she'd already be out the door.

"I'll go pick him up," I said and grabbed my keys.

If Dad wasn't in the workshop, it was a good bet he was somewhere on the three-mile route he used to jog after his doctor told him he was going to have a heart attack if he didn't stop smoking and lose some weight. When his knees refused to run anymore, he and Mom walked it together. The route was hard-wired into his brain and for some reason it was set on repeat while other things were on delete. Sometimes he'd announce that he was going and after about five minutes Mom would go pick him up. More often than not, however, he'd leave without a word.

I drove up around the hill behind the house. Boxy, white-washed mansions loomed from the inclines; absurdly massive homes only accessible via twisting veins of asphalt so narrow they should all be one-way streets but aren't. No sign of him. He couldn't have been gone that long. I remembered him going down to the TV room with Liam and Adam to hook up the PlayStation. But I didn't remember seeing him after Colleen left for the cranberry sauce.

I got to the top of the hill, then slowed on the steep decline. The turns were sharp. I didn't want to run over my own father. After each corner I expected him, and each time when he wasn't there the pit of my stomach dropped another level, an elevator plummeting to a new bottom. Still, no Dad. When I turned the last corner by the house, I couldn't believe I hadn't found him. I almost drove around again as if somehow I might have missed him. But then I realized he must have beaten me, so I parked.

I burst into the kitchen. "Is he home?"

Mom shook her head. Logan, apparently enlisted as her new helper, stood by in a flowery apron. They seemed too calm for what was happening.

"I went the whole way around. He wasn't there," I said uncertain if my mother understood the ramifications of me returning alone. Dad was lost. I was freaking out. But she wasn't. It didn't make sense. She didn't say anything. Instead she tasted a forkful of mashed potatoes.

"Mom!" I prodded. "Dad is lost."

She went to the fridge and began hunting for something, as if she hadn't heard me, wasn't listening. But when she came out with some cream, I noticed her hands were trembling ever so slightly. She was holding something in, a litany pushing against the stays of her resolve, about to burst out.

"Sometimes he goes down Ventura," she said.

"What? What do you mean? Why didn't you say anything?"

She shot me a look that I had no trouble reading. I headed back to the car, more concerned than ever. My dad was wandering alone in Los Angeles, even if it was just the Valley. What if he got hurt? What if he got mugged? What if he wasn't on Ventura like Mom thought but was who knows where?

We'd have to call the police. Start having neighbors and friends out looking for him. Guiltily I thought, "I don't have time for this." I wanted to have turkey and pumpkin pie and be on my way. I wanted to pretend my mother hadn't just asked me to kill my father. It was not okay for any of this to be happening. I had to take a nap before work. You don't call in sick at a hospital on Christmas, not unless you want the other nurses to kill you.

I got to Ventura Boulevard and realized I didn't know which way to go. Left or right? Mom had said he goes down Ventura. Did that mean toward North Hollywood or Calabasas? I took a guess and went right. Maybe he was walking to his old hardware store. As I drove the empty streets, I glanced down each side road, my heart sinking. One turn and he'd disappear, impossible to find.

When I got to the top of Chalk Hill, I could see down the boulevard all the way to Winnetka. No Dad. I kept going. Finally, after the bend, I saw a lone figure in the distance. Relief washed over me. Even from afar I recognized him. Stocky build. Striding gait. White tennis shoes. Socks halfway up his calves. He was right there. The relief grew as I got closer. I was going pick my father up and take him home. Everything would be okay, if only for a moment. I pulled up alongside him and rolled down the window.

"Howdy, stranger," I said trying to sound jovial, repeating something he used to say after we'd all moved out and he and Mom complained we didn't visit enough. But as the words came out of my mouth, I was horrified. What if this was the moment that my Dad didn't recognize me? What if today was the day that

I became a stranger to him? Every person's last moment was coming. Each of us was being erased, vanishing neuron by neuron. One day he wouldn't know any of us. And that moment, when it came, would happen without fanfare, without a goodbye.

"Bernie?" Dad said, looking up and down the street as if checking where he was. He took off his beige baseball cap and wiped his near-bald head. "Fancy meeting you here."

"Want a ride?" I made the invitation as casual as I could, as if it didn't matter to me one way or the other what he did. Dementia had given him an obstinate streak, like a two-year-old practicing "no" at every opportunity. He tapped his walking stick on the ground and checked up and down the street again.

"Sure," he said. "I'm going home."

I unlocked the door and he climbed in. I resisted the temptation to tell him he was heading away from the house. It served no purpose. He had no idea where he was going or why. I could say anything and in a minute or two it would be gone.

I took the long way home, up Wells Drive through the back streets of Tarzana and Woodland Hills. Every corner another memory: friends' houses, bike rides, hikes. He'd spent more than fifty years in *these* streets with *these* trees in *these* hills. Was it all nondescript to him now? Any street. Any tree. Any hill.

I pointed as we turned the corner. "Serrania Ridge," I said.

He looked and nodded.

"The last piggyback?" I added, hating myself for the hopeful questioning in my voice. But I couldn't help it. He always told that story here. You couldn't stop him. We'd give a collective groan and I'd shrink in my seat, embarrassed, wishing for once he'd forget, not knowing there'd be a time where I'd give anything to hear it.

Dad never let us buy him gifts for Father's Day. Instead we trudged through the hills together *enjoying* an annual hike, though I think he was probably the only one who got any pleasure out of it. Red Rock, Laskey Mesa, Caballero. I was about nine when we hiked Serrania Ridge.

It was hot. Hotter than usual. We'd gotten a late start because of me, the baby, and a missing hiking boot. Colleen, Adam, and Dad forged ahead. I lagged, complaining about the heat, the dust, my feet. I was miserable. Finally, I dropped to the ground and refused to go further. I don't know what I expected but I had every intention of not budging until someone miraculously ended my suffering.

Colleen rolled her eyes and leaned against a tree.

Adam jeered. "Stop being such a doofus."

Dad came back down the trail to witness my protest. He smiled, smirked actually, like he was holding back a laugh, knew things I didn't. He offered a hand. "Want a ride, Bumblebee?"

I nodded and he hoisted me up on his back. My solace quickly transformed into regret, my arms and legs grappling awkwardly for resting places. I was too big. I didn't fit anymore. It was obvious the instant he got me up that this would be the last piggyback ride my father would ever give me. Neither of us had to say it. We both knew.

I lay my head against his back. His scent, mixed with dirt and sweat, wafted from his shirt, offering a strange primal comfort. He carried me as long as he could and we grieved these last few moments in silence. Then, he put me down. He kissed my forehead and took my hand, giving it a little squeeze.

From the passenger seat, Dad jolted me out of my reminiscing. "Where are we going?" he asked.

I smiled to mask my anguish, amazed that he never seemed to notice the sorrow flowing just under the surface of everyone who loved him.

"We're going home," I said.

"Where's Helen?"

"She's at home."

He nodded and I wondered how long his mind would let him

hold onto the brief salvation of knowing where he was going, and that Mom was waiting for him. I'm not being flippant when I say I'd rather get hit by a Mack truck than go out like my dad. I work in a trauma/neuroscience ICU. I know exactly what Mack truck meets human being looks like. I'll take that over dementia any day. I want to go out in an instant. I don't want to disappear in little pieces, like God is crushing stars between his fingers until the whole sky is dark.

Colleen was back and making her kids clean up the living room when I returned with Dad. I took him downstairs to the TV room. Adam and Liam were racing cars on the PlayStation, looking like antiquated versions of their teenage selves. My brother was balder and heavier, but his khakis and white polo mirrored his old school uniform. Liam was still tall and thin, dressed in a plaid shirt I honestly think he had in the 90s. They were as self-absorbed as they had been as teenagers, too, oblivious to the fact that I'd been frantically searching for Dad while they gallivanted in worlds of make-believe.

Jax was on the sofa. He'd tidied up a bit since I'd checked on him, gathering his long, brown hair into a messy ponytail with a lacy, blue scrunchy that must have belonged to Laura. Dad stopped in front of him, bafflement clouding his eyes. Jax looked nothing like Colleen's boys, who all favored their red-headed, freckled father and who Dad intermittently recognized, not as individuals, but as eight interchangeable grandsons all named Lincoln like Colleen's first so many years ago.

"Who are you?" Dad said, pointing at Jax. It was a question and an accusation, like it was Jax's fault that Dad didn't know who he was. Dad's body was rigid, his finger hovering two inches from Jax's nose.

I held my breath. Jax had always been kind to my dad but they were both smoldering cherry bombs ready to pop. Just three weeks ago, when someone else had put a finger in Jax's face, he'd snapped it, plus two more for good measure. A classmate had called him an "ecofag", whatever that is, and "got all up" in his face. My son pinned the boy down, a knee to his chest, and methodically cracked bones.

"Hey, Grandpa," Jax said, reaching up and taking Dad's other hand. Dad relaxed, seemingly relieved to have been given a hint as to their relationship. He sat, their clasped hands resting in the space between them on the sofa. I relaxed as well. I walked over to the two of them, patted Jax's shoulder and kissed my dad's head, then moved to go upstairs.

Moments like these gave me hope for my son. Jax was only eight when they named the dismantling of my father's mind vascular dementia. The two of them had just found in the other a kindred spirit and were working on a house for the farm dog Jax considered his own. Like my father and Shayne, Jax could lose himself in the construction of something concrete, puzzling over dimensions, angles, stabilizations. As my father faltered, Jax exhibited a tenderhearted mercy that overwhelmed me. They traded places. Jax took the lead and guided my dad through the last project he'd ever successfully complete.

If I counted, there were probably more of these kinds of moments than the other. But the bad moments seemed heavier. They had a greater hold on me. Instead of balancing with the good, they undid them. One second, Jax was a compassionate grandchild. The next, a delinquent begging for a new diagnosis.

From the bottom of the stairs, I heard Colleen, in her lilting, super-mommy voice say, "Looks pretty good, gang. Why don't we go see if Daddy and Uncle Adam are ready to give up the PlayStation?" A few seconds later a stampede of redheads of varying heights charged past: Logan, Leland, Lance, and Lucas. My sister married an Irish Catholic named Liam Lannon and apparently thought alliteration was a requirement.

I did a double-take when Laura, my sister's only girl, came down behind her brothers, as always startled by how much she looked like Colleen at fifteen. The same long, straight, black hair and powdery, pale complexion, the eerie past wandering the halls of our present. She held up the book *Sophie's World*, my Christmas present to her.

"I like it," she said.

"I loved it when I was your age," I said just as my sister reached the bottom of the stairs. She stopped next to Laura. The lines by her eyes made it clear who was mother and who was daughter, but my sister was still beautiful. She got all the good genes. I got the ragged ones, the mousy, not quite auburn coloring, the indistinct freckles, frizz instead of curls.

"Loved what?" Colleen said. "Getting high?"

"We were talking about the novel," I said, ignoring my sister's taunt. I started up the stairs. "I'm going to help Mom with dinner."

"I'll be up in a minute," Colleen said.

"No rush," I said. It would be a lot easier to get to the bottom of what was happening with my dad without my sister in the room. "Get the boys settled. They might need to remind Adam and Liam how taking turns works."

When I got to the kitchen, Mom was clearing off one of the counters, getting it ready for the completed dishes which would be set out for self-service. Her attachment to tradition allowed for this single convenience. I started at the opposite end of the counter.

"Okay, Mom. Everyone's downstairs in the TV room. Tell me what's going on."

"I already told you."

"No, you said he's wandering off in the night, and he grabbed the steering wheel. I want to talk about the going peacefully part."

"You help people die all the time," she said.

"Not exactly. People die at the hospital because they're brain-dead and we're keeping them alive with machines. Or because they're so injured they aren't going to survive. We give them medication to make them comfortable. We don't kill them."

"But that's what he wanted. He didn't want to be like this. It isn't him."

"I know but that doesn't mean I can help him die."

"What about that girl in Oregon with the brain tumor?" she said.

"Brittany Maynard?" I asked. Mom was a dedicated reader of *People* magazine. Colleen and I had had a heated debate about assisted suicide when Brittany's story was covered. "It's not the same. You can't euthanize a person with dementia, even in Oregon and Washington, even in Europe. They have to be able to do it themselves. Dad could have put it in writing that he didn't want to live like this and had a million witnesses, but it wouldn't matter. It would be... illegal." I didn't say the word that actually came to mind, which was murder.

Her face changed, a tiny piece of heartache creeping into her eyes. I felt terrible. This had apparently been her failsafe. She'd been holding on, waiting for the moment when it was finally too much, then she thought we'd be able to help him go. Maybe she thought we'd all move to Oregon and there we could end their mutual suffering. It had probably taken everything she had to admit to me that she'd reached her limit.

"I know what you're going to say but maybe it's time for a nursing home," I said.

"No," she said. "I promised."

"I know but..."

"A promise is a promise. Just like 'till death do us part.'"

"I don't know what else to do," I said.

19

She was trapped. She'd tell you this is what she signed on for —for better or for worse, in sickness and in health—but it sucked. The three of us did what we could to help but it was never enough. We had our own lives, our own problems.

Adam lived in Washington, where he had a stereotypically nasty ex, and kids he had to fight to see. Every couple of years he dropped in for the holidays. The best he could probably do was send cash once in a while. Colleen and I watched Dad here and there so Mom could have a break: take an uninterrupted shower, go to lunch with a friend, get her hair done. It wasn't easy. We were always juggling.

Colleen homeschooled her herd and miraculously fed and clothed them all on Liam's L.A. Unified teaching salary. I worked night shift. Jax had just gotten expelled from the last school that would have anything to do with him, and his dad Shayne and I were being sued by the parents of the kid with the broken fingers. And hanging out with Dad for a few hours was nothing compared to living with him. It was like babysitting someone else's kids and thinking you know what it's like to raise some.

I heard someone coming up from downstairs and turned just as Colleen came through the door. I glanced at our mother. Was this conversation over and, more importantly, was it just for me? Had I finally—because of my unique place in the world—uncovered a situation where my mother selected me over my sister? Or was she going to talk to Colleen about it too? I wasn't sure which I wanted.

Colleen had become a Roman Catholic to marry Liam. It was a formality and total BS because she was pregnant at the time. But over the years she'd become passionate in a fundamentalistic way. We frequently argued about abortion, death with dignity, capital punishment but always in the abstract. Not about people we knew. Not about our family. It was almost like a sport and I was never convinced of her devotion. She just had a natural attraction to righteousness.

Mom's face changed. She forced a smile and asked brightly, "Do the children like the game?"

I was relieved. I didn't want to have this conversation with my sister. I didn't *want* to have it with anyone, but in a stupid way it made me feel closer to my mom, childishly glad that she'd picked me instead of Colleen. Forty-seven years old and I was still looking for my mother to put me in front of my sister, to crown me the good daughter.

"Liam and Adam are still at it. I don't know if the kids will ever get a chance," Colleen said, then walked toward me. I raised my hands like I was being arrested. She frowned. She was always fixing something on me, picking a piece of lint from my sweater, tidying me up like I was one of her kids. She lifted the charm on my necklace, the bumblebee I'd worn since my dad gave it to me for my thirteenth birthday.

"Make a wish," she said as she repositioned the clasp to the back of my neck.

The tips of her fingers brushed my skin, raising goosebumps. She looked at me. Her nose wrinkled as if the words my mother and I had shared had a particular scent that was lingering in the air. I think she sensed something was going on. I felt like a traitor.

THE PROMISE 1977

The funeral was over. Time to go. I didn't know what we were waiting for. Why wasn't Dad saying, "Let's get this show on the road" like he usually did when people lolly-gagged. The sun blazed so bright and hot I was certain the thing dripping down my back was a melted layer of skin. Funerals were supposed to be gloomy affairs, dark skies with clouds and rain. Yet there was nothing but blue above, any fragments of cloud chased off by the hot, Santa Ana winds.

The service had been short. My family—my mother, father, us three kids and our two uncles—were the only ones there, filling a single pew on one side of the church. After, we'd walked to the gravesite and stood exposed in the intense sunlight for something just a few seconds less than forever. The priest spoke more, then four men lowered Grandma Rogers' coffin into the ground.

But we were still waiting, standing in the sun as the adults wiped their eyes, hugged each other, and shook the priest's hand again and again. I no longer felt guilty for wanting to go home. All I could think about was getting out of my clammy, stiff dress and lying on the floor in our living room, salvaging whatever remained of Saturday. Maybe there'd still be time to catch a couple of cartoons or the afternoon matinee, like *Benji* or *Escape to Witch Mountain*.

Finally, after hugging my uncles one more time, Dad headed toward the car. I wanted to sprint, run so I would get the backwards facing single seat in our Volkswagen camper. Then, I wouldn't have to sit with either my eleven-year-old brother or nine-year old sister, their sweaty skin near mine. But it was too hot, and I'd already gotten scolded once for not behaving appropriately at a cemetery. When we got to the car, my brother reached for the sliding door. My father blocked his arm.

"Wait," Dad said.

We stood, huddled around him, not sure what was going on.

"Over there," he said, pointing to the side of the car. "Line up."

My mother remained next to him and I suspected the three of us were about to get reprimanded for too much fidgeting or whispering during the service. Why couldn't they wait until we were at the house? If we were lucky, one of them would turn on the air-conditioning, then none of us would care about getting yelled at.

"You too," my father said, gesturing for our mother to join us in the lineup. Dad paced in front of us, shoulders tense. Something was wrong. Dad was the gentle one, the soft-touch who could always be talked into a bag of M&Ms at the hardware store. Mom was the enforcer, the one who threw looks that hurt worse than her wooden spoon on your bottom.

But Dad had been acting different ever since the call from the nursing home informed us that Grandma Rogers, his mother, had died. He'd snap at us for minor infractions that normally only Mom policed, then sometimes without warning he'd pull us into hugs that lasted so long you had to squirm to get out of them.

Pa Rogers had dropped dead of a heart attack, when my dad was ten. My father and his two young brothers were raised by Grandma Rogers, a single mom in the 1950s. A saint in our household. But to me, a frail, old woman who didn't speak or make eye contact. A lap I was forced to sit on, a face I was obliged to kiss even though I didn't want to. The only good thing about the nursing home was the parrot in the lobby who I often sat with, listening to him repeat, "I love you," and, "Coco is a pretty boy," in the accent of the secretary at the front desk.

Dad stopped pacing and stood in front of Adam, his finger wagging at Adam's chest.

"This is important," Dad said.

Adam nodded and I wondered if he knew what was happening because I sure didn't. I was utterly confused and felt like I was going to faint or vomit.

"Promise you'll *never* put me in a nursing home," my father said.

Adam nodded again, his long, sun-bleached bangs bouncing in his eyes.

"No," my father said. "Say it."

Adam hesitated. "Dad?"

Dad's voice grew insistent. "Promise!"

"I promise."

"You promise what?"

"I promise I'll never put you in a nursing home," Adam said, his voice trembling so much it sounded like he was going to cry.

Dad moved to Colleen. I guessed she was as eager to get home as me because she looked him square in the eyes and without hesitation said, "I'll never put you in a nursing home. I promise."

I was next. The itchy lace collar on my dress scratched my neck. I wanted to rip it off. My mother took my hand and squeezed, as if it were a secret signal that I should understand but didn't.

My father towered in front me. I almost laughed. I was tiny. How would I ever be in a position to put him in a nursing home? How could someone as strong and powerful as my father ever be reduced to the state of our grandmother? The promise fell out of my mouth easily, thoughtlessly. "I promise I'll never put you in a nursing home."

I was only six. The irony was lost on me. Dad put Grandma in a home because he couldn't care for her yet we were promising not to do the same. Maybe he thought it was a covenant, somehow protective. If we all said it and there was nowhere for him to go, then he couldn't get Alzheimer's like Grandma Rogers. Or maybe he hated himself for not being able to care for her and was trying to save us from some tortured regret.

He moved to my mother, who dropped my hand.

"Bill, please," she said quietly. "Please."

"Helen, I mean it," he said, not angry but earnest, pleading. "Never."

My mother smiled, the pained smile of someone who has succumbed. "I will never put you in a nursing home, my darling. Never."

We piled into the un-air-conditioned car and rode home silently, balmy air blowing through the open windows. I stared at the green trees, still feeling sick to my stomach.

*A*fter our Christmas meal, during which Dad said, "We should do this more often," at least ten times, Jax and I headed to the The Farm, the shared living community where Shayne and I had been joined, not in a wedding but, in a pagan handfasting ceremony when I was twenty-one. We'd spent seventeen years together at The Farm. Jax was born there shaded by ancient oaks, Pam, my lay midwife, catching him as he manifested into the world already raging.

"I'm gonna call your dad and let him know we're on our way," I said to Jax who was staring out the car window and didn't seem to care one way or another what I did.

Shayne answered after a single ring—sweet, sweet Shayne, who depending on your thoughts on non-traditional religions, is either my husband, a guy I have a kid with, or my best friend whom I love with *most* of my heart, have sex with rather frequently, but with whom I can't bear to live. We never did anything to undo the hand-fasting. I don't know how. Shayne's the real pagan. I'm more neo-hippie, turned disillusioned dreamer. Facebook has no idea how complicated a relationship status can be.

"Were you sitting by the phone?" I asked. The Farm only has one phone, a landline in the main house. Nobody has cells. Even if they did, there's no reception.

"Reading. How was the feast?" he said.

"Same. We're on our way. I'm just going to drop him off and run, if that's okay," I said, even though I knew it was okay. Everything is okay with Shayne. Shayne is all soft edges—that was part of our problem. We didn't realize life was going to make one of us hard. It turned out to be me. Maybe hard isn't the right word, maybe serious is a better word. But the reality was that someone had to stop thinking that beekeeping and chicken-raising was going to save the world.

"No problem," he said, and hung up.

I glanced at the time. When there's no traffic, which is never in LA except *maybe* on Christmas, I can get from my parents' house to The Farm in twenty minutes, then to my place, a rented guest house in Santa Monica, in another thirty. I would have time for a two-hour nap before work, not perfect but totally doable. It was probably going to be a slow night anyway. New Year's is the big trauma day, not Christmas.

This year's holiday gathering had been less than relaxing. Dad wandering off was dramatic enough but my conversation with my mother raised things to an operatic level. She couldn't really think the solution to my father's dementia was death, could she? What would happen the next time I saw her? Would we pretend this conversation never happened? I hoped so.

My mind spun with possibilities. I had to slow down. Breathe. Focus on the tasks ahead. Drop Jax off. Take a nap. Go to work. Pretend to be the hero in someone else's worst day.

I glanced at Jax staring out at the trees.

"Did you have fun?" I asked.

"Yeah," he said without enthusiasm.

"Those are cool Dr. Martens Grandma and Grandpa got for

you," I said, referring to my parents as the unified team they'd once been.

"Why is Lance such a pain in the butt?" Jax asked.

I tensed. "Did something happen?"

"No, he's just..." Jax stopped. "He's so different from the rest of them."

I laughed a little, both in relief and agreement. "He certainly isn't a typical Lannon," I said. "Pregnancy is basically a genetic crap shoot. You never know what you're gonna get." I hadn't meant anything by it, but I thought I saw Jax wince, retreat further into the scenery outside the window.

"I liked that school," he said after a few seconds.

"I know you did."

"I really messed up this time."

I didn't know how I could or should respond so I said nothing. Since the finger-breaking incident it felt like there was an actual physical wall between us, a barrier I sometimes made no effort to scale. Every time something happened I felt myself pulling away a little bit more, like at some unknown future time and place he'd do something so horrible I'd have to disconnect to save myself. I felt sympathy for him. I wanted to have a heart big enough to accommodate the grace needed to be his mother, but sometimes I just wanted to run.

We drove in silence along the windy, narrow road into Old Topanga Canyon. This was still Los Angeles County but in a few moments, we'd be deep in nature, dark greens and browns filling the small canyon around us. Soon it would seem impossible that one of the largest metropolitan areas in the world lurked just beyond the hills.

The rich folks lived in the main canyon. Mansions overlooking the Valley with swimming pools designed like waterfalls cascading over cliff edges. Old Topanga still had some real people: Artists who'd inherited run-down shacks from grandparents or bought when it was affordable a million years ago.

Hippies with chickens and goats and pigs. Poets who bred dogs and lived in converted barns. Healers dealing in energy and auras.

I parked the car along the seven-foot-high wall that bordered the street-side of Calvin's twenty-acre property. The story was that his parents had been nudists and built the wall to avoid gawkers and the law. He'd inherited the place when they died in a car wreck just before he returned from Vietnam.

Calvin and Rain, his girlfriend of forever, occupied the bedrooms of the main house, a rust-colored, two-bedroom bungalow that hadn't changed since it was built. The kitchen, living room and bathroom were communal. Everyone shared meals, the phone, and the indoor composting toilet, which was preferable to the outdoor one, mostly because there was running water to wash your hands. Other living quarters with minimal amenities were scattered around the property: four trailers, two yurts, one tiny house.

Jax got out of the car, his backpack slung over his shoulder and the box with his new boots tucked under his arm. He gently pushed on the gate. In his old age, Champ, The Farm's golden retriever mix, could no longer be bothered to bark at potential intruders and instead used his body as a physical barrier across the entrance. He lifted his head just enough to determine if we were friend or foe, then lay back down. Jax scratched Champ's neck for a second, then peeled off the main path down toward the old Airstream that had served as our family home for the first four years of his life.

"Hey," I called after him, feeling like I needed to repair whatever damage I'd done. "Don't I get a proper goodbye? I'm not going to see you for a bit."

Jax came back and put his arms around me in a reluctant hug.

"Be good," I said as he disappeared down the slope again.

I work Friday, Saturday, and Sunday nights so Jax spends weekends at The Farm. Without a car, getting our son to or from school was a challenge for Shayne. With this schedule, he only had to do it twice a week.

Winter break, however, was something different entirely. Jax stayed with Shayne the entire time. My best friend Kara and I worked Christmas and New Year's—a chance for me to earn some always needed double-time—then we took a week off together after the holidays. It was a mini-vacation, actually my only vacation every year and something I started looking forward to around Halloween.

I heard a whistle from the main house. It was Shayne, standing on the steps of the enclosed porch. I walked in his direction in spite of the fact that I'd intended to drop Jax off and leave. There really wasn't anything to say about our son's situation. Getting expelled wasn't new. He'd gotten thrown out of each school he'd attended—one by one as if he were systematically moving down a checklist. What *was* new was that this school had been our last hope. We'd exhausted all resources. Getting sued was new too, but there was nothing for Shayne and I talk about. Shayne doesn't own anything or have any actual money. So really, it was just me getting sued.

"What's in the box?" he asked.

"My parents got him Docs."

"At the rate he's going he'll probably outgrow them by next week."

I nodded.

"What's wrong?" he said, out of nowhere.

Shayne's ability to read my mind or at least appear to was one of the reasons I'd never been able to untangle myself from him, that and I never gave it the valiant effort it would require. I hadn't lived at The Farm in almost ten years but he still felt like family, someone who knew me in a way others couldn't, or in a way I wouldn't let them. Shayne and Kara were the two people I felt most connected to. Shayne was all spirit. Kara, all science. The two sides of me I couldn't reconcile.

"Stuff with my dad," I said, not wanting to dredge it up after just managing to push it away. I was probably making too much of things. Nothing had really changed. Mom was simply expressing the depth of her frustration. I'd have to do more, find something that worked. I'd figure it out.

Shayne stood there, waiting for more. His unspoken inquiries ping-ponged in my head, more insistent than he'd ever be.

"My mom *kinda* asked me to kill my dad today," I finally said.

"Like... how?" he asked as if I'd said my mom had asked me to help her clean out the garage. No judgement. No cautiously camouflaged opinion. If you did something terrible, Shayne's the guy you'd call to help you dump the body—except it would take him forever to get to you with his bike and LA's horrible public transportation.

"She was thinking it was a death-with-dignity issue. Like we could get some medicine and he'd go to sleep and never wake up. He's wandering off in the night. He grabbed the steering wheel the other day while she was driving. She's crazy tired and worn out."

"There's no way to do that, right? I mean not legally?"

"No, there's no legal way," I said. But as the word legal came out of my mouth, I stopped. I thought my mother had asked me to kill my father under the mistaken belief that it was possible under the law. But was that what had actually happened? Maybe she'd simply asked me to kill my father, legal or not. My heart fluttered up into my throat, a mix of fearful anticipation and confusion. The pin on a hand grenade had been pulled. The question was whether I was going to hurl it as far away as possible to save myself or throw my body over it to save everyone else.

"There's nothing to do except wait," I said, trying to disperse the doubts now racing through my mind. "At some point, she'll have to put him in a home."

"Your mother will do pretty much anything before she does

that. She's made that pretty clear," he said, giving voice to the devil's advocate inside my head.

"I don't think she'll have a choice," I said.

"An it harm none, do as thou wilt," he murmured to himself, then looked off into the trees. "Your mom's a pretty resourceful person. Aren't you worried she'll just figure something out without you?"

My heart sank. "I am now."

THE SLAP 1987

$\mathcal{I}$t was my first day of college and only my second class of the day. I had just taken a seat at one of the desks at the front of the room when a young man walked in, tall and lanky, his long, black hair pulled back and French-braided, accenting prominent cheekbones. Although technically a freshman, a fall birthday and graduating a year early meant I was only sixteen. The class, *Theater Dialects*, was one where I was on the waitlist hoping for a spot but I wasn't quite sure how the whole process worked.

The guy crossed in front of me. He was impossible not to notice, like he was in costume for a play that only he knew we were in. He was definitely my type. Colleen called it the "heroin-hippie look." Keith Richards meets renaissance fair—lace-up moccasin boots, a brown leather vest over a dingy white pirate shirt, and baggy pants. He took a place two rows behind me. Every so often I snuck a glance in his direction unable to focus.

He appeared again that night in the student union at the freshman orientation session. I tried not to stare as he wandered the rows searching for a seat. As he approached the open chair next to me, I looked in the other direction.

"I'd be much obliged," he said mimicking the southern accent we'd practiced in the dialects class, "if you'd allow me to sit a spell, fair lady,"

I managed not to laugh. "Why, of course, kind sir."

We kept up that ridiculousness, through the entire presentation then out into the parking lot as he followed me to my car. I wasn't sure what I was doing but when he reached up and put a hand on my shoulder, my whole body tingled. I'd had sex once with a boyfriend I didn't really care about. I'd never felt anything like this.

"Wanna grab something to eat?" I asked, even though food was *not* remotely what I was thinking about.

"I'm not comfortable with the capitalist underpinnings of most culinary establishments," he said.

I stared, at a loss as to how to respond. "Is there any place you can eat?"

He thought about it for moment, then nodded. We climbed into my metallic, green convertible bug and drove to *Follow Your Heart*, a health food restaurant I hadn't heard of. We never got inside. We made love in the parking lot, cramped in the back seat of my tiny car, the windows fogging with our heat, unconcerned about anything but our desire for each other. For the first time I understood what all the fuss with sex was about. I got it. When we were done, he took out a joint and lit it. He passed it to me, then stretched an open palm in my direction. I grasped the joint, then awkwardly shook his hand.

"Shayne Sky," he said.

"Bernadette Rogers. My friends call me Bee," I added quickly, hoping he'd never get to Bernie, which was what everyone in my family called me.

He shook his head.

"No," he said. "That's not right." He took another hit off the joint and passed it back to me. He studied my face, his brow furrowing.

"*Bébé*," he said.

"Baby?" I said louder than intended.

"No, not baby," he said, mocking my tone. "*Bébé*. En Francais."

"*Bébé*," I repeated. "I'll take that."

After we finished the joint, we climbed back into the front seat. He wouldn't let me get close to his house—"Too much negative energy"—and instead had me drop him at the corner of Ventura and Wilbur. He walked from there. It was only after I watched him turn down a side street that I considered the time.

"Fuck!" It was eleven. My parents had expected me home after the orientation session ended. I'd only had my car a few months and had been a college student a single day. I was already blowing it. My parents hadn't wanted me to leave high school a year early. With Adam four years in still without a major and Colleen never going, I was their final college hope. I watched my speed as I drove along Wells back toward our house. The last thing I needed was a ticket or accident.

When I arrived, the house lights were glaring brightly but I couldn't tell if anyone was still up. I parked and quietly made my way toward the door. Then, I saw my mother's silhouette at the window.

"Where have you been?" she said stepping out of the kitchen as soon as I closed the front door behind me.

"At school," I said.

"That meeting ended hours ago."

"I was hanging out with some new friends. I lost track of time."

"Do I smell marijuana?"

"No," I said, shaking my head.

"I was worried sick, Bernadette. Worried sick."

"I'm sorry. I just…"

She cut me off. "Sorry isn't good enough, young lady."

"What do you want me to do? I can't take it back," I said with a defiant tone I couldn't control.

"Give me your car keys." She held out her hand.

"What?"

"You heard me. Give me your car keys."

"You can't take the Green Machine. It's mine. I bought it with my own money. I fixed it up."

"Your father fixed it up."

"We did it together. It wasn't a one-man show."

"Bernadette Louise Rogers if you don't give me your car keys right now, you're going to regret it."

"Fine," I said tossing the keys on the floor in front of her.

The slap came so quickly I didn't have time to prepare. My mother had spanked me when I was little with her hand and wooden spoons, but she'd never hit me in the face. I stared, taunting her fury. Everything had changed after Colleen moved out. My sister walked away. I got all the heat.

"I'm not stupid," I said, even though I hadn't been any more careful than my sister. "I'm not Colleen."

Those words were apparently worse than silence because she slapped me again, then my father shouted from behind us, "What are you doing?"

We both turned. My father was at the end of the hall, my bleary-eyed two-year-old nephew Lincoln in his arms. My mother and I turned back to each other, fixing our gazes again, neither of us backing down.

"Go to your room, Bernie," my dad said. "We're done here."

I held my mother's gaze a few seconds longer, lamely thinking I was proving a point, then stomped off to my room. I got my car keys back a few days later, after my mom realized it was a pain to drive me all the way across the Valley to Cal State Northridge every morning. We never talked about that night. It got buried in the silence that was its own form of communication in our house.

DECEMBER 25TH 3:35 PM

I made it home from The Farm in record time, the grey asphalt zooming by like when we were kids and LA wasn't overrun with cars. The house was quiet. It always seemed doubly vacant the first day Jax wasn't around, both him and my constant anxiety about him creating their own separate voids. Relief washed over me as soon as the door closed. I leaned against it and let the emptiness of the house wash over me.

It was my doing of course, so it's stupid to complain, but I got the raw end of the parenting deal. When Jax was with Shayne, I was working. On my days off, he was with me—a different labor altogether. But that's how it always is, I get exactly what I want, then nothing about it's right.

I took a breath. It felt like the first time I'd breathed in forever. Two weeks without him. Two weeks of freedom, in which I would pretend a different life for myself. Kara and I would act like we were in our twenties instead of our forties: *Rocky Horror* at the Nuart. Drinks till closing at El Coyote. The dance floor at Rage. I would experience moments, even hours, of not agonizing over the labyrinth of my son's mind.

I pulled out my phone and texted Kara: *Find me at work tonight. NEED TO TALK!!!*

The mini vacation was typically my favorite time of year not only because it was the longest stretch I was off work but because Kara and I got to hang out sans Eliot and sans Jax. During the rest of the year, Kara only stayed at my place when she'd been at the hospital all night as the weekend on-call physician, which was no more than once a month.

It was safer and easier for her *not* to drive all the way back to her mansion in Laguna Beach if all she was going to do was sleep a few hours and return. But we barely saw each other those weekends. She'd tuck into her tiny room at the back of the house —far too small for a real bedroom but perfect as an occasional crash pad—and then be gone.

During the holidays, she stayed almost two full weeks. She worked Christmas and New Year's and the baby doctors, surgical residents who were already overworked and overtaxed, got to spend time with their families. They loved her for it. They thought she did it out of kindness, but it wasn't that at all.

Eliot, Kara's husband, came from an obnoxiously wealthy family that converged in Aspen every December for a ski trip. Kara hated them, didn't ski, and, more importantly, was a bona fide trauma junkie. She preferred piecing broken bodies back together to pretty much anything else. New Year's Eve, the worst trauma day of the year, was not something anyone could make her miss, even her own husband.

I switched off my phone and set it in the basket on the kitchen table, where it would stay exiled while I slept. You can't take any chances. Too many Amber Alerts and random calls had gotten through for one reason or another over the years, waking me and making it impossible to go back to sleep.

Once my essentials were in order—blackout blinds, white noise machine, old school digital alarm—I climbed into bed. I closed my eyes, but wakefulness hummed through me, my internal clock spinning out of control, totally disoriented. After years of night shift, a haze of chronic exhaustion is my norm. Often as soon as I lie down, I'm overcome by sleep. But the inverse is a ricocheting mind, everything switched on when it's supposed to be off.

The day ran through my head in snippets: Dad looking up and down the street. Mom nodding at me. My son patting the sofa. All amidst a background of music without words, as if my mind were plotting a movie and the suspense was killing me. I fidgeted, rolling from side to side trying to find a comfortable spot, a gateway to slumber. The harder I tried, the more awake I felt.

I opened my eyes. The room was dark but not pitch black. What I was about to do was a mistake, guaranteed not to calm me. But like most bad ideas, it had a will of its own that I couldn't thwart. I got up and dug the court papers from my dresser drawer. The page corners were darkened with oil from my fingers. I leafed through them.

Of course nothing had miraculously changed since that last time I'd done this. Plaintiffs - Maria Jacobson, Mark Jacobson. Defendants - Bernadette Rogers, Shayne Sky. Damages $30,000. I tucked the documents back into the envelope and reread my scrawled note on the front: *Arbitration December 31 @ 3pm*, then dropped it back in the drawer. One more thing interfering with my poor excuse for a vacation.

I returned to bed. Jacob Marley's chains rattled in my head, warning me of things to come. I'd duped myself into thinking Highland Learning Academy, a charter school for children with behavior issues, was the answer we'd been waiting for. One more time, I'd let myself see hope on the horizon. Jax lasted eight months without a major incident. The longest he'd ever gone. But it hadn't been real. That lull wasn't hope—it was doom lying in wait.

I'd actually been asleep that day. Napping, like I was supposed to be doing now, preparing for the first night shift of the weekend. A bang had woken me, something loud enough and close enough that it made it through all my barriers. I took out my ear plugs. Voices carried in over the white noise. Shayne. And Jax. And Kara.

It didn't make sense. Kara wasn't staying at my place that weekend. And Jax was supposed to be at The Farm with Shayne or at least on the bus with him on his way to The Farm.

"Why'd he have to get all up in my face?" I heard Jax shout, then his door slammed. There was a faint tapping on mine. It opened a crack. A sliver of light widened across the room.

"*Bébé*, it's me," Shayne said. He came in, closing the door behind him. I sat up. This wasn't how it worked. I went to Shayne. He didn't come to me. I couldn't remember him ever being in this bedroom before.

"What's going on?" I asked.

He sat at the end of my bed and lowered his head. "Fight."

He didn't have to say much more. One word was enough when you were in familiar territory.

"How bad?" I asked.

"He broke some kid's fingers," he said.

We sat, basking in this new inglorious reality. It wasn't a surprise or at least it shouldn't have been. It always happened like this, no warning.

"But why's Kara here?" I asked. The fight shouldn't have been a surprise but the three of them rolling into my house together was.

"My bus got in a fender bender. We were on the side of the road forever waiting so I was late picking him up," he said. "They called her because they couldn't reach anyone."

"Fuck," I said, getting out of bed. I pulled a robe on over my sleep shirt. "She drove all the way up from Laguna?"

"I don't think so," he said, then shrugged. "I don't know."

I walked out into the living room. Shayne, right behind me.

Kara was on the couch in some fancy business outfit, not the scrubs or jeans I usually saw her in.

"I'm sorry you had to pick him up," I said, totally humiliated. Kara knew everything about Jax and Shayne and my dad. But I'd always managed to keep her separate from it. She was my confessional, never in the actual mix.

"It's not a big deal," she said. "I agreed to be your emergency contact. It was bound to happen one day."

"Thank you so much," I said, but I was grimacing on the inside. Yes, it was bound to happen one day, that's why I'd put her down. My mom was no longer available and I preferred not to have my sister involved. I'd asked Kara and once again she turned out to be my lifeline. Without her overly generous contribution to the rent, I'd have never been able to afford my Santa Monica guest house.

"As serendipity would have it, I was in the Valley," she said. "I'm doing this mentoring thing at a science magnet."

The contrast between the kids at her magnet and the ones at my son's charter—or likely his ex-charter if things went as they usually did—was stark in my mind. A bunch of wanna-be doctors, engineers, and astronauts, versus a bunch of future prison inmates. Suddenly, the alarm buzzed in my bedroom.

"Shit," I said. "I'm supposed to be getting ready for work." I walked back to the bedroom. Shayne followed.

"I'm gonna have to call in," I said, switching off the alarm. "I don't have time to drive you home before my shift starts."

I reached in my closet and pulled out a pair of jeans. I was grateful that Kara'd been there to pick Jax up but I didn't know why she'd brought them to my house. She should have taken them back to The Farm.

"We could hang out here tonight," Shayne offered.

I shook my head. "I won't have time tomorrow either. You'd have to stay all weekend and be quiet all day while I sleep. It won't work."

Kara was suddenly at the door. Everybody in my bedroom and me in a worn-out cat t-shirt and robe.

"I can take them back," Kara said. "It's not like I'm going to drive to Laguna in rush hour. I should've taken them to The Farm in the first place," she said as if she'd heard my thoughts. "I guess I figured you'd want to see him."

I stared at her blankly. It hadn't occurred to me to go see Jax. What would I say to him that I hadn't said before? All I wanted was for things to be back in order. Shayne and Jax, at The Farm. Me, on my way to work. My two worlds no longer colliding.

"It's okay," I said. "I'll call in and drive them home."

"I thought you didn't have any more sick time," she said.

She was right. I didn't. "Look," I said. "I don't want you to…"

"It's okay to let me help," she said, cutting me off. "That's what friends are for."

I quickly got ready and we all walked out together. An incongruous family photo: Shayne, as always, in a t-shirt, cut-offs and his work boots. Kara, in some ridiculously expensive designer suit, and Jax in ripped jeans and a flannel shirt, so disheveled he looked like he might be homeless.

After they'd all gotten back into her SUV, Kara rolled down the window and said, "By the way, that kid's dad was a complete nutcase. He lost his mind when I told him to go to an urgent care, not the emergency room." And as she pulled away, I'd pictured her there in her snazzy ensemble lecturing some distraught parent about misusing the emergency room. Some distraught parent that I was going to meet in a few short days at the arbitration.

$\mathcal{I}$ lay in bed a little longer but clearly I was not going to sleep. I replayed the drama of the fight a few more times, fixating on how Jax had looked as we all walked out to the car, his head hung low like a puppy who's been scolded, then my mind shifted to a new self-torture: Dad. The flimsy thread holding that make-believe together was as frayed as things with Jax. I considered what my mom had said, and Shayne. It was so much easier to believe that now she knew it was illegal, my mother would just drop it and consider a nursing home. But who knew if that were true? We'd never discussed it. She wouldn't allow it.

I rolled over and stared at the back of the clock. The worst thing you can do when trying to sleep in the day is look at the actual time. No matter what it is, it's wrong. Too early and you worry that you'll never fall asleep. Too late and you'll be angry that the time is already gone. Best to remain blissfully unaware and just see what happens.

At this point, however, I was pretty certain that no matter how much I needed and wanted sleep, my mind wasn't going to settle. I turned the clock to face me, my white flag of surrender to the sleep gods. We'd been wrestling for an hour. One more hour to go before I needed to get ready for work.

I got up and went to the living room. The computer's Google search box taunted me. If my mom were to try something, what options did she have? I typed *suicide*. Carbon monoxide, phenobarbital, pentobarbital, sleeping pills, potassium chloride, drowning, hanging, shooting. I googled, *painless suicide*. Then, *assisted suicide*.

The information was overwhelming. For every successful suicide there are thirty-three unsuccessful ones. Eight states have some form of assisted suicide for the terminally ill. Every state considers it a crime for a lay person to assist in suicide. And, of course, it is illegal everywhere in the world to murder someone, which is what it would actually be if my mother or I helped my father die. I fell down rabbit hole after rabbit hole hunting for the nonexistent, clairvoyant website that would tell me, Bernadette Rogers, exactly what to do. I needed a psychic or a Magic 8 Ball.

Then, there it was, just the answer I didn't want to see: *Britain's Oldest Killer Sentenced.* Ninety-five-year-old Jack Tindall strangled his wife of sixty-eight years. Stroke. Vascular dementia. She didn't want to live anymore, didn't want to go to a nursing home. Jack Tindall had no other options. The only way to honor his wife's wishes had been to put his hands around her neck and strangle the life out of her. Was I condemning my mother to such a fate if I didn't help? Would she go that far? Would I let her?

I kept searching, only to panic when I found myself navigating a message board and a couple of websites about how to buy Nembutal in Mexico. It was an illegal drug from an illegal source. A drug used to sedate large animals and commit suicide. Maybe the government monitored site traffic. Maybe someone was tracking my information and if anything happened to my dad, I'd be suspect number one. I freaked, erased the computer history and turned it off. It was time to get ready for work anyway.

. . .

AN HOUR LATER, I was in line behind two other nurses clocking in. Kara, already dressed in her green surgery scrubs, walked up to me. I'd spooked myself so badly with the Nembutal that I wasn't about to start talking about the situation in the hallway and Margaret Ann, this crabby night nurse, was in front of us.

She'd started a rumor a few months back about me and Kara being lovers. Little known fact: nursing is overrun with bullies. The whole thing was supposedly resolved but whenever Kara and I were together I was on the look out for a sneer or a side glance. Tonight it would have been a nice semblance of the normal but Margaret Ann clocked in without taking any notice of us.

"How's Christmas in the emergency room?" I asked Kara.

"Quiet," she said, absentmindedly braiding her long, jet-black hair.

"Oh man, you said the Q-word," I joked. Kara used the Q-word with impunity, giving no credence to the superstition that saying things were "quiet" brought on the opposite.

"Nurses and the 'jinx,'" she said, throwing some air quotes around the word. "I'm not that powerful."

"Nurses? Dude, it is *not* just nurses. Your residents are serious believers in this particular hospital voodoo."

"Really?" she said, appearing to be genuinely surprised.

"Yeah, really, and just so you know, if it gets crazy tonight, I'm telling people it's your fault," I said.

She gave me a playful head shake. I clocked in and we walked to the unit break room. The table was packed with food: stuffing, cakes, pies, and a couple of actual turkeys. Personally, I could think of nothing more depressing than this mismatched, holiday amalgamation but it made some people feel better about being at work rather than with family.

"Shoot," I said. "I was supposed to bring something."

"Benny, what's going on?" Kara said. "You texted me in all caps and now I am getting routine nonsense."

I looked at her. She could see through me almost as well as Shayne.

"It's not a break room conversation," I said.

"Jax?"

I shook my head.

"Dad?" she said.

"Sort of."

Her pager went off. She glanced at it. "Sorry, I gotta go. Werring's on tonight, so I'll be fixing everything that yahoo messes up. But if it stays"—she dramatically, but silently mouthed *quiet*—"I'll probably be able to manage dinner around two."

I nodded and watched her head out the doors on her way to the ER.

KARA TEXTED me at 2:15 am. She could meet me at the sandwich shop on the first floor, the only place open all night. I looked from the phone to Mr. Collins, the fragile, grey old man seated in the chair next to his wife's bed. I definitely wanted to talk to Kara, but I also didn't want to leave Mr. Collins. He'd been sitting there since they'd arrived four hours earlier.

Mrs. Collins had had a stroke. She was alive and on a ventilator. But her brain was swelling. Mr. Collins had to decide whether or not to let a neurosurgeon take a piece of her skull out to give her brain space to swell or to let nature take its course. The prognosis at her age was poor with or without the craniotomy. It was getting poorer by the second.

Doctors had talked to him repeatedly, but he couldn't make up his mind. Soon enough his uncertainty would become a decision of sorts. Leaving felt like abandoning him, like I didn't have the right to my thirty-minute lunch and a talk with my best friend about my own problems. Fiona, the nurse with the patients next to mine, walked by.

"Anything I can help with?" she asked.

"Perfect timing," I said. "Could you keep an eye on my pair? I want to go downstairs to eat."

The nearly deserted lobby had an eeriness to it, a silence laden with possibility. JJ's sandwich shop with its bright lights and faint tinkling of music was the only sign of life. It was like walking down a darkened street and finding the last open nightclub. Kara and a single housekeeper at the other end of the food court were the only people around. I sat down and picked up the tuna sandwich she'd bought me.

"Is Eliot skiing?" I asked, feeling like an idiot as soon as I said it. I knew Eliot was skiing.

Kara frowned. "You're doing it again."

"What?"

"Making small talk because you don't want to speak the big thing. If you're lucky, you've got twenty minutes before I have to check on that clown Dr. Werring." She held up her iPhone as if everyone's least favorite new surgical fellow was trapped inside it. "You'd better pick up the pace."

"My mom asked me to euthanize my dad today."

Kara's eyes widened. "That's a bombshell to drop on Christmas."

"I know. Then, after I pretty much convince myself that she's just emoting, Shayne says she'll probably do it on her own if I don't help. Then, I find this story on the internet about some old guy in England, who did exactly that, strangled his wife because she had dementia and didn't want to go into a home. Needless to say, I did *not* sleep a wink."

"How serious do you think she was?"

"I don't know. I guess he's gotten a lot worse recently." I told her about my father getting lost and what my mother had said about his behavior; then, explained about the promise. "It's like my dad closed and locked all these doors and we have nowhere to go."

"Your poor mom," Kara said softly. "If he had a terminal condition like cancer and was in his right mind, it would be totally different. But he's not in his right mind because of his terminal condition."

"He's not really terminal," I said.

"It's semantics, isn't it? He's not going to get better and this is going to kill him, just slowly."

We both turned as we heard shouts from the other side of the food court. Two security guards ran down the walkway toward the front desk.

"Drive-by?" I asked.

"MVA. Lots of family. Not my case."

At night, visitors had to sign in and show identification at the front entrance. With drive-bys, these visitors were sometimes gang members trying to finish a job. With motor vehicle accidents, MVAs, it could be family members who weren't allowed in because a legal next of kin hadn't been identified or because the crisis was still being managed. This particular commotion seemed under control. I turned back to Kara.

"I thought you were going to go all Hippocratic oath on me," I said. "Tell me how there's no way I can even think about this."

"Is that what you want me to do?"

"Well, right now you sound like you think I should do it, which is kind of freaking me out more."

She shook her head. "I don't think I have a right to an opinion. But I get your mom's thought process. What if he was an ALS patient who wanted to die but waited too long and couldn't physically do it himself? His wishes didn't change but now he's trapped inside a body that doesn't work and the option's gone. To your mom, nothing's changed. Your dad is the same person who didn't want to live like this but now he doesn't have the ability to do anything about it. Assisted suicide seems like a kindness."

"That's the problem. It would be murder, not assisted suicide."

"Technically, but…"

"There's no *but*. Murder simpliciter. If this was assisted suicide, I'd be fine with it, or at least I think I would, but this is figuring out how to murder someone and not get caught."

"Are you trying to figure it out?"

"Honestly, I don't know what I am thinking. You know, every nurse on that unit up there would tell you how they have a pact with someone to help them end it if they get like my dad. But how? It's not like you can get a prescription for Nembutal."

Kara raised an eyebrow.

"Yes," I said. "I got sucked into a website claiming to sell Nembutal and then some message board about buying it from unscrupulous veterinarians in Mexico."

"Nembutal would definitely be the kindest way to do it," she said.

"Kind and totally illegal."

I took a bite from my untouched sandwich. Kara glanced at the time on her phone then did the same. We ate without speaking, needing a moment for the reality of it all to settle. There were ways to do what my mother had asked. I'd just mentioned a humane and straightforward possibility. Not simple but not exactly hard either. All about risk and willingness.

"You know what really worries me?" I said. "Exactly what Shayne said. What happens if I don't help her? Am I forcing her hand? Making her try something crazy? The person he is now, that person is going to fight. He'd hurt her."

"Without that part how do you feel?" Kara asked.

"I don't know. If it were easy? Legal? Maybe. But there are these lines, right? Going to Mexico and buying the pills is one line. Putting them in his mouth is a totally different one. Then, I think about getting caught. I'd lose my license. Go to jail. I hate that I'm even thinking about that but I am. I don't know. If he'd said this is what he wanted, if he'd looked me in the eye and said this is what I want you to do."

I stopped. He had, hadn't he? He'd said it over and over again. My mother believed he meant it. Why didn't I?

"And then, of course, Shayne could be totally wrong and I'm making myself crazy over nothing," I said. "What if my mom just bucks up like she always does and I go in there talking about all this and I'm basically telling her to kill my dad?"

"Do you think you could do it?"

I shrugged. How could I know the answer to a question like that? I'd held the hands of strangers as they took their last breaths. I desperately tried to save people who couldn't be saved on a regular basis. Death was familiar to me. But that didn't mean I knew what it was like to take a life, let alone my own father's.

Kara's pager went off. She glanced at it and rolled her eyes. "Damn it," she said. "I'm gonna have to go. How did this *tonto* even graduate medical school?" She gathered the remains of her sandwich from the table.

"I'll get the trash," I said.

"Thanks." She pulled out her phone and started texting while walking toward the ER. She stopped and looked back over her shoulder. "I would go to Mexico with you," she said as if it was nothing, as if we were planning a girl trip, bikinis and sombreros. Then, she disappeared down the dark hallway.

DECEMBER 26TH 3:00 AM

$\mathcal{K}$ara's words, "I would go to Mexico with you," were running through my head when I returned to the unit. To get to my patients on the far side, I had to walk past twelve rooms. The outer wall and door of each was glass, allowing the nurse to observe her patients from the computer station outside. The beds faced outward, propped at forty-five degrees, a standard to decrease pressure in the brain and prevent pneumonia, but it made the place look like a macabre laboratory in the dim light; nurses watching specimens on display, charting every twitch. A peculiarium.

This dystopia was my familiar. Wrists secured to beds. Tubes taped to faces. A space pulsing with beeps and buzzes. Screens of colored lines—heart, blood pressure, oxygen, intracranial pressure—dancing along in self-importance as if they alone were relevant. Families must feel like they have been dropped into the center of a mad scientist's experiment.

I arrived at my computer station and immediately Fiona approached with Gene, the charge nurse. Gene was big, both tall and broad, with a flat top haircut so sparse at the crown it was like a ring around his head. He was a giant next to tiny Fiona,

51

with her skinny arms and bleached pixie cut. But he was more cuddly teddy than dangerous grizzly and he was good at what he did. Things ran smoothly when Gene was in charge.

"Any progress?" I asked Fiona.

"Not really." She tipped her head in Mr. Collins' direction. "He doesn't seem any closer to making up his mind."

The doctors had talked to him twice before I'd gone to dinner, trying their best to help him to understand the complexities of what was happening. In a few fateful moments, his life had shifted, gone from picking what channel to watch to making the hardest decision of his life, one that likely didn't have a right answer. He was paralyzed.

Fiona shook her head. "I mean, come on. How old is she? Seventy? How can you never have thought about dying?" She said it not with coldness, but with the cynicism of someone too intimate with this kind of death, someone who has to get in line to do compressions knowing it's wrong.

"They thought about it," Gene said. "They just didn't think it was going to be today."

One of Mrs. Collins' alarms began beeping. I slid open the door and stepped in. Her blood pressure was fluctuating over wider ranges, maybe an indication that the swelling was reaching her brain stem, or maybe nothing. I silenced the alarm and watched to see if her blood pressure would go up again. It didn't. I adjusted her pillow, shifting her head so that she was straighter and appeared more comfortable. Her white, almost-translucent hair framed a tiny face that in spite of the tube secured between her lips held an eerie half-smile.

"We'll have to turn her in a few minutes," I said. I'd explained our routine of shifting sides every two hours to prevent pressure ulcers before but it was an easier way to open a conversation than saying, "So how about that craniotomy?"

"Can she hear me?" Mr. Collins asked, his voice so quiet it seemed to evaporate in the air before it reached me.

"I believe she can hear you." It was my stock answer. Plenty of patients had told me things they'd heard in the room when they were unconscious, zonked on sedation. They can hear you, no matter where they are, and if they can't, what difference does it make? Mr. Collins turned to his wife.

"Honey, I don't know what to do," he said and then waited as if she was going to respond.

I let the space fill with silence before finally saying, "Are there any questions I can answer to help you decide?"

He looked at me, his eyes puffy and red against pale and withering skin. He was older than her. I could see it now, maybe ten or even fifteen years older. A few straggling wisps of silver hair stuck out from his shiny scalp, leaning to the left as if too exhausted to stand on their own.

"What do I do?" he said, asking the one question I truly couldn't answer. The same question no one could answer for me. I took his hand. Part of me wanted to say, "I don't know. It could go either way," but another part wanted to shout, "Set her free. Let her go." I smiled softly, trying to convey compassion instead of pity. But I felt both.

"Only you know what the right answer is for you and your wife," I said. "One way to look at it is that you're on a road. The destination's been set. You don't get to pick that part. The thing you get to choose is how you travel down that road, what your wife's final journey looks like. She can go peacefully."

That was what my mother had said, wasn't it? "You could help him go *peacefully*." I did know how to do that: a morphine drip. That's what I wanted for Mrs. Collins, an opioid-padded slumber to help her slip seamlessly into that other world. But stepping out of the way so death can come is not the same as bringing it with you. Tears welled up in Mr. Collins' eyes. He squeezed my hand, then let it go to take his wife's hand again.

"What happens if they turn off that machine?" He pointed at the ventilator, as if it were the source of his dilemma. I'd already answered these questions for him and so had the doctors. Now, I was hunting for different responses, ways to say the same thing, find the words that would reach him.

"It's hard to predict," I said. "Your wife may be able to breathe on her own for a little while. But if she doesn't have the surgery, her brain will continue to swell. Eventually it will push so hard against her skull that part of it will come out through the hole at the bottom and she'll die."

"Will it hurt?" he asked.

"No," I said. "We'll make sure she's comfortable."

As I was speaking, I felt the stark contrast to my father's situation. He hadn't been given this kind of chance, a moment where my mother could have said, "Let him go. Let nature take its course." His was a slow chipping away rather than a sudden, total destruction. Did that chipping away hurt? Probably not. Not him anyway. But her. The one thing he never would have wanted.

"Does she need the surgery?" Mr. Collins asked.

"Even with the surgery, her brain will be severely damaged. She may not be able to speak or walk or feed herself. The surgery might keep her alive. But it may not be the kind of life she would want. Only you know if she'd want to take that chance. No one can predict exactly how much damage has been done, but the stroke was significant."

Mr. Collins' head fell forward onto his wife's hand and he cried. I stood behind him debating whether to give him space or to bring up her code status one more time. She needed to be "do not resuscitate" but he'd left her "full code", the standard default for most patients. If her heart stopped, which would happen when her brainstem herniated through her foramen magnum, I would push a button to call the code team. I would start CPR. We'd assault her body with chest compressions, tubes, drugs. All of it futile because her brain couldn't be fixed.

Not every stroke was like this one, certain to eventually bring death. You couldn't know until the CT scan, and even with that you couldn't be sure exactly what the outcome would be. It was the worst game of craps in the world. Mrs. Collins might come out with her life but with unbearable limitations that made it seem less than life. Not much of a win.

I backed out quietly. Sitting at my station, I watched him talk to her, maybe still hoping that she would give him the answer. I'd seen it before with other couples. She was the decision maker, the one that kept everything together. He hadn't expected to be here with the weight of the world on him. He was supposed to go first. I thought of my father and understood too well Mr. Collins' predicament. If I could ask my dad, it would make it so much easier. If I knew with absolute certainty what he really wanted me to do, I could do it. Or at least I thought I could.

THE NEXT TWO days passed in the haze that twelve-hour night shifts become, a bubble of life drifting through a darkened world. There's just enough time to get home, take a shower, sleep, and start all over again. When I'm working, the hospital world moves to the forefront, life exists only between those walls. Everything else recedes.

Kara and I barely saw each other, our two worlds running parallel. Hers, in the operating room. Mine, on the unit. Except for her towel in the bathroom and a half-finished coffee on the kitchen table, I might as well have been alone in the house.

Mrs. Collins died at 6:00 am on my last shift. Mr. Collins never made any decisions, but he never left her side either, seeming to sleep upright in his chair waiting for the answer he never got. As the alarms went off, I climbed up on her bed, clasped my hands together on her chest, and began pumping. I pleaded with my eyes, but Mr. Collins seemed numb, backing away from the bed as the room filled with people.

Mrs. Collins' fragile ribs snapped beneath my hands. The code was pointless. No matter what we did she was going to die.

I wanted to beg Mr. Collins, "Just say stop and we'll stop." When families see what a code really looks like, they often end it. It isn't like the movies where people sputter and cough, then open their eyes. It's brutal and desperate. This was the opposite of Jack Tindall, the English man who'd strangled his wife, this was hanging on when everything was telling you to let go.

Mr. Collins did not end the code. He vanished from view, absorbed into the background, as if willing himself to be there and not be there at the same time. I didn't understand. The decision was so obvious to me. But I'd been here so many times. Mr. Collins had only been here once. He was waiting for something life wasn't offering, something I wanted myself, certainty. How long do you wait until you realize no answer is coming?

The code seemed to go on forever. Another nurse took over CPR. I felt sick to my stomach. We do this too often, code people we shouldn't. Fight when there is nothing to fight for.

Dr. Ivanov called it after twenty minutes, and the team dispersed. The room looked like an accident scene, fragments scattered across a highway. I covered Mrs. Collins' body and straightened her head on the pillow. I tossed used supplies and wheeled out the crash cart. Only when things looked almost exactly like before, did Mr. Collins return to his place at her side. I was exhausted and facing at least an extra hour of charting before I could even think about leaving.

"Take as much time as you need," I said but I wondered if there would ever be enough time. He was still there when I left. I don't know how long they let him stay or how they got him to leave.

At home, I climbed into bed without taking a shower, dropping my scrubs on the floor and falling into the softness of my mattress. I closed my eyes. My body still felt like it was doing compressions, rhythmically pounding Mrs. Collins' chest as I drifted off to sleep.

In my dream, she got the morphine drip. I stood at her

bedside, turning the drug up and up and up, knowing that I was crossing a line, no longer just making her comfortable but actively trying to kill her. But I was calm, like the opioid was coursing through me, making me cold, numb. Then, suddenly just before she died, she grabbed my hand. She shook her head violently back and forth screaming, "No! No! No!"

REUNION 2009

I sensed someone come up behind me. It was 4:00 am and I was rushing through my patient charting. I'd been a nurse for just under two years and had only been off orientation in the ICU a month. Thirty minutes into every shift, I was two hours behind. I was trying to get everything I'd done all night into the computer before the doctors started coming by. True rounds happened on the day shift but in the early hours the residents and fellows would check the charts, then come by to ask questions. The more they found in the chart, the less likely they were to talk to me and make me even more behind schedule. Maybe I'd get out on time for once.

"Any changes overnight?" a vaguely familiar female voice said.

I turned around expecting to find one of the residents but there was Kara, one of my best friends from high school. I stared. I recognized her but my mind wouldn't believe it was her. It wouldn't let me place her here, like her green scrubs and white coat were a disguise and someone else was underneath it all.

Kara and I had been part of a best friend triad with another girl, Jenn. We spent virtually every lunchtime of junior year jammed in the backseat of Jenn's mustang. It was *Three Stooges* meets *Charlie's Angels*. I was the quirky one with kinky hair and thrift shop clothes, always looking for a punchline. Jenn was tall and blond but not girly, a beach bum who could kick your ass. Kara was the pretty one, dark hair and eyes, and gullible in a way that made people underestimate her intelligence. She was constantly swearing at us in Spanish, which was the funniest in the world when you were three near-grown women jammed into a tin can.

"Bernie?" she said, appearing to be having a similar problem recognizing me in the moment. The last time we'd seen each other was at my hand-fasting seventeen years earlier. Jenn hadn't come. She'd stopped talking to me when I became a pagan. Kara and I had simply lost touch, drifted out of friendship as adult lives pulled us in different directions.

"You're a nurse here?" Kara asked. She was almost the same as I remembered her, just a few grey hairs mixed in with her black mane. I got up and hugged her.

"I am," I said. "And you look suspiciously like an MD."

"I just took an attending position."

Terri, my nursing aide, popped her head out of our patient's room. "I've got other stuff to do," she said.

"Sorry. I'll be right there," I said.

"Can we catch up later?" I said to Kara. "I have tons to do."

She slipped me a post-it with her phone number.

WE MET for drinks a week later at El Coyote on Beverly, the quintessential LA watering hole where you are as likely to have someone pull a gun on you over a parking spot as you are to run into someone famous. We made small talk like strangers on a blind date as we waited for a table: "I wonder how old this place is." "Parking around here is crazy." "Hope it doesn't take long to get a seat." If we stayed in this zone, the night was going to be a bust.

A hostess beckoned us with a wave. Candles flickered in red glass holders on each table as we followed her to our seat. *One drink and I'm outta here,* I thought. Whatever had made us friends in high school appeared to be gone. We weren't the same people we had been. We sat in awkward silence until the two golden margaritas we'd order arrived. I was bringing the drink to my lips when Kara finally said something.

"You're so smart," she said. "Why didn't you become a doctor?"

I set my glass down in disbelief. "Really?" I said, pulling out my old acting skills to feign indignation. "Are you really asking me that?" I couldn't believe she'd actually spoken those words. She was a rabbit setting its own trap.

"What?" she said, confused.

"That's like the number one question you never ask a nurse. It implies a) that doctors are better than nurses, b) that every nurse wanted to be a doctor, and c) that nurses are dumber than doctors."

She shifted uncomfortably in her seat. "I didn't mean it like that. I meant..."

I cut her off, amazed she was falling for it. "It's a different job, you know. You don't go up to a hairstylist and say, 'Why didn't you become a doctor?' You don't go up to a mechanic and ask, 'Why didn't you become a doctor?'"

"Okay, okay," she said, putting up a hand to stop me. "Point taken. I'm sorry. Let me try again. Tell me how you came to be a nurse?"

I took a deep breath. "Well," I said, then gave a long pause as if I were generously forgiving her. "I really wanted to be a doctor."

For a second her face stayed confused, then we both laughed so loud and hard I thought someone was going to ask us to leave.

It was like old times. Me, the snarky funny one. Kara, my favorite victim. We were back to where we'd been in high school, so close it was like we were related. We only had to fill each other in on the details.

"Okay," she said, when we finally pulled ourselves back together. "I'm a moron for asking that question. But the last time I saw you you were barefoot, in a homemade wedding dress and everyone was drinking that stuff." She scrunched her nose.

"Mead," I said.

"Yes, mead. The journey from there to here has to be interesting."

"Well, last time I saw you I was barefoot in a homemade wedding dress and you were *not* going to medical school so same question right back at you."

"You first."

I didn't know how to begin. How do you cram decades into a few sentences? I'd opened, then immediately closed a Facebook account a few months ago when someone sent me a post called, *What have you been doing for the last ten, twenty, thirty years?* The unspoken expectation to make everything seem great had crippled me. The truth for most people—or for me anyway—was there was no plan. I had no idea how I ended up where I was.

"Okay, Handfasting 1992. Shayne and I are living at The Farm in our Airstream. Total pagan-hippie heaven, growing our own food, raising animals, everyone sharing everything."

"It was that old guy's place, right?"

"Calvin. He lets people live there in trailers and tents in exchange for work. He's a small-time actor, commercials, and bit parts, then he's got this place. The dream was I write plays and Shayne acts in them. He did some Shakespeare stuff at the Will Geer theater, then about seven years ago, they actually put on one of my plays."

"How cool," she said.

"It was. We were all high, thinking it was the beginning of everything but then it kind of turned out to be the end. After about four years of nothing else happening, I realized that was my moment. That was it. Then I got pregnant, and I don't know, everything seemed wrong. I started nursing school right after Jax was born."

"Cute name."

"Until you try to say Jax's truck or Jax's blanket. Then, it's a mouthful."

"How old is he now?"

"Almost four," I said. "It started to seem crazy to be living in a trailer. There's another family with kids but I don't know. I guess the whole pagan thing turned out to be Shayne's and not mine. And the communal living was…"

I stopped. I'd rented an apartment in West LA a month earlier and I wasn't sure myself what was going on. I didn't know if I was leaving Shayne or The Farm or both. I looked at Kara sitting across from me suddenly struck by how much I needed someone other than Shayne or my family. I wanted to tell her everything. But what if it was too much? What if I dumped too much madness on her at the first sitting and snuffed out our momentarily rekindled friendship?

I forced a laugh. "You know what? There was just too much dirt. It was like we were camping all the time. I wondered, 'Am I gonna live in this trailer for the rest of my life with this kid and all this dirt?'"

She smiled tentatively, as if she suspected I was leaving something out. "So, you went to nursing school, then you and Shayne moved to West LA?"

"I moved to West LA."

"Divorced?"

"Never legally married so I can call it whatever I want."

"Separated?"

"I'm separated but I might have forgotten to mention it to Shayne."

Kara had been sipping on her drink the whole time I was talking. My margarita was still full. I picked the glass up. The sweet and sour mixed on my tongue. I really needed a drink. I've really needed a drink like every day of my adult life.

"Boo-yah. Beat that, mofo," I said rehashing a ridiculous thing I used to say in high school, pretending that everything I'd said was funny, and that I didn't feel totally pathetic.

"Hard act to follow." Kara seemed to be proceeding cautiously, tiptoeing through the minefield of my failures. "So, starting point, your handfasting, which was by far the most unique event I've ever attended."

"You're welcome," I said, dipping my head in a little bow.

"I finished college and had no idea what I was going to do. After about six months of smoking pot and watching *Knight Rider* reruns at my parents' house, I went back up to Portland to see some university friends, and I met Eliot at a party."

"Eliot?" I said.

"Husband." She flashed me a ring with a stone so big it could have its own TV show. "He'd just started medical school. He kinda talked me into it."

"He talked you into medical school?"

"Pretty much. It's not much of a stretch. I was a biochem major. Everybody I knew was going."

"I didn't know you wanted to be a doctor."

"I guess I didn't know either but it runs in the family," Kara said. I'd forgotten that both her parents were doctors. "It's a good fit," she continued. "Especially trauma. The hours can be tough but I love it."

"Kids?"

"Nope. Not in our plans."

"Never?"

"I don't think we're kid people."

"Good call."

"You mean, you agree that I'm not a kid person?" she teased.

"No, but kids are not always what you expect."

The waiter arrived and asked for our orders. I took my time mulling over the menu, stalling. Hoping my words would disappear, dissolve like the salt on the rim of my margarita glass.

I wanted to believe it was a phase, a long one. Terrible twos progressing to terrible threes on steroids. Jax had zero structure. But I was noticing how different he was from all the other kids. He would get possessed by rage, suddenly exploding, using anything within reach as a weapon. Sometimes he hurt other people but mostly he hurt himself, banging his head against the wall, literally—blood-drawing, concussion-forming banging.

I'd finally really grasped what I was dealing with a week earlier. We were at Serrania Park. Jax climbed to the top of the slide but instead of going down, he turned around and stood there. I waited, wondering if he wanted me to help him down. Then, without a sound, he flung himself face forward off the ladder, as if trying to fly. He plummeted to the earth like a sack of potatoes. I thought he was going to die. He smashed into the sand and started screaming.

I ran to him and picked him up. His face was scraped up, sand imbedded in his cheeks. A trickle of blood ran out of his nose and his right wrist was crooked, obviously broken. He was crying and letting me comfort him. But he had a look in his eyes, a glint of satisfaction, that terrified me. He'd done exactly what he'd intended to do. I was a pawn in the game, whatever it was. I'd started to cry, too.

Kara and I ordered food and a second round of margaritas. The waiter walked away. I fiddled with the menu pretending I was deciding on something else.

"And?" she said.

I could feel my heart pounding in my chest. This was the moment of truth. I was alone. I needed someone. A friend.

Someone who was mine, not enmeshed with Shayne and the sprites that animated his world.

"I think my son is..." I paused. I'd never put it into words before. He was young, maybe too young for the label I was about to give him. But I, more than anyone, knew that something wasn't right. "I think my son is mentally ill."

December 28th, 1:00 pm

I was forcing myself, with limited success, to focus on my upcoming evening out with Kara as I pulled up in front of my parents' house around one. We had three nights off before New Year's Eve, then five after that. But Mrs. Collins' death and my dream about her had left me unsettled. And Shayne's words kept nagging at me. As much as I hated to admit it, his intuitiveness and refusal to pass judgement on others sometimes led him to see things I missed. I couldn't imagine my mother doing something on her own because regular people didn't do that kind of thing. But they did. Jack Tindall had. He was desperate. Was my mother?

I squinted as I got out of the car. Even with shades the afternoon sun was too bright. I hadn't been in full daylight since Christmas and this first day off, where I got only a few hours of sleep before trying to rejoin the daytime world, was always a tough start. I came around the car only to stop abruptly at the path to the front door. The top half of one of my mother's cacti was lying across the first step. One section of the enormous plant had snapped in the middle, too much height for its thin core. It looked like a discarded limb, adding a grim quality to what was already feeling like a strange day. I carefully stepped around it and walked into the house.

Colleen and I had each planned to spend half the day with Dad so Mom and Laura, Mom's only granddaughter, could bond over lunch and a mall trip. I found my sister and father at the kitchen table, a partially-eaten stack of finger sandwiches and a photo album in front of them. I immediately felt tense.

This life had slipped into the background while I was at work. It was hard to believe that earlier this morning, I'd been trying to save Mrs. Collins. The hospital world was somehow easier to cope with. Bad stuff happens to other people in the ICU, not me. There, I am the strong one, the one who knows what's going on, the person with answers. In the real world, I'm answer-free.

"That's your son Adam on his fifteenth birthday," Colleen said.

"I know my own son," Dad snapped.

Colleen sighed then pointed at me as I came through the door.

"Look who's here," she said feigning surprise, as if she hadn't seen me through the window and waved just a second ago.

"Hi, Dad," I offered as brightly as I could manage. "Browsing photos of the good ol' days?"

Dad looked back and forth between me and Colleen and said, "I'm going to take out the trash."

"Good call," I said as he stood up and headed to the bedrooms downstairs. Trash was another mainstay, like walks. He took the trash out about twenty times a day.

"Same?" I asked as I sat down next to my sister and pulled the photo album toward me, flipping through pages without focusing on the images.

"He seems to have a shorter fuse. I think he's gotten mad at me more today than he has my whole life. I had to go out front and take five."

Dad came back into the kitchen and Colleen handed him a small plastic bag from under the sink. I wondered if she'd made fake trash for him like I did. He always seemed so disappointed when he found empty bins. He headed out the front door with his prize.

"Mom told me he's getting worse," I said. "He's taking walks at night."

"She didn't say anything to me." I thought I heard an edge in her voice, like if Mom hadn't mentioned it to her it couldn't possibly be true. But I was pretty groggy, the edge was probably me.

"I think it's new," I said. I'd been ruminating over whether to tell my sister what my mother had said. Telling her and not telling her were equally troubling options. But if I was going to start trying to convince Mom to put Dad in a nursing home, my sister would need to understand why.

The rusty creak of the mailbox made us both turn to look out the open window. Dad checked inside the box, then snapped it shut. He disappeared from view then reappeared with a broom and began sweeping the street between my car and the curb. The fervency in his actions was new. Everything was turned up a notch.

Colleen checked her phone. "I'm gonna have to get going soon," she said. "The kids are with Liam's parents and they'll start melting down soon."

"The kids?" I asked. Colleen was not one to bad-mouth her kids.

"Liam's parents. They can only last about four hours with the little ones these days."

I could only imagine. Colleen's never-ending supply of children wore me out from a distance.

"Isn't Liam on Christmas break?" I asked.

"He and Adam decided to go on a hike." She smiled, but I heard a hint of resentment. Our brother Adam always made time for the fun stuff when he was in town: Get-togethers, hikes, roller skating. He was rarely around when bad stuff went down. He'd never spent more than ten minutes alone with Dad once the dementia was apparent. He'd say things that made me want to hit him like, "It's really tough to see Dad like this," as if it weren't hard for me or Colleen or Mom. My sister and I were going to have to be allies, a situation neither of us would relish. But what choice did I have? If I wasn't going to figure out a way to euthanize my dad, then this was the only answer.

"I need to tell you something," I said. "But you can't get all Catholic on me." The statement had sounded more innocuous in my head than coming out of my mouth. I wasn't intentionally trying to provoke her but the adversarial relationship came naturally to me. I waited for her to get defensive, but she didn't. "Mom asked me to kill Dad."

"What?" she said. "For real?"

"I think so. I'm pretty sure she thought it was a death-with-dignity issue, like Brittany Maynard."

"Who the heck is Brittany Maynard?"

"That girl with the brain tumor who moved to Oregon so she could kill herself," I said. Clearly she'd forgotten the argument we'd had, lending more credence to my theory that she cared more about being right than the content of a discussion. "You know, *People* magazine. Assisted suicide."

She nodded. The front door opened. Dad came in, grabbed a set of keys from the key hooks and went back out front. A few seconds later I heard a car door slam. I stood up to look out the window.

"Is *The Club* on the truck?" I asked. We hadn't been able to get Mom to sell the truck or even hide the keys but we had extracted one concession from her, an anti-theft device called The Club on the steering wheel. That way Dad could have the keys but not drive. Amazingly, it worked. The battle shifted away from my mother to the vehicle, which he was convinced was broken.

My sister nodded. "He took me out to 'fix it,'" she said with air quotes, "about ten times this morning."

I looked around but couldn't see him. Then, I caught a glimpse as he disappeared down the left side of the house, taking the side way down to the backyard.

"He's going to the workshop," I said, turning back to my sister who was staring at me. "What?" I said after she just kept staring.

"You know you can't do that," Colleen said.

"I didn't say I was going to. I'm just telling you what happened," I said, thankful I hadn't mentioned Mexico.

"You aren't God."

"That's really not something you need to remind me of," I said.

"It's not the same as that girl. It's not the same at all."

"I know. Trust me."

"Life is sacred."

I stopped myself from responding. We weren't getting anywhere and in a way I agreed. Life is a gift, amazing and fragile. But she and I weren't talking about the same thing. We drew the life line somewhere different. She was talking about a heartbeat, but the heart is the greatest liar of all. A heart is nothing without a brain and not just any brain, the good stuff, the stuff that makes you you. Your memories: A first kiss. The smell of your new baby. Everything taken for granted until it is slipping away.

"I'm not talking about doing it," I said. "I'm trying to tell you that Mom is really stressed. I don't know how stressed. I'm worried she might do something crazy."

"Like?"

"Like put a bag over his head."

"Would that work?" she said with astonishment.

"In theory. But someone would have to hold his hands down or drug him or something."

"You've been thinking about this."

"In the abstract, yes. But if she tries something, he'll fight her. That's what I'm scared of."

"What do you do at the hospital?" she asked.

"What do you mean?"

"Don't you help people die?"

"People die there but we don't kill them. Nursing is mostly about *not* killing people."

"But if they are brain-dead?"

Her choice of words surprised me. Just a few months earlier we'd argued about a teenager who'd been declared brain-dead by a hospital in Oakland, but whose mother rejected the concept and kept her on life support at home for five years. The poor girl had finally physically left this world earlier in the year. Colleen wouldn't even use the phrase brain death in that discussion. "Life is not a mental construct," she'd said. "Life is an all or nothing deal. It's in God's hands."

"We let patients die naturally," I said. "We don't kill them. We remove manmade things that interfere with their ability to die the natural death that God intended."

Colleen frowned, her turned-down mouth looked just like Mom's. "I'm trying my darnedest to have a conversation with you and not bring my religious beliefs into it just like you asked. Can't you stop doing that and be civil?" she said.

She was right. We needed to be on the same team and we were arguing. She was playing as fair as she could manage and I wasn't. But I'd had this conversation with her in my head a bunch of times and it was like some of the words just had to come out. I knew I shouldn't say them but they already existed and had to get free.

"I'm just tired," I said. "I've only slept like four hours."

"Are there special medications?" she asked.

"You mean at the hospital?"

"No, like what that girl did. Assisted suicide."

"Yeah, it's completely different. They give them, I don't even know for sure. Probably pentobarbital."

"Is that something you can get?"

"Me? Or do you mean can anyone get it?"

"Would Mom be able to get something like that? Is it legal? You said you were worried she'd try something. Is that something she could try?"

"It's legal in the sense that a doctor can prescribe it but it has to be for a legitimate reason. And you can't use it to kill someone. That's the illegal part."

Colleen didn't answer. She stared at me for a long time, then stood up and pulled out the coffee maker. I paused. The conversation had derailed. I had to get us back on course.

"We have to talk about nursing homes," I said.

"We can't send him to a nursing home. We promised."

"I was *six*."

"A promise is a promise," she said.

"You were *nine*."

She shook her head.

"You realize that you're saying no and no, right?" I said. "You're not offering any solutions."

Colleen turned the coffee machine on and sat back down at the table. She pulled the photo album toward her and flipped through the pages. The room filled with the thick, rich smell of coffee. I inhaled deeply as if the scent alone might wake me up. I didn't say anything else. Apparently, neither my mother nor my sister considered youthful naïvety a valid excuse for not taking that promise seriously.

Colleen turned the photo album toward me and pointed to a picture of Dad and Mom from when they were stationed in San Diego with the Navy. They were kids, married only a few months. Dad, twenty. Mom, eighteen. The picture was blurred, taken while they were dancing. There was motion to it, like a film clip about to move forward. I couldn't quite make out their faces, but the whole image was alive with joy.

"She," Colleen said, pointing at the youthful figure of our mother, "promised him."

I nodded.

"We don't know the people in that picture," Colleen said.

I stared at those young lovers. They'd shared a whole world without us. They made promises we never knew about, whispered hopes and dreams from pillow to pillow in the night. They knew each other in a way we never would.

"I get it," I said. "That's my point. Do you want to come over here and find them both black and blue because she's tried to save him the only way she thinks she can?" I stared, waiting for the light to click on, waiting for her to get it.

Something in the front of the house caught my eye. Dad stood by the mailbox, in his bare hands was the broken piece of my mother's cactus. He was trying to jam the top back onto the bottom.

"Crap. Dad's got Mom's cactus," I said.

Suddenly, the phone rang. Colleen and I both jumped.

Colleen checked the number on the screen. "It's Mom."

"Tell her everything is fine." I wasn't about to have my mother give up her day with her granddaughter because of a cactus. I could handle a cactus.

*W*hen I got outside to Dad and the cactus, he looked at me, perplexed.

"This thing's gotta go there but it won't stay," he said.

"Let's work on that." I tried to sound agreeable. Questions about what he was doing or why would only irritate him. "I wonder what tools we need."

"I have tools in my workshop," he said.

"Good call."

He put down the cactus, and we headed back into the house together.

"Grab some tweezers, will you?" I whispered to Colleen who was talking to Mom and pouring my coffee. She gave me a thumbs up. I held my breath as Dad went down the death stairs facing forward, something he forbade us to do as kids.

In the workshop, he sifted through boxes looking for who knows what, while I hunted down work gloves. His hands were most certainly filled with cactus spines, but he didn't seem to notice, his sensations dulled by the same poor circulation that was starving his brain.

"This will work," he announced, holding up a two-foot piece

of rebar that had been painted white, a victim of last summer's infamous painting spree. One afternoon while Mom remained blissfully unaware, Dad had picked up every one of her garden statues and painted them white. They were souvenirs from family camping trips and the few retirement adventures they'd managed in their RV before dementia hijacked their lives. Dwarfs, butterflies, turtles, saints, fairy houses transformed into ghost memories that haunted the yard.

I showed him the gloves. "I think we need these, too."

He gave me a thumbs up. "We need those."

To someone unaware of his dementia, the moment might have seemed normal—except the part where we were fixing a broken cactus. But he hadn't said the word "gloves." He was playing along, acting like he knew what was happening when he didn't. He was good at it. But he had no idea why I was suggesting gloves. He probably didn't remember what they were called nor where they fit into the world.

Whenever I noticed these lapses, I wondered when my siblings and I would become something he couldn't place, when he would forget what we were called and not be able to fit us into whatever remained of his world. Who would go last? Adam, because he was the oldest? My sister, because she was the most present? Me? How could it possibly be me? The youngest. The black sheep. A role we had each auditioned for but I, the pagan dancing around the May pole on Beltane, had won in spite of everything.

Colleen met us at the sliding glass door and handed me the tweezers.

"Everything okay?" I asked Colleen, careful not to say Mom or Helen. My dad hadn't shown concern about my mother's whereabouts yet, and I didn't want to start the cascade of questions. Colleen nodded. I held Dad by the wrist. "Why don't we go have a cup of coffee while I get those stickers out of your hands?"

Dad turned over his hands, little cactus spines shining in his palms. "How did those get there?"

"I don't know. But I'll take care of them."

The three of us sat at the table. My sister passed me my mom's reading glasses and held a flashlight over my father's hands while I pulled out stickers, setting them one by one in the saucer Colleen had set at the center of the table. The light in her hands trembled. I reached out and held it steady.

"It's not for us to decide what life is worth living," she said.

"How'd those get there?" Dad said again, oblivious to our exchange.

"You picked up a cactus," I said bluntly. Colleen glared as if I'd shared the bigger secret we were actually discussing. "Can you get me a lamp or something?" I asked. "This is gonna take a while."

A few moments later Colleen placed an old desk lamp on the table between us, its base plastered with faded stickers. She plugged it in and bent the arm until the beam pointed at my dad's hands. I stared at the thing, incredulous.

"Where'd you find *that*?" I asked.

"Mom uses it for embroidery."

I wondered if the relic meant anything to her. Was that ancient desk lamp entwined with the events of that night so many years ago or was it just another thing Mom couldn't throw away? Did Colleen even remember?

"Where's Helen?" Dad suddenly asked.

"Mom's at the mall with Laura," I said.

"I don't think Helen should be hanging out with that Laura," Dad said. "The neighbors never liked her."

Colleen got up and collected her stuff. "I really have to go," she said. "Do you want me to talk to Mom?"

Part of me did. Let her try to deal with the whole mess, conjure some mythical answer between *no* and *no*. But my mother had asked me. I was the one my mother had reached out to. Maybe it was because I was a nurse. But she'd asked me for a reason. I wasn't going to let it go that easily.

Our parents always tried to treat us equally but I always felt Colleen was Mom's favorite and I was Dad's. It wasn't anything specific. It was the pride and pleasure in her voice when she talked about Colleen and Liam and their kids, how she looked at them. It used to drive me nuts when Shayne and I were trying to get pregnant and didn't seem to be able to. We'd be at a family gathering and my sister's gaggle of kids would be running around and I'd catch my mom gazing at them. Their mere existence giving her joy. My sister made kids by accident. It took me years of effort to make one and when I finally did? Well, I couldn't even get that right.

"I'll talk to her," I said.

"Okay," Dad answered. Colleen kissed him on the cheek and left.

I tediously pulled the never-ending supply of spines from his hand. Every couple of minutes he said, "How did those get there?" or "Where's Helen?"

I answered truthfully again a few times but then starting making things up: "I think a porcupine came in the house." "Mom's in the backyard." "You were sewing." "Mom's at the hardware store." Each answer got the exact same response: "Oh." Then, he returned to peering at the tweezers as I pulled out the stickers that seemed to be multiplying in his palms.

Once I almost said, "You have dementia, Dad. You're losing your mind." But I didn't. I'm not sure whether it was because I was afraid he would understand and be sad or if I knew he wouldn't understand at all and would just say, "Oh."

"Do you want to go for a walk?" I offered once I thought I'd gotten all the stickers out. The sun might help reset my internal clock and taking him out was likely easier than preventing his escape later. By the time we were halfway up the hill though, I was out of breath. Dad, not even winded, charged ahead, maybe forgetting I was there. At seventy-five with dementia, he was in better physical shape than me.

"Dad! Wait," I called.

He turned around and in that moment he looked completely present, not lost, not surprised to find me there. Me, the baby lagging behind. Me, the whiner, the weak one he doted on. More than anything I wanted him to say, "Want a ride, Bumblebee?" then to lift me up, carry me, to be my indomitable father rescuing his baby from the treachery of life. But, of course, he didn't. He couldn't, neither literally nor figuratively. I was on my own.

Once we were back at the house, I took him down to the TV room. I'd decided to learn a game on the PlayStation so Jax and I could play something together. Colleen and I had jointly purchased the system. Technically, it was Mom's Christmas present but it was really for the kids. With Dad's dementia, it was harder and harder for them to visit. This way they could hopefully have fun even when Mom wasn't completely available to them.

Dad sat on the couch watching me trying to figure out the game. After a little while, he put his hand out for the controller as if he wanted a turn. I gave it to him. He made no connection between the device in his hand and what was happening on the screen and instead set the controller on the ground and nudged it toward me with his foot. He laughed. I nudged it back. Soon we were both laughing as we pushed the controller back and forth between our feet.

It felt wonderful. I couldn't remember the last time we'd laughed together, the last time we'd both connected with something in a shared reality and laughed. Could the hours he spent disconnected be canceled out by a single moment of joy? Maybe Colleen was right. Maybe these moments had an immeasurable value.

"Dad?" I said.

He looked up at me. Everything we'd just shared, the happiness, the laughter, hung in the air. I felt the connection, like he was there, like he could hear me, truly hear me.

"Are you happy?" I asked.

He stared as if pondering my question, carefully considering his answer. I half-expected him to smile and say, "Of course not, Bumblebee. This is exactly what I didn't want. Do whatever you have to do to make it right." If he said that, would I do it? He picked up the controller and handed it to me.

"Where's Helen?" he said and as if in response, the front door creaked open upstairs.

"We're back," my mother announced.

"TV room," I shouted, feeling as if she'd interrupted his answer to me but knowing that it was a delusion, that the answer was as far away as it had been three days ago on Christmas.

Dad glanced around the room, unable to connect the distant voice to anything. Mom came in. Anxiety rose off her, steam from a kettle, as she fussed over Dad like she needed to make sure I hadn't damaged him while she was gone. For Mom, the only thing worse than being with Dad was being away from him.

"Did you have a good time?" I asked the question to the room, not really directing it to either of them. My niece Laura nodded but was hanging back, a strained smile on her face. I thought I understood. She'd grown wary, protective of herself. Don't get too close. Don't need Grandma Rogers too much. Don't want her. Grandpa needs all her mothering and grandmothering energy.

Colleen's first four kids had known different grandparents. Laura was really the one who experienced the total shift, who saw my dad change and then watched my mother shape herself around that change. Sometimes I wondered if she felt gypped. I know I did.

"Mom, I need to talk to you," I said.

"It's been a long day. Can we talk another time?"

"I don't know if it can wait. It's about what you said on Christmas."

My mother looked from me to Laura. It was like a hologram of my sister hovering. I knew we couldn't have this conversation in front of her. But I didn't know how much time I had.

"I'm tuckered out," my mom said. "I was hoping you could take Laura home for me."

I stood there, wondering if she knew what I was actually asking. She spoke so often not in words but in gestures and looks that she expected us to interpret. Right now, she seemed content, happy to have my father to fuss over. Maybe all my worry was wrong. Maybe I'd let Shayne put ideas in my head. I considered pressing the issue but I was tired and that imaginary world where I had no problems, the one with Kara and drinks and loud music, was waiting for me.

"So, everything's okay?" I said.

She looked at me, a slight confused expression on her face. "Of course."

I hugged and kissed both my parents goodbye. Then, Laura and I left. But as we pulled away I wondered if I'd let it go too easily. For just a second, I'd felt sure. But the more I thought about it, I wondered if I'd just fooled myself.

THE SECRET 1984

*a*dam, Colleen, and I watched silently as Mom placed dinner plates in front of us, a Swanson potpie at the center of each, like a prize on display. Frozen chicken potpie was our standard meal when our parents went out without us. Mom rounded the table, kissing cheeks.

"Be good," she said, then left with Dad.

As soon as their car pulled out of the driveway, Adam picked up his plate and disappeared without a word. He and Dad had finished his studio apartment the day before and the three of us had spent the afternoon carting boxes of stuff to our now separate spaces. For the first time in our lives, Colleen and I had our own rooms. I was thirteen, Colleen, almost sixteen, and Adam, eighteen.

A few minutes later, the thumping of muffled rock music reverberated through the floor, as if a giant creature were pounding its way through the earth below the house in rhythm to Quiet Riot's "Come on Feel the Noise." Suddenly, it stopped.

"Thank God for headphones," Colleen said.

I split the lightly browned piecrust with a knife. Steam rose from the crack. I blew to cool the always dangerously hot gravy. Colleen poked at her food with a fork, then stood up and dumped the whole thing into the trash. She put her index finger to her lips.

"Shh," she said.

After putting away her dish, my sister stood at the end of the table and watched as I picked off pieces of crust and lined them up at the edge of my plate to save for last. The crust was the best part.

"Seriously?" Colleen said and rolled her eyes. She started to leave, but then turned back. "I'm gonna need that lamp back, okay? It wasn't a gift."

She walked out and left me alone. Her snottiness couldn't dampen my excitement. I'd been waiting for my parents' night out the whole week. When I was certain Colleen was in her room, I grabbed a matchbook from the drawer by the stove and slipped it into my pocket. My stomach twisted as I sat back down at the table.

The pie's heat forced me to eat slowly, which was good. Hopefully, my siblings would be well-occupied before I ventured out on my mission. Once I finished eating, I headed to my new room, checking to see that my sister's door was closed. I reached into my pillowcase and retrieved the gold jewelry box that my birthday necklace had come in. I opened it. Two cigarettes rolled from side to side.

Three weeks in and ninth grade was a budding disaster. I'd been moderately popular in middle school, the much-appreciated class clown who knew just how far to take a joke without getting into trouble with the teacher. I'd expected high school to be the same but they teased me for my uncontrollable mass of frizzy, brown-red hair and my makeup free face. I'd earned a solid spot on the geek squad. A drastic and instant image change was the only way to salvage things. For the bargain price of a dollar, Keith Munster, who spent the school day leaning against the back wall of the gym smoking, sold me two cigarettes. I was going to take the express lane to cool.

I peered out of my room to confirm that my sister's door was still closed then bolted through my parent's room to the back stairs. The grass was wet. My Vans were damp and cold by the time I got to the far end of the backyard. I looked up at the house expecting my brother or sister to be in pursuit of me, the tense energy of my exploit having alerted them somehow, but the house remained quiet and dark.

I tucked behind the coop that Adam had dubbed the Chicken Hilton and pulled out my contraband. Like a good salesman, Keith had demonstrated how to hold, light, and pose with a cigarette. I imagined myself with him, taking long, seriously cool drags as the other kids reconsidered their ridiculous first impressions of me.

The dry paper stuck to my lip and the bitter tobacco smell assaulted my nostrils as I struck a match. I stared at the glow until the flame almost burned my fingers, then lit the cigarette and took a shallow drag. I immediately began hacking. My throat burned as if I'd inhaled fire itself.

I held the cigarette away from my face and coughed. It felt as though layers of tissue were stripping off and being expelled. I tried again, inhaling as shallowly as possible. Saliva flooded my mouth. I was going to vomit. I tossed the cigarette to the ground and crushed it under my shoe as I retched. When I finally stopped, I hadn't actually vomited—just dry heaved.

A lump of nausea hung in my throat like a hairball. I felt terrible, sure that come Monday, somehow all the kids would know. They'd know my failure as certainly as if I wore a sign around my neck that said, "GEEK." I looked down at the barely smoked but totally smashed cigarette, clear evidence that I indeed lacked some vital element of cool. I emerged from behind the coop, spitting to purge the aftertaste.

I was just about to cross the lawn when I saw someone hop

our fence and start up the stairs. I almost screamed, but then recognized the figure as Liam, my brother's best friend. He must have forgotten that Adam had moved into the studio that afternoon. My sister stepped out onto the balcony. She took him by the hand, and they disappeared into the darkness of the house.

I climbed the stairs, thoughts swirled through my mind, unhinged by light-headedness. All I wanted to do was get back inside and pretend the smoking thing had never happened. I reached for the sliding glass door. Locked. I tugged harder. But it was definitely locked.

"Great," I said.

Of course, my sister had locked the door. How would she know I was outside? As far as she was concerned, Bernie the dork was quietly reading in her room as usual. I mulled my options. Adam was definitely less likely to tattle than Colleen.

I walked to the studio door and knocked. No answer. Chances were he was still blasting out his eardrums with heavy metal. That's probably why Liam had to go upstairs. I knocked harder. Still, no answer.

"Bonehead!" I shouted, kicking the door.

I crept around the side of the house, the dirt path packed and smooth from three months of Dad and Adam working the extra space into livability. The front door, of course, was locked too. I dutifully checked under a few pots like in the movies, even though I had no reason to think my parents kept an extra key that I didn't know about.

I considered the doorbell and its faint, warm glow. I needed to get inside before my parents came home, and I had no real sense of what time it was. If Liam answered, I was set. He wouldn't rat me out like my sister. And there was a good chance that he was right there in the kitchen raiding our fridge. It was like they didn't have food at his house.

I rang the doorbell. The seconds ticked by. I began to feel nauseated again. Finally, the door opened. My sister frowned down at me, appearing taller than usual because of the step up into the house.

"What are you doing outside?" she said.

My stomach turned. "Nothing," I said.

She made a show of sniffing the air. I pushed by her and ran to the bathroom, locking the door behind me. I leaned over the toilet and gagged. Once again, the nausea didn't develop into anything. It stayed lodged in my throat, a nagging sickness caught somewhere between my stomach and mouth. I brushed my teeth and got in the shower.

Only later, when I was lying on my bed in clean pajamas, did I start to feel better. I tucked the jewelry box with the remaining cigarette in my underwear drawer and thought about the situation. I'd barely had two puffs on the cigarette. Had Colleen actually smelled it or was my mind playing tricks? And if she did suspect, would she tell?

I grabbed the lamp from my desk. In the room swap, I'd been left with a single, weak, overhead bulb that my dad was going to replace with a fancy fixture and fan. Colleen had temporarily loaned me the lamp to do some homework.

I went down the hall, lamp grasped in front of me. I swung open the door to my old room and stopped cold. Liam was stretched out on top of the ruffled pink comforter and Colleen was sitting on him moving up and down. They were both naked.

I'd seen girls and boys at school making out. Once I'd even seen a boy reach under a girl's skirt, both of them glaring at me with scorn as if I were invading their private space rather than them groping in public. But I was not ready for this. I stood there, mouth agape, head spinning. Liam was *Adam's* friend. He spent so much time at our house, people thought he was our brother.

"Bernadette," Colleen said more calmly than she should have been able to manage. "Please close the door."

I did as I was told and walked back to my room, still gripping the lamp. I sat on my bed, a new sick feeling twisting through me. A few minutes later there was a tap on the door. Colleen walked in, wrapped in a pink bathrobe, soft and fluffy as the Easter bunny. She sat next to me, unrattled, as though she'd caught me rather than the other way around.

"Are you okay?" she asked.

I didn't say anything, keeping my eyes fixed on the stickers on the base of the lamp: Snoopy in his goggles and scarf ready for a Red Baron adventure. Curious George and his mischievous smile. Hello Kitty with her red bow.

"Liam and I were having sex," Colleen said.

"I *know* that," I said. "But why? Liam is Adam's friend."

"Liam and I are in love. People who are in love like to make love. We are going to get married and have lots of babies. We're going to spend our whole lives together." She said it with such conviction that I felt like the fool missing an obvious truth.

Colleen took the lamp. She set it on the desk and plugged it in, clicking it on to make sure it worked. Her face glowed in the momentary spotlight, illuminating not my childhood playmate but someone else, an almost adult emerging from its cocoon.

We'd been inseparable when we were small. Colleen doted on me like I was a living doll, dressing me up, braiding my hair, directing me through tea parties. At school she was my quasi-mother, scolding me for roughhousing with the boys, ensuring I didn't toss the apple from my lunch. We'd begun growing apart when she went to junior high. We saw less of each other, but it was more than that. We were growing into people separated by more than time.

Colleen leaned forward and brushed the hair out of my eyes. I shook my head so it fell back to the way it was.

"Are you going to tell Mom and Dad?" she asked.

I should have had the upper hand. I'd caught my underage sister having sex with my brother's best friend while our parents were out. She should have been beholden to me. I should have been able to extort promises, demand anything. But I didn't. I couldn't. My heart raced. It felt like the ground beneath my feet was shaking but it was me, trembling all over. I could barely look at her.

"If you don't tell them I was smoking, I won't tell them about you and Liam," I said. Colleen raised an eyebrow. "I swear," I added.

She hadn't asked for a promise. I gave it away freely. I wondered if she'd actually known about the smoking. Maybe she hadn't or maybe she didn't care. She stood up and walked to the door.

"You can keep the lamp," she said over her shoulder and left.

Two months later, one day shy of her sixteenth birthday, Colleen announced that she was pregnant. She and Liam were married at a family-only ceremony in his parents' backyard, Colleen's still slim figure draped in a white satin dress picked from the JCPenney Outlet, huge puffs of fabric billowing at her shoulders. She finished tenth grade just before their son, Lincoln, was born. They managed not to have another baby until Liam got his teaching license. With a little help, they purchased a modest three-bedroom house in Chatsworth and embarked on exactly the life Colleen had described that night: two people in love making lots of babies.

At thirteen, I held my sister's future in my hands and traded it for two poisonous puffs on a cancer stick. I never told anyone that I'd known and that secret I held weighed me down more than Colleen, like it was my fault, like I'd been the one in that bed. I'd picked sides, betrayed my mother and chosen my sister. But what else would a thirteen-year-old do?

For a while, I was terrified that my mother would find out. I thought I felt guilty. If I'd told, my parents would have stopped them. Colleen wouldn't have dropped out of high school and never gone to college. Everything would have been different.

But over the years I realized it wasn't really guilt, it was jealousy. Having a baby at sixteen didn't ruin my sister's life. It was the first step of filling a happy home with perfect little children just like she'd said. I never knew if I'd done the right thing or the wrong thing and Colleen still ended up the winner.

a s I drove Laura home after her shopping trip with my mother, we chatted about her intention to follow in Liam's footsteps and become a teacher. I don't know why but it always seemed weird to me that Liam went to work every day to teach other people's children while Colleen taught their kids at home. Then again, it kind of fit, just because she thought Liam was good enough to teach other kids didn't mean she thought others were good enough to teach hers.

I dropped Laura at the end of their driveway, not venturing close enough to encounter my sister. I didn't want to talk to her again. I didn't want to tell her that I hadn't really spoken to our mother, not in the way I'd intended. I felt reasonably sure my mother wasn't going to do anything, definitely not immediately, and maybe not at all. I was going to take the night off, stop making myself nuts with all the possibilities. But it was going to be an uphill battle.

Once Laura was safely inside, I pulled away and called The Farm. After about twenty rings, I gave up. I'd be there before anyone answered and arriving without warning was probably better anyway. It was certainly easier than explaining an unplanned detour across the Valley to have sex with my maybe-ex-husband as an antidote to stress.

The main house appeared empty when I arrived, so I walked down the gently sloping hill to the trailer that Shayne and I had shared for seventeen years. So much of my life was connected to The Farm that it always felt a little like coming home. Jax was born on the bed in the main house after twenty-four hours in labor walking the property with Pam at my side. Pam, who with her partner Freedom, had birthed and were raising their two children here. I'd expected that life for Shayne and me. The shift away from it had been gradual, something changing ever so slightly day by day until now it felt like a different person had lived that life, not me.

I found Shayne sitting on a tree stump outside the trailer salvaging seeds from a pile of winter squash guts. He was barefoot, wearing his favorite cut-offs and a long-sleeved green t-shirt from some auto parts store, his long hair pulled into two fishtail braids, one on either side of his head, likely Pam's handy work. I smiled. I don't know how it's possible but it's like I love and hate Shayne with the same intensity. I don't recognize that young girl so head over heels in love that living in a trailer and writing plays seemed like a life plan but I miss her desperately.

"Surprise, surprise," he said, mimicking a lyric from *X*, my favorite LA band. I took the stump next to him and reached into the cold, stringy mess to help. Our matching bracelets, exchanged at our handfasting, sat at the same place halfway up our arms pushed out of the way.

"Where's Jax?" I asked, trying to be nonchalant though it was not the first time I'd showed up unannounced with the primary intent of sex and nothing else. Great sex was one reason our relationship had lasted as long as it had. After I left The Farm, I dated a few guys but they all offered mediocre copulation skills or complications I didn't want merged with my own: The respiratory therapist whose kid had cystic fibrosis. The cop who asked every two minutes if I was having a good time. The guy from the gym who was so focused on his image in the mirror while we were having sex that I might as well have not been there.

"Riding with Calvin and Rain," Shayne said.

I nodded. Calvin and Rain were all the kids' hippie grandparents, teachers of vital skills like bread making, sock darning, and tie dye. Jax had never hurt anyone at The Farm except me and Shayne and, of course, himself. His relationship with Pam and Freedom's kids was much like his relationship with his cousins. He viewed them as oddities, creatures he couldn't relate to and from whom he fortunately kept his distance. One of the reasons I'd thought it so necessary for him to go to school was the precarious nature of things. What would happen if he did hurt one of those kids? What would we do then?

After a few minutes of sitting next to each other working the seeds, Shayne winked at me. We washed our hands in a bucket of water and went into the trailer, heading to the back bedroom, which was just the size of the mattress it contained. Without any pretense or fussing, we climbed onto the bed and kissed. After all this time, Shayne still started slow, caressing my breasts through my shirt, squeezing my ass over my jeans, like we were high schoolers, and he was testing things, unsure if today was the day we'd go all the way. I gasped as he reached under my shirt and his cold, bare hand touched my belly. I felt like someone deprived of water getting their first sip.

He scooted further up onto the bed and pulled off his shirt and shorts. Physical labor kept him thin and muscular. Most of his body was brown from a summer and fall spent outdoors. But a pale, peach band of skin started below his navel and traveled a few inches down each leg, the negative of his shorts. He lay there waiting for me like he was posing for a photograph, the blue tie-dyed bedspread his background.

I pulled off my own shirt and bra, my worries temporarily paused, the real world abandoned. This was exactly what I was looking for. We entered a place where all that mattered was our bodies. For the briefest of moments, our coupling would solve everything while, of course, solving nothing at all. He pushed inside of me, filling an emptiness that no one else ever seemed able to.

Afterwards—thirst slaked—I drifted into the fantasy that almost always called to me after Shayne and I had sex. We could get back together. I would come back to The Farm. We'd home-school Jax. Everything would be fine. Sometimes the fantasy lasted minutes, sometimes a whole afternoon. I ignored all the things that made me leave and basked in the temporary enchant-ment of the moment.

"How was your dad?" Shayne asked.

"My father is the last thing I want to talk about right now."

"Got it," Shayne said. He turned on his side and petted my hair. "Rain's got this shaman coming in from Australia tomorrow. He's gonna be here for a few months."

"Cool," I said. Rain was an herbalist. She often arranged semi-nars and events with other healers as a way to generate cash.

"I wanted to ask you something," Shayne said. "Promise you'll hear me out."

"I don't know what we're talking about so…"

"Just don't blow me off," he said, with an unusual hint of irri-tation in his voice.

"Okay," I said, confused. I couldn't care less about some Australian shaman. It was nothing compared to everything else on my mind. Mostly I didn't discuss alternative beliefs with my former land mates. Their lives went on the same as before I'd left. There were different WWOOF volunteers crashing in the yurt and Pam and Freedom's children were getting bigger. But mostly it was as it had been. I'd been out there with them, drumming and chanting, praying, offering the gods cake and flowers. I'd believed it all. They still did. It wasn't their fault I'd changed.

"Rain talked to this shaman about Jax and…"

I groaned.

"Man, *please*. Try to keep your negative energy in check for like five seconds." We were still lying naked side by side but the intimacy I'd felt was rapidly evaporating. I waved my hand for him to continue. "He wants to do this coming-of-age ceremony on New Year's Eve at the ocean. The ocean is really important to them."

"I've heard New Year's is a big aboriginal holiday," I said, making no attempt to contain my sarcasm.

"It's not gonna damage him," Shayne said.

"So why not do it and just not tell me about it?"

"That would be wrong, and you have to be there. We both have to be there." He squeezed my hand. I shifted my position and got my hand loose without actually pulling it away from him.

"I'm working New Year's. Double-time. Remember that thirty grand we don't have?" It was a stupid thing to say. The double-time I'd earn on the holiday would barely make a dent in the money we were going to owe Mark and Maria Jacobson for their son's crushed fingers.

"Bee, please."

"I'm not going to be involved in any hoodoo."

"Come on. It's not black magic. It's a coming-of-age cere-mony. I'm not off in fantasyland thinking this is gonna fix him. But if it helps one tiny bit, great. And if it does nothing at all? Well, no harm, no foul."

I got up from the bed and started to put my clothes back on. My whole purpose for coming had been negated by a couple of sentences. I didn't want to go to any ceremony. I didn't want to watch whatever this soothsayer cooked up for my son, genuine or not. How many times had I hoped something would be differ-ent? A new book. A new school. A new therapist. Hope is not a victimless crime. Hope can be a lie. It doesn't heal nor save. It's not innocuous. It can do harm.

Shayne propped himself up on one arm and watched me

dress. "It was his idea," he said. "That's the only reason I brought it up. Rain told him about the shaman and Jax *asked* if the guy could do something for him."

I wanted to be mad, to accuse Rain of filling my son's head with nonsense in my absence. But I knew it wasn't true. She was especially careful about Jax and his mental health. She promoted healthy eating, hard work, and adequate sleep, and that was about it when it came to our son. I tucked my shirt into my pants and straightened my hair out as much as I could in the tiny mirror in the hall.

"*He* asked for it?" I asked.

Shayne nodded.

I sighed. It was easy to see the sides of Jax as dichotomies: the compassionate soul who could be gentle with my father and the madman who could snap a kid's bones. But they were not disjoined. They were one.

Jax could see something in himself that needed repairing and that was important. I couldn't ignore it. Maybe it was his first insightful step toward change, a different life. If he believed, then maybe the ceremony could change something. No magic, just the placebo of his own belief.

"I'll think about it," I said and headed for the door. "Either way, I'll pick you up Monday at two for the arbitration."

"Please think about it *for real*," he said.

"I will."

I was heading toward the gate to leave, when Jax came rushing toward me from the barn, Champ lumbering behind him in the distance.

"I thought you were off riding," I said.

"Did Dad talk to you about Allambee?"

"Allambee?" I asked.

"The guy... from Australia... the shaman guy?" Champ finally caught up and lay down in the dirt at Jax's feet.

"Yes, he did," I said. It wasn't actually possible but Jax seemed taller than when I'd seen him three days ago. The bottoms of his jeans were a little too high up his boots and his t-shirt was right at his belt line. An early growth spurt had kicked in a few months ago and showed no signs of being done. His arms and legs were long and skinny but his face was full, chubby baby cheeks and a forehead dotted with pimples. His loose hair hung messily around his head. He looked a lot like Shayne, only slightly less refined.

We stood there a few moments in silence. He'd had never been much of a talker, more a brooder, everything trapped inside of him, tamped down like gunpowder, waiting for the flint. Or maybe Shayne had prepared him for the possibility that I wouldn't react positively. The plan had been to drop in and out, enjoy a quick fling and run. A diversion to take my mind off things. It was turning into something else entirely.

"Are you gonna come?" he asked.

"You want me to?" I asked even though I knew he did. He'd come running down the hill to find me after all. This I couldn't ignore. If I'd wanted to pretend that it was Shayne or Rain, I wouldn't be able to. This was my child asking me directly. How exactly could I refuse?

"Yeah, it's, you're my mom," he said, as if we both needed to be reminded that we were forever intertwined, his cells, like all children, physically more mother than father. And me, my brain harboring pieces of him, so no matter where I go he is within me.

"True, I'm your mom," I said trying to sound playful, lighten things up.

"So, uh, it's on New Year's and Dad... you and Dad... I want you and Dad both to come." His breathing was rhythmic and predictable between his words. "Could you *please* come?" he implored.

I remember the first time I participated in a code at the hospital. I didn't feel anything until it was over. A part of me automatically turned off. No fear. No sadness. You compartmentalize.

Narrow the world to the count of chest compressions, the shock of the defibrillator, the pushing of epinephrine.

I had a natural talent for it. Before me was a life in irreparable demise and I saw only the steps, the methodical, systematic actions that needed to be done. There's an algorithm, a limited number of paths. Pulseless V-tach? Do this. Asystole? Do that. It's the opposite of real life. In that single moment it's so simple: an answer for every question.

Standing there with Jax, I felt exactly like I did in those moments when the code alarm first went off. My emotions were switched off and I was hunting for steps, looking for that answer. Mentally ill kid wants aboriginal shaman to do coming-of-age ceremony? What's the algorithm for that?

"I'll do my best," I said.

I left The Farm, heading toward the Pacific Coast Highway. I'd already missed the sunset but I always took PCH when I wasn't in a hurry. There are few things as beautiful as the California coastline: The expanse of the ocean on one side and the majesty of the Santa Monica Mountains on the other. No better way to get a sense of where tiny you fits into the cosmos.

Shayne was supposed to have been a distraction, instead he'd given me something new to worry about. I didn't want to go to some aboriginal coming-of-age ceremony but I didn't have a reason. Not a good one, anyway. Mostly I wanted the world to stop conspiring against me. But only a crappy mom wouldn't make an effort to get there, which probably meant I was going.

I turned off Old Topanga onto the main canyon road, which winds and twists more and more the closer you get to the coast, the mountains making you work for what you are about to see. It feels perilous, a glance away from the wheel and you might tumble over an edge or crash into oncoming traffic. Then, there's this moment when a tiny piece of ocean emerges from between the mountains and expands up and out in front of you, until it's the never-ending horizon.

When we were teenagers, Kara, Jenn, and I would drive to the beach every Friday night. Jenn would pick us up in her Mustang and we'd cruise too fast through the canyon, Jim Morrison howling, "Break on through. Break on through," from the tape deck.

We had a secret spot, about a mile north of the canyon where you could climb out onto this massive chunk of cement, a remnant of an old pier. When the tide came in, it was like you were sitting in the ocean. It made you feel small but in the right way, a piece of something bigger, a spark in some divine fire. The waves crashed around us, drowning out the hum of the vehicles on the highway. We didn't drink or smoke. We just sat and talked and made the kind of magic only young people with all of life in front of them can conjure.

WHEN I GOT HOME, I found Kara on the couch, wrapped in a robe with a towel around her head, sipping coffee and browsing her phone. She was just out of the shower, her cheeks still pink from the heat of it.

"Perfect timing," she said. "I was going to braid my hair, but it looks so much better when you do it."

Kara set her phone on the couch, then disappeared down the hall returning with a comb and hair ties. In addition to a useless ability to hold entire conversations in pseudo-Elizabethan English, years of Renaissance Faires had left me, like Pam, a master of braids. I kicked off my shoes and sat on the couch. She grabbed a pillow and plopped herself down on the floor between my knees. Her black, satiny hair cascaded down as she unraveled her towel turban. I started combing.

No matter how often I'd braided other women's hair, I always found something sensual in it. It's sisterly and motherly but also intimate. An exposed neck. Fingers pulling through slippery smooth strands, untangling them. Being so close that you can hear each other breathe.

"I researched some assisted living places in the Valley with memory care units," Kara said. "There's a list on the table."

"You didn't have to do that," I said. I didn't want to get into the topic of my father. "But thanks."

I held the comb in my mouth and finished up the Dutch braid. Kara jumped up and checked it in the bathroom.

"Fabulous," she said, coming back down the hall. "I wish you could do my hair every day."

"You couldn't afford my day rate."

Kara was always attractive but pulling her hair up transformed her, the angles of her cheekbones and her nose were clearer and more defined. She was beautiful. This weird mix of emotions bubbled up: envy, awe, gratitude. I felt intensely close to her but also a little jealous. She engaged in my problems because she didn't have any of her own. No money issues. No kids. No parents with dementia. Sometimes it seemed a little unfair.

Suddenly, her phone rang. It was Eliot. I grabbed it before she could.

"You are not stealing her back this year," I said, playfully. Last year, he'd unexpectedly come home early after hurting his ankle. Kara and I had still gone out a few times but she'd spent most of the mini-vacation taking care of him.

"Not to worry, Benny. I'm not," he said.

"Good. I'm in desperate need of some R&R."

Kara chatted briefly with Eliot then hung up. She headed toward the kitchen.

"I got donuts at Primo's," she said.

I sat at the table and pulled a Bacon Crunch donut from the box. She poured me a cup of coffee.

"This is literally the best thing that has happened to me all day," I said.

"I think that might be a little sad."

"It definitely is."

We sat quietly for a while, enjoying the decadent treats. This was what I'd been wanting all day. A momentary pause, something rich with pleasure and nothing else. Then like an idiot, I told her about the coming-of-age ceremony.

"You're going," she said, when I told her I hadn't committed.

"I'm working," I said.

"You're kidding, right? Call in sick."

"I don't have any sick time left, and it's a holiday. I'll probably get written up," I said but I knew was grasping.

"I'd say this is worth the risk. Can't you get someone to cover for you?"

I felt terrible. Why didn't I want to go? Did I lack some motherly component that my sister had in excess? Did he need something I couldn't give? I always thought I was reacting to him. Was he reacting to me?

"You know the only thing I've wanted all day long is to put all this crap out of my mind and have a couple of hours where I pretend I have a normal life. Is that too much to ask?" I said, a little more sharply than I'd intended.

"No, I get it," Kara said. Then, we sat in an awkward silence trying to enjoy the donuts and coffee.

"You know where we haven't been in ages?" she said after a while, rather obviously changing the subject.

"El Coyote?" I asked.

"Barney's. I'm dying for a bacon-wrapped hot dog."

"After this?" I said.

"I've actually been thinking about it for days."

"That's a different kind of sad," I said.

She nodded. Her cell phone rang and she glanced at it.

"I've gotta take this," she said and headed toward her room.

I decided to throw myself into getting ready. If I was going to pretend to be a carefree woman out on the town, I should look the part. Kara and Shayne were right, of course. I had to do my best to attend the coming-of-age ceremony. One night off was all I was asking.

As I walked down the hall, I stopped at Jax's bedroom. His door was slightly ajar. I pushed it open. Jax's bed, a mattress on the floor, had a dark blue blanket messily pulled over it. A clean pile of laundry and a stack of library books sat near the head of the bed. He'd tacked an array of pictures with no discernible connection to each other on the walls: a perfume ad with a white horse; a photo of Yosemite; some athlete I didn't recognize. I always thought it was like he understood the idea of decorating but had no personal feelings attached to it. He just knew you put things on the wall.

His space managed to be simultaneously spartan and messy. His few possessions scattered haphazardly. The minimalism of life at The Farm was something we both brought with us. So much so that Kara sometimes joked that it looked liked we only used our rooms part-time too.

I walked in to take a closer look at a black and white comic he'd drawn, slightly misproportioned superheroes. He was no savant but he had natural abilities. With diligence he might get somewhere. But where was somewhere? I'd tried to get there and it turned out to be nowhere. I'd been floundering ever since.

WHEN I FINALLY EMERGED FROM my bedroom in my favorite cocktail dress, I found Kara's door open. She was sitting on the edge of her bed fidgeting with the buckle of her sandal. She'd gone for all black — loose pants and a silky tank.

"Wow, you pulled out the red dress," she said. "Trying to get laid?"

"Been there, done that," I said.

"I know you don't want to talk about this, but that was Teddy Ivanov. She's got a condo in Baja that she offered to let us use."

Teddy was one of the other attending physicians at the hospital. She'd been Kara's mentor in her trauma fellowship.

"You didn't tell her anything, did you?" I asked.

"I kept it simple: 'Bernadette and I are going there to buy drugs.'"

"Not funny."

"A little funny?"

"You'd still go with me?" I said.

"I wouldn't let you go by yourself." Her slight laugh reminded me of Colleen.

"You think I can't handle it?" I said.

"No *cabrón*. I *habla* the *Español*."

She rummaged through her purse and then, frustrated, dumped the contents on her bed. She sifted through everything until she found the cherry Chapstick she always wore.

"Why is this so easy for you?" I asked. She was too casual. We were talking about killing my father, but she seemed unconcerned about the possible ramifications. "I'm losing my mind and you're like a cucumber." She didn't answer for a second. When she did, her voice was quiet and serious.

"I suppose the simplest explanation is it's not my father. I'm not going to be there. It's between you and your mom and ultimately in some way your dad. That's who you're beholden to."

She gathered all her stuff back into her bag before continuing. "And I guess the more I think about it, the more I believe you and your mom should have that power. I've seen a lot of bad things in my career. This isn't bad. You're trying to honor the wishes of someone you love. You're trying to end a suffering. I'm not encouraging you but if this is what you decide I want it to be as easy and safe as possible."

"Then, why look up the nursing homes?"

"It's another choice. You need all the information. I don't think me helping you get Nembutal is going to be the deciding factor in whether or not you use it. There is a big difference between having the option and doing it. Not all the people who get prescribed medications for assisted suicide use them. Something like thirty-five percent don't. Mexico is about giving yourself options."

"One second I think my mom is absolutely right, then the next I think she's insane. I want to be sure and I'm just not. It's only been three days since she asked me about it, but it feels like a lifetime."

"I only brought it up again because, honestly, out of nowhere Teddy offered me the condo. I just thought since we have the week with Eliot gone, we could go after New Year's," she said. "You know how hard it usually is for me to get away."

My stomach twisted like if I agreed the next step was killing my father, right then and there. No turning back. No undoing it. It was stupid. Just like she said, even if I had the medication, I didn't have to do anything with it. I could have it just in case, a possibility. We might not even be able to find a place that would sell us Nembutal but anxiety tingled through my body.

"I can't make this decision right now," I said. "Can we please go back to pretending like I have no problems?"

She put up a finger. "For one night only."

AN HOUR LATER, we were eating bacon-wrapped hotdogs at Barney's, deliberately not talking about Jax or my father, which made them loom even greater in my mind. At ten, we hit the dance floor at Rage, a club in West Hollywood. I threw myself into the pounding rhythms, dancing with Kara, then with anyone, guy or girl, who came into my space. The music was electronic, no words or just an occasional inspirational phrase repeated.

I tried to lose myself in the beat, but there was something behind the music, an undercurrent that kept catching my attention, something hidden beneath its showy surface. I wanted to dance away my thoughts but that echo kept pulling me in like I was supposed to understand it and didn't.

Around midnight, I was dehydrated and exhausted. I took a seat at the bar. The bartender smiled at me with the headshot-ready face of an actor. He put a glass of water in front of me and leaned in.

"What's your poison?" he asked.

"Can you make a Sidecar?"

"Can I? I think the question is will I?" he said.

"Pretty please?"

"Anything for a lovely lady." He winked and gave me a flirtatious grin, then disappeared down the bar, skillfully grabbing a glass and bottles from the shelves without looking at them. I turned to find Kara in the crowd. She was dancing with two men who looked too young to be in the over-twenty-one club. Both with crew cuts and white t-shirts. They looked so similar I thought they might be siblings until they leaned into each other for a long, not-so brotherly kiss. Kara waved at me from the dance floor, then headed in my direction.

"What do you do?" the bartender asked, setting my drink down in front of me.

"Nurse," I said, as Kara sat down and swung her arm around me.

"Nice!" he said. "Two hot nurses out on the town. Not a care in the world."

I didn't correct him on either account.

THE BITE 2012

I was late. I'd told Shayne I'd pick Jax up at three. It was five and I was just arriving at The Farm. Even laidback Shayne would notice, not that it would matter. I'd slept through the alarm. Maybe because subconsciously I knew it was a holiday and Jax was with Shayne, not waiting for me at his new school. Champ met me at the gate, first bristling as I dared to enter his territory, then bowling me over with affection when he recognized me. I heard voices from the main house and headed in that direction.

So many things had changed in the last few months. I was still adjusting to my new Friday, Saturday, and Sunday night work schedule. On Mondays instead of sleeping a full eight hours, I napped until about one in the afternoon. That way when nighttime came around, I might be tired enough to sleep with the rest of the world. With this new arrangement Shayne only had to figure out how to get Jax to school on Monday mornings and home on Friday afternoons. I could do the rest.

I'd moved too, rented a guest house in Santa Monica. It was a little more than I could afford, but Kara was paying a quarter of the rent to very occasionally occupy the small guest room. It put us in a better school district with smaller class sizes. The old school in West LA had been below average and Jax's kindergarten class, way overcrowded. I thought things might get better in the first grade but they'd only gotten worse.

In kindergarten, they attributed Jax's issues to adjustment and age. In first grade all the tolerance disappeared. Every time I got called into the principal's office, I felt judged, like the principal suspected I ran a meth lab in my apartment and that was the reason for all Jax's issues. It didn't help that half the time I showed up barely conscious, having been awoken after only a few hours of sleep.

I was glad I moved him mid-term. The new school seemed to be working. Jax had been put in a special education class with other children having difficulty with traditional school settings. I was hopeful. We were two months into the second semester of first grade and all seemed well.

A rich, savory smell overwhelmed me as I opened the patio door and entered the communal house. Shayne and Jax were sitting at the counter, a fresh batch of cookies in front of them. Rain and Pam were in the kitchen each working over a pot on the stove. The scene was very Norman Rockwell if you didn't look too far into the details.

"This place smells great," I said.

"I made cookies!" Jax announced with satisfaction.

Rain looked up from her pot. "He did indeed and now we're making the most of a bumper crop of onions. Caramelizing," she said, pointing to herself. "Canning," she said, pointing to Pam.

I sat next to Jax and took the cookie he offered. I smiled at Shayne but didn't move in for a kiss or a hug. I'd just started dating a respiratory therapist and was trying to give it a fair shot. Jax jumped up from his seat and started hopping, imitating a rabbit or a kangaroo.

"I want to make something else," he said.

"I want another cookie," I said. He hopped over to the table and handed me another cookie then bounced off in a different direction. After a little more conversation and a lot more cookies, I picked up my bag.

"Buddy, it's time to get going," I said. "Got to get enough sleep for school tomorrow."

"I want to make something else," Jax said. His tone made me tense. I was reading a parenting book that emphasized identifying the moment that things started down a negative course and diverting. This was it.

"I hear you. You want to make something else. How about you help me make dinner?" I said, doing what the book advised: validate feelings, avoid confrontation, give options. "We can make spaghetti or mini pizzas!" I forced a little too much faux enthusiasm for the mini pizzas and Shayne stifled a laugh.

"I hate school," Jax said.

Shayne reached out and tousled Jax's hair. "Everybody hates school, little man," he said. "But that's where you learn crap."

It wasn't the most convincing argument but at least he was trying. The plan had been to homeschool Jax but like so many things, it felt apart when it came to the specifics. Like co-sleeping. I'd been a committed co-sleeper until I was in bed with my actual child, getting climbed on and shoved all through the night. I ended that fairy tale when Jax was one and he accidentally kicked me in the nose so hard I thought it was broken.

"Help me pack these yummy cookies so you can have one every day with lunch," Rain said handing Jax a paper sack. Jax took the bag and began helping Rain count out the cookies by school day. I smiled gratefully. For a woman with no children, Rain was a natural peacemaker. It looked like we were going to get through the moment.

A few minutes later Jax, Shayne, and I were walking to the gate together, Jax holding the cookie bag in front of his chest gripped tightly with both hands. We were about halfway to the gate, when he threw himself to the ground screaming. For a second, I thought he was having a seizure. His whole body writhed and shook. But the screaming was wrong. It was definitely a tantrum. Shayne and I observed for a minute, neither eager to jump in. Champ came running over, first trying to nuzzle into Jax, then backing off and sitting down as if watching a show.

I tried something I'd rehearsed from the parenting book. "Jax, you can walk yourself to the car or I can carry you." Jax continued screaming. "I'm going to count to three," I said. "If you aren't walking to the car at three, I'll carry you."

I noticed Shayne grimace as I said it, but I was committed. I couldn't go back now. I'd given him options. Now, I had to follow through. The book said not to repeat the choices but I honestly wondered if he'd heard them over his wailing. I repeated my ultimatum, then started counting, "One… two…"

Before I got to three, Jax flung himself at me. He pounded with tiny fists and kicked. He was small so it seemed like I should have been able to contain him, but the impact of his blows hurt and there was a fierceness to the attack that I couldn't negotiate with. Our unbalanced motivations gave him the advantage: I was trying not to hurt him, but he was desperately trying to hurt me.

"That's not gonna help anything, little man," Shayne said. He put out his arms but had no better luck navigating the ball of fury between us. "You gotta stop."

Jax didn't stop. Finally, I got hold of each of his wrists, dropped to my knees, and from behind wrapped myself around him. The book said that when he was emotionally out of control, he was actually terrified. By embracing him, I was keeping him from hitting me but also soothing and reassuring him. He was supposed to resist a little but then eventually, the book said, his body would relax and he'd melt into tears.

I prayed that it would work, that somehow his mother's arms around him would subdue whatever this was that burst forth. He raged, then I felt a shift, a distinct change in his body. I couldn't believe it. The book had been right.

Then, his teeth sank into my arm. Pain seethed through me. I gripped tighter. I didn't know what else to do. What would happen if I released him? His head shook back and forth, like a rabid animal trying to tear the flesh from my bone.

I could hear Shayne—"What are you doing? You gotta stop."— but it was as though Jax and I were enclosed inside our own sphere of madness, the rest of the world disappearing. Shayne tried to pry Jax's mouth off but he didn't let go and began kicking furiously, which made his teeth sink deeper. I didn't realize that I was screaming too until Champ started howling along with me, our voices rising together in agony.

Suddenly, Calvin's burly body stormed toward us from the barn, his golden-red dreadlocks flapping like wings. He reached into the fray and with two massive arms grabbed Jax by the back of the neck and shoulder and pulled him up and out from my hold. He held Jax out in front of him like a mother wolf picking up a cub by the scruff of the neck. Jax went limp. He'd been ignited, consumed everything burnable, then died out.

Blood oozed down my hand. A flap of skin the size of Jax's mouth hung loosely off my arm. It seemed impossible that someone so small had done so much damage. Rain ran out of the house with a first aid kit. She wrapped my arm with a clean cloth and then an ACE bandage. We piled into The Farm pick-up truck. Rain driving. Shayne and me next to her in the front seat. Calvin and Jax in the flatbed. The emergency room wasn't crowded. We sat in a group waiting to be seen, Jax lying across Shayne and Calvin's laps, all his energy dissipated.

The bite required thirteen stitches. The physician's assistant who sewed it up looked at me suspiciously when I said my seven-year-old son had bitten me. I knew I couldn't be the first person whose kid had bitten them but the severity was probably unusual. After I was stitched up, he warned me of things I already knew. The flap might not reattach and could die, leaving a large, deep scar. He told me to wait. He'd be prescribing antibiotics.

I sat there alone, staring at the puffy egg-shaped wound, touching the border where it was numb from the lidocaine. After a little while, a tall man with short black hair that was a little too shiny stepped in and introduced himself as Raymond Geoff, psychiatrist.

"The PA told me your son did this to you," he said.

I nodded. "Sometimes he loses it," I said.

"Loses it?" he repeated. His face was flat, without emotion or contour. He was the first psychiatrist I'd ever talked to about Jax. I was pretty sure he wouldn't be the last.

"He has a temper and lashes out," I said. "Sometimes he hurts himself. A couple of months ago, he scratched his leg up really badly with a sharpened stick."

"How does he do at school?"

"The principal has me on speed-dial," I said, then stopped. Smart quips weren't going to help and more importantly I wasn't supposed to be talking to a mental health professional without Shayne present. We'd agreed on that much after the counselor at his old school had tried to convince me that Seroquel was the only answer.

"Because?" Dr. Geoff encouraged.

"Well, let's recap kindergarten, he ran away twice, got in an insanely major fight for a six-year-old and threw a chair at a window until it broke because the teacher made him play the triangle instead of the drums," I said. "In first grade, the other parents banded together to help us find another school." Dr. Geoff face didn't change. I sensed that he didn't believe me.

"I'm not fucking kidding," I said.

"I know you're not. Is he medicated?"

"He's never seen a real doctor, just that idiot counselor at school. His dad's granola-man. He doesn't believe in psychiatry, or medicine, or any of it. He thinks we're going to walk down the aisle at Whole Foods and find an herbal remedy for psychopathy."

"You think your son is a psychopath?"

"Look," I said shocked that that particular word had slipped out of my mouth. The hostility toward Shayne was unexpected, too. He was a good dad. He hadn't run when things got tough. "I'm not sure I know what that word means in psychiatric terms. I'm not diagnosing him. But something's wrong. That I know."

It had been more than three years since I'd first said to Kara that I thought Jax might be mentally ill, but we hadn't done anything about it. I'd hoped that school would have an impact—the structure, the teachers, the other kids. Most of all I'd hoped that someone would understand, be able to relate to what we were going through, and help.

What happened instead was meeting after meeting with the principal, sessions with a school counselor who compared not wanting to start a six-year-old on antipsychotics to child abuse, then the letter from the other parents, basically a petition explaining all the reasons Jax had to go. Almost every kid's parent had signed it.

After we talked a little longer, Dr. Geoff suggested a two-week, in-hospital evaluation that was mostly covered by my insurance and conveniently had an open spot for a kid Jax's age. When I came out and told Shayne, he didn't resist. I didn't see how he could. But I saw the hurt in his eyes. Just like me, he wanted to help but didn't know how.

A couple of hours later, we watched silently at the intake area as Jax changed into his hospital-issued pajamas and slippers. We wouldn't be able to see him again until visiting hours the next day. We said our goodbyes, then two techs led him away. As the doors were about to close behind him, Jax turned and looked at me.

He seemed unafraid, maybe a little excited even, energized by something inside that had been dormant and was suddenly ablaze again. It was that same sickening glint I'd seen just before he'd tried to fly off the slide at the playground. I was the pawn; it was his game. And I knew then that somehow I'd have to love him, while at the same time protecting myself from him. I'd have own duplicity, my own two worlds, whole in neither.

Jax came out of that two-week stay with the first of many diagnoses—oppositional defiant disorder—a grab-bag classification that came with no wonder medication to treat, just the promise of a thirty-dollar co-pay for twice weekly therapy that would last indefinitely, three thousand dollars a year. After a few months, I figured we might as well have gone to Whole Foods.

DECEMBER 29TH 10:00 AM

*J*pulled into my sister's driveway and double-checked the time on my phone. Exactly 10:00 am. Just like we'd agreed, but Adam was nowhere to be seen, not ready to "jump in the car and take off" like he'd said he'd be. I don't know why I expected he would be on time. He never was.

I honked the horn. We had some leeway. But the 405 was an unpredictable beast, and I wasn't going to pretend I wasn't annoyed. A few seconds later Colleen stepped out the front door in jeans and a white t-shirt splashed with paint. Barefoot, she walked gingerly toward the car. I rolled down the window.

"He's still packing up his stuff," she offered with a little headshake.

"Estimated time of arrival?"

"Who knows? Want to come in?"

"That'll just encourage him to take longer," I said.

She nodded. After Dad's official diagnosis in 2013, we'd fallen into a pattern of Adam staying with Colleen and Liam rather than our parents whenever he came into town. Less disruption to their daily routine made Dad easier for Mom to manage. My job was chauffeuring him to and from the airport.

"Did you talk to Mom?" Colleen said.

"Kind of. She was tired and didn't want to get into it."

"I'm going over there this afternoon. I'll talk to her."

"Can it wait?" I asked. The last thing my mother needed was someone getting sanctimonious about the value of life.

"Aren't you the one who's worried she's going to take matters into her own hands?" Colleen asked. "Why would I wait?"

I hesitated. I wished I'd never brought Colleen into the whole mess. She was only complicating things. "I got the sense she understood what I wanted to talk about," I said. "I think things are okay for the moment." I *had* gotten that feeling, but I wasn't sure I believed it. I mostly wanted it to be true and didn't want Colleen making Mom feel guilty.

"Bernadette, you could overthink an ice cream cone," Colleen said. "Sometimes you just have to do what needs to get done."

I took in a deep breath. She always knew, or at least thought she knew, the right answer. I second-guessed myself so much it was like a hobby. Colleen didn't say anything else. The silence shifted from empty to awkward. I wished she'd stayed inside.

"Did you talk to Adam about it?" I finally asked.

"Why would I do that?"

"Doesn't it seem like we should?" I said.

"What's he going to do? His life's up there. He's not going to drop everything to help with Dad."

She was right, but the comment irritated me. Adam had escaped, left us behind years ago. Mom emailed him a couple of times a month. He and Liam kept in touch via Facebook and occasional phone calls. But he had a new life that was disconnected from us and his childhood. Every few years he dropped in at Christmas or Thanksgiving with a laissez-faire attitude and we all reconnected in that weird way you feel automatically close to someone with whom you share a history. But then, he vanished into that other world where we were far-away relatives, nothing to worry about in the present.

"Maybe he could send money?" I offered.

"For what?"

I didn't say what I was thinking, which was a nursing home.

"It's only going to stress him out to know about stuff he can't change," she said. "He's got his own problems. He's trying to get his custody arrangement revised." She shook her head, then added, "Divorce is terrible for children."

A clamoring at the front door stopped our conversation. Adam, his Hawaiian shirt untucked on one side, came out dragging a beat-up suitcase. Its wheels screeched loudly as he came closer. He threw an arm around Colleen and kissed her on the cheek, then dragged his case to the back of the car, slamming the trunk so hard that my little Honda bounced.

"I'm going over at three," Colleen said to me as Adam climbed into the passenger seat. "You can come if you want."

I started the car and pulled out. An afternoon visit to my parents' house was going to make an already hectic day crazy. After the airport, I had to stop at the hospital to find someone to swap New Year's schedules with and Kara and I were heading to *Rocky Horror* at the Nuart at midnight. But I didn't see that I had a choice. Once Colleen decided something, it was going to happen. I'd been no better at convincing her to consider a nursing home than I had my mother, and I still hadn't made a decision about Mexico. About the only thing I knew I could do was be there for my mother.

As we turned onto Highway 118, Adam announced, without any precursors, "Dad's worse. It's really hard to see him like that."

I mumbled agreement. I considered telling him what was going on. Keeping it secret was like punishing him for leaving. It wasn't as if he knew when he took his internship in Seattle at twenty-three that Dad would get dementia. Colleen and I could have left too. We just hadn't and now we were deciding that he didn't even need to know what was going on with his own parents. But talking to him wasn't going to make any difference in things either. We weren't going to drive over to our childhood home and get everything sorted out because Adam was around. He didn't have a solution. He'd be one more opinion. Probably one that wouldn't help.

"Whoa," Adam said, picking up the stack of CDs below my radio. "I haven't listened to *X* in a million years."

He popped the CD out of its case and slipped it into the player. And like that we weren't talking about Dad anymore. John Doe called to us from the past, "Well, hello everybody and welcome to the Whiskey-a-Go-Go on the fabulous Sunset Strip." Drums pounded, and my brother cranked up the only band we'd ever agreed on.

Traffic was clear, and we made it to the airport before the double-album was over. I entered the airport circle as the last song came on. Cars darted in and out of the traffic flow as we made our way to his terminal. I pulled into an opening at the curb and left the engine running. We sat listening to the final words of "Johnny Hit & Run Pauline" like we used to when we were young, and it seemed sacrilegious to cut off a great song just because you'd arrived somewhere. When the song was over, we got out.

"They were a great band," he said, pulling his case from the trunk.

"They still are. I saw them last year on their fortieth anniversary tour."

"Forty years? Man, I hate it when bands get old," he said.

"How would they not get old?" I asked.

"You know what I mean."

"You mean you wish we were all still kids," I said.

"Probably," he said, slamming the trunk too hard again. "Well, thanks for the ride. It was good to see you."

"Good to see you, too," I said. My heart sped up. I was about to let him leave without telling him anything. I knew that would be it. I wouldn't email him or call him, he just wouldn't know and it would turn out however it turned out. We were going to cut him out of an important decision about his own father. That wasn't really fair and maybe, just maybe, he'd help me convince them on the nursing home. The person behind us honked, the tail end of his truck sticking out as he tried to jam his vehicle into a space that was too small.

"Mom asked me to euthanize Dad," I blurted. "She wants to put him out of his misery," I said, knowing I was using all the wrong words.

"What?" Adam said. "Put him out of his misery? Like a lame horse? You're joking, right?"

"I'm not. I told her I couldn't help her, and now I'm worried she's going to try to do it on her own."

"What do you think she's going to do? Poison him with Drano?" he said. "Mom's not going to do anything like that. She needs to put him in a nursing home."

"She won't. We promised."

"We promised? What are you talking about?"

"At Nana Rogers' funeral," I said. He looked at me like he had no idea what I meant. Somehow it hadn't been etched into his memory like the rest of us. "You don't remember? Dad made each of us promise *out loud* that we wouldn't put him in a nursing home."

My brother's face didn't change. He didn't appear to suddenly remember, to be shaken out of the stupor that led him to a different childhood than mine. He was saying exactly what I'd wanted him to, but it was all wrong, his ease, the lack of concern, everything.

Adam shrugged. "He was upset. He felt guilty because he put Nana in a home, but what else was he going to do? Unfortunately, that's what nursing homes are for. That's why they exist."

He checked his phone, but we both knew he had plenty of time. The traffic had been good. "Damn, sometimes I'm so glad I don't live down here. You and Colleen can be so melodramatic."

"This isn't easy," I said.

"Of course, it isn't. Getting old sucks. But people don't kill their spouses with dementia. That's crazy. Find a decent place and put him there. It's pretty straightforward."

I didn't know how to respond. In his mind, the solution was simple. Put Dad in a nursing home. But he was getting on a plane in a few minutes. He wasn't going to have sit with our mother and sister and convince them.

"And what if she won't?" I said.

"She will once it gets bad enough. They should have been saving for this," he said, self-righteously.

"Are you saving for it?" I asked.

"For Mom and Dad?"

"No, for you. Do you set aside money every month to pay for a nursing home when you maybe get dementia like your grandmother and your father? I'm not. I can't. I can barely pay the fucking bills."

His expression soured. This wasn't what he wanted out of his seven days in Southern California. He wanted a bit of sunshine, a hike in Runyon Canyon, a bike ride on Venice beach.

"Look, I'm gonna go," he said. He leaned in for a weak embrace, then walked through the automatic doors back to his other life. I watched until I lost him amongst all the people mulling in the terminal.

"Asshole," I shouted and then got back in the car.

A traffic snarl between the airport and Westwood made it slow going. The total opposite of what we'd had coming in. I didn't make it to the hospital until one and I was more stressed than ever. It was a different place in the daylight, bustling with people and noise. Night shift is the shadow world, where things seem less solidified, like your hand might pass through whatever you try to grasp.

I photocopied the schedule from the notebook at the front desk and ducked into the break room. The only way I could justify *not* going to Jax's coming-of-age ceremony was if I could honestly say I'd exhausted every possibility. First, I'd try to find someone to switch with. If that didn't work, I'd ask the manager for the night off. I wasn't going to call in sick. That's where I would draw the line. Or at least that's where I was planning to draw the line, but between Jax, Shayne, and Kara, I didn't know that I'd be able to.

I highlighted everyone who was off New Year's Eve then everyone who was on the night of New Year's Day. If I worked the night of the first into the second, Kara and I would still have time to go to Mexico, if that's what I decided. But after my conversation with Adam, I wasn't sure. Maybe he was right. Maybe it was totally crazy to even be considering.

Only three people were highlighted on both lists. Fiona, who I knew had asked for the night off to attend her sister's wedding. Jolene, who'd only been on the unit a few months. And Margaret Ann. I dialed Jolene, who, not surprisingly, had plans. I looked at Margaret Ann's number and shook my head. Of course, Margaret Ann would be on the list. Of course, I'd have to reach out to my least favorite co-worker and ask for a significant favor that I didn't even necessarily want her to grant. The only person I could imagine wanting to call less was Maria Jacobson, the parent of the kid Jax had attacked. The phone rang four times before anyone picked up.

"Hello?" Margaret Ann's voice was lined with misgiving. Either she had my number in her cell and couldn't figure out why

I was calling, or didn't and thought I was a telemarketer preying on her.

"This is Bernadette from work," I said. Margaret Ann was silent. My presence on the phone, as unimpressive to her as in person. "I know this is short notice and a holiday and everything, but I was wondering if you could work New Year's Eve for me and I'll take your shift the next day... on the first?" I waited for a response but nothing came. "You actually get more hours OT on New Year's Eve," I added trying to sweeten the deal.

Because we worked opposite ends of the week, I'd managed to have only a few conversations with Margaret Ann in the years we'd worked together. I wasn't sure if gaps were the norm or if she was giving me the silent treatment. I waited until it seemed ridiculous not to speak. "I'm really sorry but my son asked me to come to an event at the last minute and..."

"Your son?" she said as if prior to that moment I wasn't human and having a child transformed me. I'd woken her out of her trance by giving birth twelve years ago.

"He's twelve."

"Don't you always work New Year's with..." She paused again and I wondered if was looking for choice words to describe Kara or if she was still marveling at the existence of my son. "... Dr. Fink?"

"I was planning to but then my kid asked and it's something really important to him otherwise I wouldn't have bothered you."

I looked down at the schedule, searching for other options. Everything came with complications. If she said yes, I'd owe her and I'd have no excuse not to go to the ceremony. If she said no, I'd have to ask for the day off and irritate my nurse manager, maybe endanger my job, or I'd have to disappoint the three people I cared about most. Wasn't anything as simple or straight-forward as everyone seemed to think it was?

"You know," I started to withdraw the request, but Margaret Ann cut me off.

"I can do that. I don't have any plans."

"Thanks," I said, trying to sound thankful rather than leery. I had to be missing something. Everything was falling into place too easily. I hung up feeling as if I'd set in motion a trap for myself, but I couldn't understand how.

*A*rriving at my parents' house after ninety minutes in LA traffic wasn't exactly a relief. Colleen's beat-up minivan sat in the driveway behind Dad's truck. Every house had so many cars *not* stored in their garages that the city had made one side no parking, otherwise no one could get through. I had to drive up and around the corner to find a space almost two blocks away, which gave me time to mull over the new, less than helpful, information I'd obtained.

After calling Margaret Ann, I'd contacted the three assisted living places on Kara's list closest to my parents' house. As it turned out, my father didn't need a nursing home. He needed a memory care unit in assisted living and it was a lot more expensive than I'd thought. Housing and feeding someone, and keeping them from wandering off, came with a price tag between four and five thousand dollars a month, fifty to sixty thousand dollars a year.

I didn't know what I'd expected but it was less than that. Someone like Kara with two generous six-figure incomes and no kids could afford that. Our family couldn't, at least not for very long, and there was no way to predict how many years someone like my dad might be there. Convincing my mother and sister to even consider a nursing home was difficult enough without the hefty price tag.

I tucked my notes about the assisted living places, scrawled on the back of the work schedule, in my bag and headed toward my parents' house. I'd already filled out the needed form at work to swap schedules with Margaret Ann but I hadn't let Jax or Shayne know I'd be attending the coming-of-age ceremony. As I walked, I called The Farm. Rain answered after a couple of rings. Jax was helping Calvin repair the barn roof so I didn't have her get him.

"He'll be so pleased," she said after I told her I'd be coming. The sincerity in her voice made me feel guilty for ever having considered not going. My sister was right. Not only could I complicate an ice cream cone, I'd make myself feel horrible about it after the fact.

I found my mom and sister at the kitchen table having tea when I arrived.

"I didn't know you were coming," my mother said. "Would you like some tea?" She got up to pour it before I had a chance to answer.

"Where's Dad?" I asked. I hadn't seen him out front and didn't hear him anywhere in the near vicinity.

"Gone for a walk." Mom pointed to her phone. "The regular route," she said as if we'd established some code system for the different paths he took. I leaned over to see the little picture of my dad on the Friend Finder app on my mom's phone. I sat down across from my sister and my mother set a tea cup in front of me. I decided to jump right in, feign my brother's certainty about the nursing home.

"I got some information about assisted living places with memory care units," I said. I pulled out the list. Colleen shook her head ever so slightly.

"No nursing homes," my mother said.

"Technically, it's not a nursing home. It's assisted living with memory care," I said. My mom and sister gave me identical disappointed looks.

"It's the same thing," Colleen said.

"Look, there really aren't any other options. At some point very soon we'll need this information." I pointed to the paper. "There are two that are less than five miles away for about five thousand a month."

"Five thousand *dollars?*" my mother said. I refrained from making the obvious smart-ass joke but I wondered what else she thought I might be referring to other than dollars.

"I know," I said. "It's expensive but I guess that's what all that hard work was for, right? Not the way you wanted to spend your nest egg but at least it's there."

Colleen and Mom shared a glance. It meant something but I couldn't tell what. My sister was quieter than usual and I couldn't shake the feeling that I'd come in too late, that they'd been talking for hours without me and I was being indulged. I plowed ahead, trying not to be dissuaded by my ever-present sense that my sister was outdoing me.

"Not to be rude, but how much do you guys have saved?" As I asked it, I felt as crappy as I'd judged my brother to be. Colleen stood up and for a second I thought she was going to walk out, like asking my mom how much money she had was so offensive she couldn't bear it. Instead, she walked over to fridge and pulled out a packet of cookies, which for some unknown reason Mom has always stored in the fridge. She put a few on a plate and brought them to the table.

"No nursing homes," my mom repeated. "Absolutely not."

"Just humor me," I said. "You must have sold the hardware store for at least five hundred thousand, right? You did a couple of trips in the RV but it was almost new when you sold it, right? I wished I hadn't said it but it wasn't like it was a surprise to anyone. We all knew what had happened. "So maybe four hundred and fifty saved?" I asked hopefully. "That's maybe eight years."

Mom and Colleen shared another glance. I felt like they were speaking in signs.

"What?" I finally said. "What am I missing?"

"We put that money aside for the children for college," Mom said. "Thirty thousand each."

I let her words sink in, at first not quite understanding which children she was talking about, then getting it: her grandchildren. Adam's two. Colleen's nine. My one. I hadn't heard anything about this college fund, but Colleen would have known about it. Three of her children had been to college. Only Lincoln, her first, wouldn't have benefited from this impromptu scholarship. He'd joined the Air Force at eighteen to take advantage of the GI Bill and had been immediately deployed to Afghanistan. The years of worry about his safety could have easily made this decision seem logical.

"And you can't get it back?" I asked.

"That wouldn't be fair," she said.

"It's kind of a unique circumstance, right? We have to roll with the punches," I said. I waited for her to answer my original question. "So, can you get it out or not? Is it in an education trust or something?"

My mom nodded.

"How much is left outside the trusts?" I asked.

"A little under two hundred," my mom said.

I did the math in my head. She could pay for a few years but if that was everything she had, nothing would be left for her if she needed it.

"What do you get from Social Security?" I asked.

"About two thousand," she said. "I thought we'd have enough. The house is paid for. It seemed like so much money."

I wanted to scold her about savings like Adam had. After Grandma Rogers, how could they have not considered this possibility? But who knew what this kind of care cost back then and what was the point in bringing it up now?

Suddenly, Colleen popped in. "I don't know why we're even talking about this. This isn't what Dad wanted."

"You remember what Dad *did* want, right?" I said. I thought about Kara and the condo in Baja. I pictured myself wandering into some Mexican pharmacy with her, buying Nembutal, bringing it home, and then what? Adam was right. It was crazy to even be thinking about it. It was something from a movie, not something I could actually do. A nursing home was the only thing that was rational. But everything about it felt wrong.

"You keep saying no but what else is there? I get that Dad didn't want to go to a nursing home. But this is what nursing homes are for. It's why they exist." It sounded just as cold coming out of my mouth as it had out of Adam's.

"You wouldn't understand," Colleen said.

"What do you mean I wouldn't understand?"

"You and Shayne aren't together anymore," Colleen said.

"How is that relevant?" I asked.

"I just mean it's different," she said.

Suddenly, the doorbell rang. We all looked at each other startled. I got up. Dad was expectantly waiting at the front door even though it was unlocked, something he'd never done before.

"That vehicle is blocking my truck," he said, pointing at Colleen's minivan.

"It's Colleen's. Why don't you come in and tell her about it," I said, gesturing for him to come in, which seemed strange since it was his house. I followed him into the kitchen, relatively pleased that the confrontation was headed in Colleen's direction.

"Your vehicle is blocking my truck," Dad said to Colleen, his tone sharp.

"It's always so crowded now that you can only park on one side of the street. That was the only spot," she said. "I'll move it in a couple of minutes."

"You should move it now," Dad said, pounding a fist on the table for emphasis. I had the same sinking feeling in my chest that I got when Jax was digging in, and I knew we were heading toward an unstoppable disaster. Colleen turned to Dad and studied him for a second before responding.

"Okay, Dad," she said. "I'll move it right now. Let me find my keys."

Dad watched intently as Colleen got her purse and shook it, her keys clanking inside. She reached in and pulled them out.

"Ta-dah," she joked, trying to change the tone. Dad didn't crack a smile. He followed her outside.

"We *need* to talk about what you said on Christmas," I said to my mom as soon as they were both outside. "For real."

"I understand," she said. "You can't."

"And neither can you," I said. "I'm worried you are going to try to do this alone and he's going to hurt you because he doesn't understand."

She went over to the window, pushing aside the cherry print curtains. She'd made them years ago when I was a kid, some women's club project. She sat at this kitchen table, the sewing machine whirring away. It was a set: curtains, apron, oven mitts, festive and cheery. Life seemed simpler then, easy.

I got up and stood beside her. Dad was on alert in the driveway. Colleen's van was gone; she'd probably have to drive all the way around the block hunting for an open place like I had.

"It's not a real option," I said but it felt like a lie. My best friend, who was a doctor and spoke Spanish, was willing to go with me to Mexico to buy a drug that could do exactly what my mother was asking. Kara and I had a place to stay. We had time off together. Every needed piece had fallen into place. Was it a sign or a warning? The universe capriciously tempting me down the wrong path? Or a bounty I was too foolish to appreciate?

My mother sighed. "It's not right. He shouldn't have to be like this. There should be a tablet you can take. Everyone should have that choice. It's just like cancer." We stared out at my Dad who appeared to be losing interest in standing guard and was glancing around for something to direct his attention toward.

"Do you remember when we put Tina down?" my mom asked.

I nodded. I was ten when they put our fluffy, white Cockapoo to sleep. Her body was so riddled with tumors she could barely eat and drink. We'd all been there in the exam room, when the veterinarian suggested it was time to let her go. But it was my mother who stayed with her. My mother who held that sweet dog as she took her last breath, while the rest of us waited in the lobby crying with our father.

"It was a kindness," Mom said. "She was suffering. I held her and she went to sleep." I put my arm around her. "I can be kinder to an animal than my own husband," she said quietly.

"I know you want to keep your word," I said. "But..."

"This isn't about my word," she said a little curtly. "He didn't want to be like this. This was his worst fear and he trusted me to make sure this never happened. But there isn't any way to do that. I thought you'd know how. You're so smart and strong. You never just took what life handed you. I thought you'd be able to..."

Her voice drifted off. My dad puttered around the driveway looking for purpose. If you'd told him this was what was going to happen, then handed him a pill to end it all, he would have. He would have lain down on his bed, his family all around him, and taken that pill. He would have been better off. We all would have been. Dad gave up on the driveway and turned to come back into the house.

"When did you get here?" he asked when he found me in the kitchen.

My mother offered him tea and cookies and he joined us at the table. I watched her watching him, her face a mix of love and resignation. My heart was breaking. He didn't want this. She didn't want this. My mother had asked me for help because she thought I'd know what to do. And I did. I was failing her and there was Colleen standing right by her side, maybe not helping, but at least defending her.

I pulled out my phone and texted Kara, "I want to go to Mexico."

DECEMBER 31ST 12:00 PM

I woke up at noon on New Year's Eve under the covers but still in the clothes I'd been wearing the night before. I was only getting out of bed because I had to be at the arbitration by three. I couldn't risk being late but my hangover would have definitely preferred a few more hours of sleep.

After the *Rocky Horror* show on Saturday night, Kara and I had followed a group of revelers to a local bar and stayed until closing, tumbling out of an Uber around four, mangling songs from the film as we made our way into the house. We'd been a drink or two shy of full-blown hangovers but spent a fair amount of Sunday morning regretting the final round.

Sunday evening was supposed to be the antidote: Chinese take-out and a series of tear-jerking chick-flicks. But one of them, a film about a quadriplegic man who ultimately ends his own life, reminded me too much of my father's situation and spoiled the cure. We stayed up late again, sharing a bottle of wine, which mostly I drank, and talking until neither of us could keep our eyes open any longer, the keys to the Baja condo on the table between us—a silent conspirator.

I climbed into the shower. The hot water against my skin

helped dampen the nausea rumbling in my belly. Alcohol wasn't improving anything, but getting tipsy seemed perfectly rational whenever I considered the path ahead: arbitration, coming-of-age ceremony, trip to Mexico to buy a drug to murder my father. The wine temporarily slowed my ricocheting emotions and made it easier to stay on the surface of things.

After the shower, I put on the business dress I'd worn to my interview at the hospital but it was stiff and dated. I'd look bizarre next to Shayne. More than a decade at a job with a uniform left me at a distinct disadvantage when picking out clothes. All I had was scrubs and casual clothes. I changed into a pair of tidy jeans and a long-sleeved black blouse, then gathered the legal papers and got ready to leave.

As I headed for the door, I noticed Kara's door ajar. Unlike me, she'd made it into her pajamas but was sprawled over the top of her blankets. I lingered a moment awash in feelings of gratitude and connectedness. I couldn't believe there was someone in the world who would do what she was going to do with me, that I had that kind of friend.

I gently pulled her door shut. New Year's Eve was always rough. She needed her rest. It would start slow, around midnight, a few car accidents, some gunshot wounds. By one in the morning all the operating rooms would be filled, surgeons using the same skill to piece back together drunk drivers and their victims, usually not aware which was which.

I grabbed coffee and a snack at Coffee Bean, then headed north on PCH. Just past the first light, the traffic halted abruptly. A river of red lights glared in front of me. The disadvantage of the ocean to the left and mountains to the right is that if there is an accident, there's nowhere to turn.

The man in the next car gripped his hands to the wheel and grimaced, as if his dark suit and neatly knotted tie had tightened around him, crushing his insides. "God damn it!" he shouted so vigorously I heard him through both our closed windows. I glanced at my phone. I had plenty of time. After years in trauma, I refused to get angry in traffic, late or not. I never want to be the asshole whose first thought is, "Damn, I'm going to miss spin class," instead of, "I hope everyone gets out alive."

I slipped in the The Doors' first album, the one Kara, Jenn, and I used to play over and over as if the band were ours alone, communing with us across time. The CD was half over when a trickle of cars started coming through heading south. The northbound traffic inched forward. Whatever was going on had only just happened. It took another fifteen minutes before I reached the scene.

A burgundy Jeep Grand Cherokee lay on its side on the right shoulder and a smashed up blue VW Bug with one door ripped off was in the center of the southbound road. The cops were letting cars pass in the far lanes, but the wreck was still there where it happened. Two young women, maybe twenty, were sitting on the bumper of the ambulance, wrapped in blankets, one pressing a bloodied white cloth to her forehead, the other resting her head in her hands.

I saw myself in those girls. Kara, Jenn, and I had driven so many times down this highway, too fast, too wild, too sure of ourselves and our invincibility. It could have been us any one of those nights, but it wasn't. Just luck. Nothing but dumb luck. When you're young, you think you're the main character, the heroine of your story. As you get older, you realize you're actually the jester juggling everything while someone offstage keeps throwing more balls into the mix. Or, in my story, knives.

Traffic surged forward after the accident, faster but heedful. The cautionary tale of the accident, enough to keep reckless habits in check, for a mile or two at least. I don't know that we live better, those of us who daily witness the alacrity with which the universe brings our endings. But we understand viscerally that death is always there, a dark silhouette lurking, its scent part of the wind.

When I arrived at The Farm, the main house was empty and Champ was nowhere in sight. I headed down the gently sloping hill to the trailer. Shayne's work boots were tucked under the steps. I didn't knock. Even if I didn't own half the trailer, I probably wouldn't have knocked. The Farm wasn't that of kind of place.

"Shayne?" I called as I opened the door, not really trying to find him so much as letting him know I was here. He was stretched out naked on the mattress in the bedroom, taking advantage of what was apparently a teen-free moment. He greeted me but barely moved, patting the mattress next to him. I sat and he took my hand in his. It could have been an invitation for sex, but it didn't seem like it. His penis lay flaccid against his right thigh.

"How come you aren't hanging out with the shaman?" I asked, making special effort to control my tone so I was just starting a conversation rather than flooding the space with my infamous negative energy.

"He took Jax on a hike. He's been giving him a different challenge every day and working on the songs he'll need for the ceremony. The kid built his own hut yesterday," Shayne said. "It's pretty cool."

I nodded, keeping the less polite things that jumped into my mind to myself. Building a hut wasn't exactly a real world skill Jax would be needing.

"We're going to the ocean later, right?" I asked.

"We'll head out after we get back."

"It'll be cold," I said.

"We'll build a fire."

"You can't build a fire on the beach," I said a little too sharply.

"Cal reserved a couple sites at Leo Carrillo."

The last time I was at Leo Carrillo I'd been pregnant with Jax, about to burst. Freedom and Pam and another couple who used to live at The Farm had been there with us. Freedom and Pam's children were tiny. River was about three and Delilah one, and just walking. After I settled into a chair a few feet from the fire, I'd watched the children play. The sand was cool between my toes. Waves crashed in the distance as the sun set on the horizon.

River and Delilah dragged sticks along the ground, drawing shapes. Their golden blonde hair fell in soft ringlets, River's down his back and Delilah's all around her cherub face. I dreamt about my own baby, imaging a life of limitless possibilities.

It seemed apropos that thirteen years later I'd be there again, pleading with spirits I no longer believed in to repair a son who was broken in a way I wasn't sure was fixable. The infant the stork had dropped on my doorstep was so very different from what I thought I'd been promised.

Shayne put my hand to his mouth and kissed it, then pulled me down on the mattress next to him. But instead of making an advance, which was what I was expecting, he nestled me against his shoulder. We lay there comfortable in each other's embrace, our preparation for the battle ahead.

THE CLINIC 2003

"*I*'m not a fertility specialist," Dr. Newman said taking a seat across from me and Shayne. "I did this as a favor to Calvin."

The office was spacious and tidy, but the furniture was out-of-date, what you'd find at an estate sale for someone who'd lived in the same house their entire life. Dr. Newman was out-of-date too, haggard and worn like a hide tanned in the sun too long. A perky bowtie peeked out from under his white coat as if trying to convince us otherwise.

"We appreciate it," I said. The LA Free Clinic where we usually got our healthcare didn't offer anything non-essential. Dr. Newman, who'd served in Vietnam with Cal, could occasionally be called upon for more specialized needs, outside regular hours, cash payment only, and always with the reminder that he was doing you a good turn. After eleven years living on The Farm, we were used to making the most of what was available.

"Did you find anything?" I asked. I was jumpy, not able to sit still on the green vinyl two-seater bench Shayne and I were crammed into. I hadn't exactly been trying to get pregnant. I didn't have a calendar marking out the fertile days or a thermometer to measure my morning temperature. But I'd never done anything to not get pregnant. Even that first time—our steamy get-together in the back of the Green Machine—I'd been playing Russian roulette. After more than fifteen years and no pregnancies it seemed certain that the game was rigged. One of our chambers wasn't properly loaded.

"No," he said. "I didn't find anything that would interfere with your ability to produce offspring."

"There's nothing wrong?" I asked, shifting so Shayne's sweaty leg wasn't pressed against mine.

"No, but, as previously stated, I'm not a specialist."

I turned to Shayne for reassurance. This was crazy. We'd wasted our time and precious money. Dr. Newman didn't know what he was talking about. We had to find someone who did. But Shayne's face didn't reveal anything about his thoughts. It was a blank canvas that wouldn't be painted on with my newly found desperation. I turned back to the doctor.

"How can there be nothing wrong?" I said. "In all these years, I've never been pregnant. We have sex all the time."

Shayne reached for my hand, but I pulled it away.

"*Bébé*, it's okay," he said.

Dr. Newman smiled. I think it was meant to be sympathetic, but it seemed smug, like he'd given us ample warning that this was how it was going to turn out and we'd refused to listen. "I suggest you see a fertility specialist."

"We don't have insurance," I said, wondering how he'd managed to forget that we were seeing him precisely because of that.

"Fertility isn't covered by insurance," Dr. Newman said.

"There's no money either," I said, exasperated. Why else would I be sitting in an overheated office when it was technically closed, getting care that was clearly past its expiration date? "You can't help with anything?"

A gust of chilly air landed on us from the air vent above our heads. The whole time we'd been in the clinic, the air conditioner had been switching on and off, struggling to fight off the summer heat and mostly losing.

"The starting point for most people is artificial insemination," Dr. Newman offered. "It's a few hundred dollars if you're using your own sperm donation." He gestured in Shayne's direction, as if it might not be clear who out of the two of us would be donating sperm.

Shayne stood up abruptly. "Thanks, Doc," he said, thrusting a hand out to shake, something totally out of character. With Shayne it was usually either a hug or a cold shoulder. I followed Shayne out without a glance in Dr. Newman's direction.

"He's a jerk," I said when we stepped out onto the sidewalk in front of the strip mall where Dr. Newman's family practice was located. It was blistering hot, and unusually humid. Sweat beaded on my skin almost instantly. We'd parked the car far on the other side of the lot, in the dirt under the trees, hoping the shade would keep it cool. The car had overheated twice in the last week, and it didn't have an air conditioner.

"He didn't do anything," Shayne said.

"Exactly," I said.

"If it's meant to be, it will happen. You don't mess with the cosmos."

Sometimes talking to Shayne was as frustrating as talking to my sister. He'd fall back on the universe as often as she'd fall back on God. He didn't seem to care that something was clearly wrong, and we didn't know what it was. We walked together under the overhangs in front of the stores, the only available shade. We were together but apart, an arm's length between us like a couple having an argument, even though technically we weren't disagreeing.

"It's not fair," I said. "She doesn't even try, and babies fall out of her like she's a Pez dispenser." I didn't have to explain who I was talking about. Our next stop was a baby shower for my sister's sixth child. Every time I turned around, I was bumping into Colleen's yet again pregnant belly. "What's wrong with me?"

"Everything is just as it's supposed to be," Shayne said. "It can never be anything else. You don't will life into existence."

I didn't answer. He was wrong. People willed life into existence all the time. They got together and said, let's make a baby, and then did. My sister created a whole life filled with babies by the force of her own certainty. Why couldn't I?

But the truth was, until now babies had never been at the forefront of either of our minds. Shayne wanted to be an actor. I wanted to write plays, with fictional characters that did my bidding, not make babies where the roles would be reversed. For someone who should have been acutely aware of the ramifications of unplanned pregnancy, I approached sex without much concern about outcomes. In spite of my sister, or maybe because of her, Shayne and I were cavalier, doing what we wanted when we wanted, devotees of providence, not science.

Then, suddenly I was thirty-three years old and didn't have any children. It was like I'd been napping, and I woke up old and infertile. As soon as I began to think that I couldn't have a baby, it became the most important thing in the world, like this essential right had been stripped from me and everyone needed to know I wouldn't tolerate it. As we approached the Green Machine, the same car I'd been driving since I was sixteen, Shayne handed me the keys. The shift dress I was wearing didn't have any pockets and I hated purses.

"Was that there when we parked?" I said, pointing to a dark puddle of fluid under the car with a rainbow glint of oil.

"I don't know," Shayne said, then hopped over the side of the convertible like he was a teenager. Even in the shade with the top down, the leather seats of the car were so hot they burned the back of my legs. I turned the key. There was a grinding screech, the howl of a machine being murdered.

"That sounded bad," Shayne said.

I tried the ignition again. Nothing.

"Why now?" I pounded my hands against the steering wheel. "Why at this exact minute does this piece of shit have to stop working? Why not before we left for the appointment? Why not yesterday?"

I got out of the car, slamming the door behind me, not checking to see whether Shayne followed. I looked at the signs along the mall, trying to judge by the names which staff might let me use the phone. I picked Happy Feet Shoes, the only one that didn't sound like a chain.

When I came out of the store, Shayne was under the hood poking around. I shook my head. Shayne could build fences, hoe vegetable gardens, and repair just about anything on The Farm. But cars were not in his skill set. As long as we stayed on Little House on the Prairie, he was my hero. A covered wagon, he could probably fix, but to him the Green Machine was a futuristic beast speared and bleeding on the open plains.

"My dad's coming," I said when I was close enough for him to hear. No one had answered at The Farm so I'd called my parents. We were only five miles from their house and the baby shower would start in a couple of hours. Shayne stepped back from the vehicle and brushed his hands together as if he'd actually done something.

"I won't do anything artificial," he said, articulating the word artificial deliberately, syllable by syllable. "We're not having a test tube baby."

I knew that a test tube baby and artificial insemination were not the same thing. I suspected Shayne did too, but for him they were on a continuum of interference with the natural world. My knowledge about what else might be available from a fertility specialist was limited.

The Farm was insulated. We didn't have a TV. Information filtered in via old-fashioned means: newspaper and radio. Our human interactions were governed by our needs. What we couldn't grow, we bartered from other folks who didn't partici-pate in society in the "normal" ways either. We dove in dump-sters with freegans. Had conversations at farmer's markets about lentil and chickpea recipes, how to build chicken coops from free wooden pallets, and the best way to winter vegetables through the off seasons. How to make babies when nature didn't want you to had never been a topic.

"It doesn't matter," I said. "We don't have money for it anyway."

"If it's meant to be, it will happen," he said.

"I'm pretty sure you said that already."

The eucalyptus tree above us rustled but the breeze was hot and brought no relief. I didn't tell him about the redheaded, freckly teen manning the deserted shoe store. He'd pushed the phone toward me, his eyes filled with suspicion, then observed as I dialed. He stood too close, deliberately in my personal space so he could listen. I was under surveillance as if he thought the whole thing was a ruse and I was going to tuck some Hush Puppies under my arm and take off at a gallop. The phone rang and rang at The Farm. I hung up and called my father.

I felt useless. Helpless. I was a grown woman, married, trying to have a baby, to be a parent, and there I was calling my daddy to rescue me from the life I'd created for myself.

My father arrived about ten minutes later. He leaned under the car and looked around. "Oh, Bumblebee," he said, his voice filled with admonishment and doom. "You cracked the block."

"What does that mean?" I asked.

"That's it. Kaput." He sliced a hand across his throat like an imaginary guillotine. "There's no fixing it." It felt like a pronouncement about the car and me. I was one more thing beyond repair.

DECEMBER 31ST 2:40 PM

*S*hayne and I arrived at the lawyer's office in Old Calabasas twenty minutes before the appointment for the arbitration and parked directly in front of the door. The suite occupied the first floor of a steel grey building with white shutters and a front porch with carved posts. It was meant to look like a restored old house, something singular saved from destruction like the glorious oak the parking lot was shaped around. But it felt like a movie set, as if you'd walk through the door and find it was only a facade.

We hadn't really spoken during the drive. The space between us awkward, filled with its own density. There was no strategy to discuss. We had nothing to offer or trade. We were going to take our place at the table, poker players with a whole lot of nothing in our hands. I didn't want to spend any more time in the office than I had to so I sat in the car gripping the steering wheel like a child pretending to drive. Shayne broke the silence.

"Can you give up parental rights?" he asked.

The statement was so unexpected, it was like he was speaking a foreign language that I was just learning, and I had to take my time deciphering it. Did he mean me? Or was it a generic "you" as in, *Is it possible for people in general to give up parental rights?* Or was he referring to himself?

"What are you talking about?" I asked.

"You know like if you were giving him up for adoption."

"Me? You mean if I were giving him up for adoption? Why would I do that?" Anger pulsed in my chest. "Do you think this is my fault?"

"I don't think this thing is going to go our way," he said, not answering my questions and seeming too nonchalant for what he was suggesting. He stared out the front window as if mesmerized by something in the distance.

"Are you fucking high?" I asked.

"Of course not."

"Then, why are you suggesting that I put Jax up for adoption? You think not having me as a parent will fix him?"

He turned to me, his brow furrowed in denial, his head shaking. He put his hands up like he was surrendering. "No, no, man, that's not what I meant. I was just thinking how businesses go bankrupt and they get off the hook for their debts. What if you weren't his legal mom on paper? You're his real mom. No one cares what it says on a paper, right? But maybe that's a loophole we could use so you don't have to pay." He stopped as if waiting to see what I thought, then added, "Only if we lose."

I stared at him, wondering if he could possibly be serious. His logic wasn't exactly wrong; big corporations ran away from their responsibilities all the time. But it was naïve. A half-baked, last-ditch effort to avoid the inevitable. I couldn't help wondering if there was something more underlying it all, an unspoken motive, an assignment of blame.

In the end, we had done artificial insemination to conceive Jax. After a few too many glasses of wine at Colleen's baby shower for Laura, I'd cried to my mom about not being able to get pregnant and Shayne being unwilling to do anything about it. It felt like tattling, like in seventh grade when I told Adam a boy had called me a name and he beat the kid up. It was exactly what I wanted but it was tainted, a reminder that I wasn't able to do what needed to be done myself. I needed someone to do the tough work for me.

My mother insisted on paying for the treatments and a few days later my dad took Shayne out for a beer. Neither of them ever told me what transpired that night but the next morning Shayne told me he was willing to try "assisted" insemination. His face had been pale when he'd said it, unmistakably a man doing something he felt was wrong.

"I DON'T THINK me giving up parental rights will work," I said. "There are no loopholes for people like us." Shayne nodded earnestly as if I'd spoken an undeniable truth. "We need to go in," I said.

A woman in a crisp, white suit adorned with gold buttons looked up at us as we entered the office, then turned away. Her face was framed by large, golden-brown curls, soft but also locked in place like hair on a new doll. I presumed she was Maria Jacobson, the other boy's mother. There was no one else in the waiting area. A black briefcase-style handbag rested on her knees. She had an air of tidiness, organization, the kind of person who keeps all her documents in manila folders with neatly printed labels.

I immediately regretted my choice of clothes. It wasn't a professional vibe. Shayne was worse, frayed cut-offs and an Ocean Pacific t-shirt that looked as if it had been rescued from a dumpster, which it very likely had been, and his work boots. He looked exactly like what he was, a goat-milking, commune-dwelling pagan, and occasional actor. The receptionist smiled warmly, without giving any indication as to whether I was as out-of-place as I felt.

"Bernadette Rogers?" she asked.

"Yes."

"Shayne Sky?"

"You bet," Shayne offered too eagerly.

"Mr. Cornwell will be right with you. Can I get you some water?"

"Yes, please," I said, then cringed when she returned with two plastic bottles. She offered one to Shayne. I waited for him to tell her that she was destroying the planet with consumption but thankfully all he said was, "None for me."

My hand trembled as I reached for mine. My brain couldn't stop it. I surveyed the room for something to focus on. The glint of Maria Jacobson's white shoes caught my eye. Bleach-white, patent leather low heel pumps, right-out-the-box shiny. I was baffled. Really? Who has white shoes? This woman asking for all the pennies I didn't have to my name lived in a world that was so predictable she could wear all white. How did you find such a place? No blood from unexpected sources. We didn't stand a chance. We wouldn't be getting any breaks from someone with white shoes.

The office door opened and all three of us looked up. Cornwell, the court-arranged arbitrator, was younger than I'd expected but there was no mistaking him for anything but a California lawyer. He was tanned to just the right hue. His black hair, slick but not greasy. He grinned and there was not a wrinkle in sight, not on his face or his navy-blue, tailor-made ensemble.

"Come on in," he said.

The three of us stood in unison. Shayne gestured for Maria to go first, which she did. Good sign? Bad sign? Who knew? I looked down as I went through the door and another pair of luminescent shoes glared up at me. Cornwell's were grey but just as polished as Maria's, sheltered from the real world. They were on the same team. Team shiny shoes. Shayne and I were doomed. I might as well sign over my meager IRA without protest.

Cornwell took a seat at his large antique desk. "The purpose of our meeting today is to attempt to reach an agreement between parties without the ordeal of court time," he said. "Often an arbitrated agreement saves both parties money. Court decisions don't always go the way people think that they are going to go."

I wondered if the comment was boilerplate or if it was specific to me and Shayne. Did he think we expected to walk out unscathed? Did he think I didn't know, better than anyone, my son's flaws?

"If everyone is amenable, we'll start with agreed upon events." He continued without actually stopping to confirm that anyone was amenable. "On November 16, Jax Sky and Leonard Jacobson, both minors, were in an altercation approximately twenty feet from the property line of Highland Learning Academy, where they were both students."

The school had persistently pointed out that according to the policy we'd all signed, they could not be held accountable for an event that had occurred *off* campus and *outside* school hours. That same fact, however, hadn't stopped them from expelling both boys: Leonard for instigating the fight and Jax for taking it to a whole new level.

Cornwell continued with the summary of the altercation and Leonard's injuries, every so often jotting a note on his papers when one of us commented. Maria's cell phone buzzed. She pulled it out of her pocket and began texting, her thumbs flying across the screen with practiced skill. Cornwell paused. Maria stayed fixated on her device, seeming oblivious to the fact that we were all watching her, waiting.

The whole thing was taking too long. I knew what Jax had done and that, indirectly at least, it was my fault and so my responsibility. If I'd had $30,000, I probably would have just paid it. But I didn't and neither did Shayne. Any tiny reduction would help. Maria's phone buzzed again. She hissed through her teeth at it and then looked up at Cornwell as if she'd only just realized he wasn't speaking anymore.

"May I continue?" he asked.

She nodded but kept the phone on her lap.

"Police were not contacted by either party. No formal charges have been made through law enforcement."

It was a detail I hadn't thought about before. Now it seemed important. I understood why Shayne hadn't called the cops. Cops were the establishment. Cops were fascists who imprisoned the masses. I couldn't imagine any scenario in which Shayne would call cops. But why hadn't the Jacobsons called the cops? Maria shifted in her seat but offered nothing.

"My understanding is that there are extenuating circumstances?" Cornwell said in a way that was both a question and a statement. The room went quiet, the low buzz of traffic on the street outside now apparent. Maria sighed and flipped her phone over as if someone might be watching her through the screen.

"Leo is on probation," she said. Her voice was the antithesis of her appearance, rough and raspy, like she'd started smoking in grade school. "The last thing I need is another chat with L.A.P.D." The acronym was inflected with the disdain and hostility I might have expected from Shayne or Calvin.

I glanced over at her and instead of the enemy in the white suit I'd seen in the lobby, I saw myself. The lines around her eyes from too many sleepless nights. The tension in her shoulders, her muscles pulled tighter and tighter like a rubber band about to break. She was a mother at a loss, just like me, exasperated by the life she brought into the world, not understanding how she'd ended up desperate for answers that nobody had. Our eyes met and she offered something like a smile, a grimace turned up at one side. I suspected she'd just had the same realization I'd had. She and I were on the same team. No one else understood like we did, felt like we did, suffered like we did. The fruit of our loins putrid instead of ripe.

"Look," she said, talking directly to me. "We've got crap insurance. I don't even know why we bother with it. We were better off on Medicaid. This whole thing was his dad's idea and his dad is an ass. Pardon my French. The genius thought you were some hotshot doctor, which clearly you're not." She waved her hand up and down as if to indicate how obviously I was not a physician, hotshot or otherwise. "No offense," she added quickly. "I just need someone to pay the medical bills, $5,750."

Cornell didn't speak for a second, maybe unsure she'd finished. Then, he scrawled the number down in large print on a paper and turned it toward me and Shayne. He leaned far back in his chair and said, "Ms. Rogers? Mr. Sky?"

Shayne took my hand and squeezed as if we were a unified front and he'd be pulling a checkbook out of his torn back pocket and writing those digits down.

"I can do that," I said. "I can totally do that."

We all sat together in the office while the receptionist prepared the papers. Cornwell made small talk, telling us about Leonis Adobe, the historical building across the street. I told him about going there as a kid when there was nothing else around but fields. Maria ignored all of this, furiously texting and occasionally sighing and *tsking* at her phone.

After all the papers were signed, we stood up. Cornwell shook my hand, then Maria's. Shayne pulled him into a hug, which the man allowed but clearly didn't appreciate. Maria and I stopped in front of each other. I wanted to hug her too, exchange phone numbers, remind us both that there were other people in the world who understood. A small few but they were out there. Instead I shook her hand. As we moved toward the door, she reached into her bag and pulled out a golden name plate that she affixed to her suit. It was a uniform, not a statement at all. Cosmetics counter? Health spa? I held the door open for her.

"Thanks," she said quietly as she passed.

"Thank *you*," I said and I wished I had the $30,000 to give her.

*L*ater that afternoon at The Farm, I helped Rain load the shaman's rental car, a bright blue Chevy Impala that did nothing to alleviate my skepticism about the evening ahead. A dubious adventure with an aboriginal shaman awaited but I was actually in a good mood. The arbitration had turned out better than expected. Yes, Jax was still Jax and my father still had dementia but one thing, one significant and concrete thing, had improved. I intended to be happy about it as long as I could manage.

We took three separate vehicles to Leo Carrillo. Rain, Cal, Jax, and Allambee rode in the shaman's rental. Freedom and Pam drove The Farm pick-up with their kids and four WWOOF farming volunteers in the flat bed. Kara and I had been sharing a series of texts about the arbitration that kept being interrupted by the mountains. I let Shayne drive my car so I could respond. Some delayed messages from her came through as we exited the canyon and hit PCH: "Great outcome!!" "Tonight won't do any harm. Trust me. I'm a doctor."

I still wasn't eager to go to the ceremony, but Kara and Shayne were right, it probably wouldn't do any damage, at least not to Jax. I didn't have to buy into it. I could just sit there. Play my part without getting too caught up in things.

I set my phone in my lap and looked out at the Pacific. All my life, the ocean had made me feel better, no matter what was going on. I was a grain of sand on the shore, minuscule compared to the vastness of the sea, the planet, the universe. I didn't have to do or be anything, and no matter how overwhelming things might seem, my decisions and actions were invisible compared to the breadth of human history.

I tried to hold on to the peace that thought gave me as we drove but instead my mind drifted to Jax and what lay ahead after the ceremony. We didn't have a school. We didn't have a plan. Sharing that moment with Maria Jacobson made me understand more deeply the isolation caused by my son's actions. We'd never juggled play dates or debated over which birthday party to go to. People like to pretend otherwise, but they treat kids like Jax differently. If he had a hole in his heart or cancer, we'd be drowning in sympathy. Kids with cancer are sick. Kids with mental illness are bad. So much for staying happy.

THE TWO SITES Calvin had reserved were next to each other, the fire pits side by side. We all parked. The WWOOFERs with their shaggy clothes and hair piled out of the truck and headed toward the beach. The night with whatever it had to offer was getting closer. I moved to get out of the car, but Shayne reached out a hand to stop me.

"I didn't want to forget to tell you," he said. "Thank you."

"He's our kid," I responded. It came out flat and vague, which was better than what I'd been feeling, which was obligated and a little trapped.

"He *is* our kid," Shayne repeated, nodding as if I'd said something more profound. "We got lucky today. Next year is going to be good."

I almost laughed. Next year Jax would be thirteen. A testosterone storm was lurking on the horizon bringing *more* not less, *worse* not better.

You know, an unexplained sense of impending doom is an actual warning sign of a pulmonary embolism. It's not something supernatural like a premonition or an omen. It's likely an aspect of the body's own self-awareness. The body perceives the ticking time-bomb of the clot drifting through the bloodstream about to settle and wreak havoc. All it can do is give a momentary warning, a last gasp, before it succumbs. I felt like right now was our last gasp.

"Sometimes I feel like therapy helps," I said. "But then, maybe just as often, I'm not sure. How many diagnoses are we going to try out before puberty?"

"He's been doing really good here," Shayne said. "Maybe we should homeschool him."

"Maybe we should medicate him," I said, more snidely than intended. Shayne shifted in his seat. I didn't actually want to have a discussion about psychotropic medications. I was only slightly less skeptical about it than Shayne. Our options were narrowing, but bathing Jax's still developing brain with powerful drugs wasn't a leap I was going to take lightly.

In nursing school, all my young female classmates had clamored over limited clinical rotations in labor and delivery. I volunteered to take psych. The last thing I wanted was to spend my days around happy new moms and their flawless offspring when I had my own screaming infant at home, nothing able to calm him. But psych was its own kind of depressing. Patients wandered the halls, some near stuporous from medications, half treated their illnesses and the other half, the side effects. I didn't know if medicating Jax would prevent that future or cause it.

"You know we've known each other for more than thirty years," Shayne said, as if I hadn't said anything about medication.

"It can't be that long."

"It is. We met in nineteen eighty-seven. It's a really long time." He paused as if we both needed to process that information. Then, he reached over and squeezed my thigh. "Do you remember that first time in the Green Machine? You were so spontaneous and ripe, like a strawberry."

"A strawberry?" I said, laughing. It was a ridiculous analogy. "I don't remember ever being like a strawberry."

"You know what I mean," he said. "*Bébé*, you say stuff with your words, but then you do other stuff with your body and your heart. And you know, you left, but you never *really* left. So, I was thinking, there aren't any more schools, right? Maybe you should come back... to us, to me, and we could homeschool him here, together."

He took my hand and kissed it, holding it against his lips. I was dumbfounded. In all the years I'd been coming and going, knowing I could show up and lie down beside him, he'd never asked me to come back.

"I've been waiting for you to come back on your own," he said, "but maybe you need me to ask so I am."

"You've been waiting? It's been like ten years."

"Nine," he said. He fiddled with his hand-fasting bracelet. Through all of it, neither one of us had taken them off.

"I didn't leave because of him," I said, even though it didn't answer his request.

"You needed your space. You needed to do your thing. That's okay."

"I was never pretending," I said. "I loved you. I loved this life. I just feel like I turned out not to be the person I thought I was."

"Maybe you don't need to think so much about who you are," he said. "Maybe you just need to be who you are."

We didn't look at each other, instead staring out the windshield watching preparations for the ceremony. Calvin piled wood in the fire pits. Rain walked the perimeter of the site waving burning sticks of sage. The shaman and Jax swept the dirt with makeshift brooms made of tree branches. It was like the opposite of television, all the action on the outside of the glass, the figures inside still and quiet.

I'D STARTED INVESTIGATING education programs a few days after the Green Machine died outside Dr. Newman's clinic. I'd traipsed through my first degree without bothering to get any advice from anyone, especially not someone as unimaginative as a career counselor. This time, I attended a career advisory session. I felt like a fool. The room was filled with pimply, borderline adolescents fidgeting in foldout chairs that creaked and scraped the linoleum, nails across a chalkboard.

We completed self-assessments and aptitude tests, then received a list of ten potential careers. Next, we were supposed to talk to an advisor about the classes we needed to prepare for those jobs. I'd been honest with my answers and there was not one practical thing on the printed-out list in my hands. Not one thing that regular people actually did to make a living.

I stood up and walked over to the only table managed by a woman at least as old as me. Her short black hair was pulled back into a minuscule ponytail. Her strong jaw gave her a no-nonsense edge.

"First degree?" she asked.

I shook my head.

"Liberal arts?" she guessed.

"Theater," I said. I was a type she recognized, disillusioned dreamer falling back to earth. She sorted through the stacks of papers in front of her and held one out to me: Bachelor of Science in Nursing.

"Nursing is the most financially worthwhile bachelor's degree you can get," she said. "Unless chemical engineering strikes you?"

I shook my head.

"As a second degree program, you could be done in eighteen months."

I took prerequisites while I was pregnant and started nursing school a few months after Jax was born. Fifteen months later, I was an RN in a nurse residency program. Three years after that I was signing my first ever lease on an apartment.

It was a long, drawn-out departure that, just like Shayne was saying, never resulted in me actually being gone, our lives not joined but intertwined, tangled, that new world I left him for never quite living up to expectations either. I touched my bracelet, then the scar on my arm, a half-moon of small human teeth. Shayne kissed my hand again.

"I love you," he said. "You may not love me but I never stopped loving you. One, only, forever."

Suddenly, Jax popped up in front of the windshield, startling us both. He waved at me furiously, clearly eager and excited, looking more child-like than adolescent. They were both trying to get in and I was trying to keep them out.

I smiled and waved back. That's when I felt it. As hard as I'd tried, hope was shimming its way between the cracks in my facade. I had wanted to be a bystander, an observer. I didn't believe but in that moment I found myself wanting this evening to be something I knew it couldn't. I wanted the same thing that I'd wanted since watching my three-year-old son fling himself off the ladder of the slide: a simple solution, an answer I could grasp in my hands, a wand to make everything better.

"You know how they say insanity is doing the same thing over and over but expecting it to turn out differently?" I said. "I feel like I've been doing that my whole life. I keep waiting for a moment where I'm sure about something, where I know exactly what to do and I know it's right. I feel like everyone has that but me."

"There's no such thing as certainty. It's a wild ride. You just hang on." Calvin had said that at the handfasting, just before the knots were tied that joined Shayne and me as life partners.

"I don't *not* love you," I said. "But I can't say I love you like you're saying it to me. I don't know what to do, but I know I can't decide anything right now. I'm sorry."

Shayne and I sat for a few more minutes in silence. Then, with a smile on his face, he said, "It's okay. I know you. You're always a bit of a downer." He got out of the car. I stared out the window and watched him join the family he'd made for himself. I loved them too in the same way I still loved Shayne. I never stopped. It just got complicated, so different from what I thought it would be. My phone buzzed in my lap.

"Don't be a sour puss tonight," read Kara's text. "It's not any weirder than shit you used to do."

I smiled ruefully and texted back, "Too late."

My phone buzzed again. Kara's next message was a string of New Year's emojis: fireworks, a party hat, and a glass of champagne. I stared at the message until the phone's light went off and all that was left was the black screen shining back at me.

DECEMBER 31ST 6:30 PM

The night closed in, bringing a chill as we finished our preparations for the ceremony. Pam and Freedom had settled on their blankets and shared dinner with their kids. I helped Rain arrange some crystals and a basket of plant cuttings along the length of the picnic tables, while Shayne and Cal tended the two fires. Jax and Allambee sat at a distant table. Allambee talking and Jax listening intently, his face a mere foot from the shaman's.

Allambee wasn't what I'd been expecting. But then the "typical" aboriginal person I was looking for, a man with dark skin and hair, white stripes painted on his face and a cloth covering his genitals, was something right out of *National Geographic*. Probably not real at all or at least not current and likely to make his way to Malibu.

Allambee *was* dark-skinned but with silvery-white, chin-length hair. He was thin and sturdy, like Shayne, a body used to hard work. He had a calculated, natural appearance and an outfit that might have been purchased right out of the display window at Tommy Bahama's: beige linen shirt, dark khakis, and genuine Birkenstocks.

Once we'd all taken our places around the fire, Jax and the shaman moved toward the group. The shaman stood between the two blazes and spoke. "I am Allambee," he said, his voice less whispery and gentle than it had been when I'd introduced myself earlier. "Tonight, we will share in Jax's story to help him move from boyhood to manhood and take responsibility for himself in the world."

Jax stood beside him, his face glowing orange in the fire light. He was nearly as tall as the shaman. His long hair hung down his back in a loose braid. He looked serious but young, a mishmash of grown-up and child, just as likely to engage in serious conversation as to climb up on a picnic table and do a Tarzan imitation. Allambee raised his arms to the sky. The flames undulated in front of him as if under a spell.

"We came from the stars," he said. "We are spiritual beings. Our bodies are physical vessels. They limit us. This is our human experience. We are visitors. We arrive. We observe. We learn. We grow and love. Then, our vessels return to our mother earth and we return to our home in the sky.

"Jax has been betrayed. His vessel is corrupted. It makes him be someone he doesn't want to be. But each of us is provided with exactly what we need to learn our lessons. A man accepts these challenges with no pride, no vanity. He is wide awake. He creates his path with heart, not head.

"Tonight, we help Jax become, take control of his vessel, make him the driver not the passenger on his journey. He must be reconciled. He must make his path. Paths do not exist before us, they are left behind us."

Allambee turned to Jax and they began singing together. Jax did his best to keep up, stealing glances at a worn paper in his hand. I felt a little better. It was starting generically enough, the kind of thing you read as a teenager and think is the most amazing thing in the world but as a grown-up seems sparse on the details.

An ocean breeze blew in. Without thinking, I slid closer to Shayne and snuggled up against him, then wished I hadn't. I didn't want to give the wrong message. He put his arm around me and squeezed my shoulder.

The song finished. Allambee signaled to Jax. My son held his paper out in front of him, his hands trembling. He cleared his throat and walked toward me and Shayne. He knelt and bowed. A section of his hair fell forward covering part of his face. I felt turbulence in the air, raw emotion radiating off him.

"Mother. Father." Jax deliberately fixed his gaze on each of us as he said the words. "I'm sorry for the hurt I've caused you. Sometimes I am not who I wish to be. Sometimes I feel like I am in another world watching myself from afar unable to control my actions."

I fought back tears. He was talking about the exact duplicity I saw played out in front me so many times. Good and bad, each vying for control, demanding to be the dominant force. A boy transformed into a maniac.

"There are many paths, many worlds," he said. "I have been following paths that are mixed and woven around each other, fighting to straighten them. I must make my own path. Tonight, we will call to my true self and bring him back here to stay. We'll banish the other self to that other world where he belongs."

Jax stayed kneeling in front of us and Allambee began to chant. The chanting, the fire, and the darkness seemed to create a kind of spell around us. I felt myself being pulled in, feeling the power of all that might be.

When the chant was done, Jax stood up and took a place next to the shaman again. Allambee told us that each of the grown-ups would now take a turn and tell Jax what we expected from him as a man. He would start with Pam who was to my right, go around the circle to Shayne, then end with me.

Jax walked over to Pam and knelt in front of her. "I'm the first person who laid eyes on you," she said. "Only your mother has known you longer." She glanced over at me and smiled, her face embodying the calm that made her an excellent midwife. "This world can be a cruel place. But I don't believe in cruel people. Cruel actions, yes. But not cruel people. Be kind. Men should be kind." She leaned in and kissed him gently on the forehead.

Jax moved to Freedom. "You know how they say, 'Love makes the world go round?'" Freedom said. "That's what life is all about. Love. There isn't anything more important. You gotta love your family. Your mom, your dad, us. Family isn't just the people you're related to. Life is all about love." Freedom awkwardly shook Jax's hand and patted his shoulder. Jax moved to Rain, who spoke of compassion for all creatures.

When he got to Calvin, my body tensed. All of a sudden, I realized I was going to have to say something to him and it was going to have to mean something. The only way any of it had even a chance of helping was if we all meant it.

I didn't believe Jax was some out of control almost-teen trying to transform behaviors under his control. It was more than that. There was something wrong with his brain, crossed wires, messed up connections. His mind floated in a bath of the wrong neurotransmitters. Too much cortisol? Too little serotonin? A toxic concoction bestowed on him by the die roll called conception.

I didn't have the power to change that. And after all I'd seen of medicine, I wasn't convinced they did either. But I was his mother. Wasn't it my job to try again and again no matter how much it exhausted me? If not me, then who?

Jax knelt in front of Cal. The burly man who'd welcomed me and Shayne into his enclave had become my son's de facto grandfather when dementia forced my dad to abdicate the role. Calvin made an overly dramatic show of clearing his throat. We all laughed a little, releasing some tension. Calvin rested one of his big workman's hands on Jax's shoulder.

"Everybody does stupid shit," he said, looking directly into my son's eyes as if he might be able to reach his soul through a stare. "Everybody is an idiot once in a while. But a man takes responsibility when he's an idiot who does stupid shit. He makes it right and does his damnedest not to do the same stupid shit again."

Everyone smiled and Cal pulled Jax into a long hug. They both wiped tears from their eyes as they broke their embrace. Pressure pulsed inside me. I wanted to say something like that, meaningful and honest but also simple. I had no ideas.

Jax moved to Shayne. They sat looking at each other awhile, then Shayne started to cry. He croaked a few words through his tears. "Be strong," he said. "I love you." Then, he pulled Jax to him for a hug, holding him and patting his back as if they were good friends who wouldn't see each other for a long time.

Too soon Jax was kneeling in front of me, beseeching me with big, brown eyes. To do what? Play along? Or find the words to heal him? I was his mother. I was the reason he existed at all. I'd wanted a baby so badly. How could I abandon him?

I took his hands in mine and pulled them close to my chest. I did not let myself cry. I did not let myself believe in magic. But I did let that wall I'd been building crumble a little. I let myself hope, hope that somehow he'd find a way to do what I was about to ask, that this was the first step. I leaned forward and pulled his head close to my mouth so I could speak directly into his ear, words just for him. His hair smelled the same as it had when he was a boy, a scent likely only Shayne and I would recognize.

"This isn't your fault," I whispered, "but it is your problem to solve. Don't hurt people. Please don't physically hurt any human being again, including yourself. If you can do that, it will change everything."

He nodded. His face seemed full of understanding. I wanted to say more, ask for more. But when I tried to think of one thing I needed from him more than anything else, that was it. It wouldn't be easy. It wouldn't come quickly or naturally. But if he could do it, it would be enough.

After I spoke, Jax and Allambee sat together between the two fires. They swayed back and forth connected by Allambee's hands on Jax's shoulders. The shaman guided us through another song and chant, repeating the lines again until we had them, then led us onward into the verse. When the chant finished Allambee stood up and motioned toward Jax. Jax stood and began removing his clothes. When he was standing in just a loincloth, I glanced back at Shayne to see if he'd known this was coming but his face revealed nothing.

Allambee walked over to the picnic tables. He removed his shirt, set it on the bench and picked up two small clay pots. He returned to the fires. He dipped his fingers into the pots, then painted black and white symbols on Jax's chest. Jax tipped his head forward and Allambee poured the thick liquid over his head so half his head was white and the other half, black.

"Now, we will go to the sea," Allambee announced and began walking through the darkness to the ocean. Everyone got up, shaking the sand from their blankets and wrapping them around their shoulders. Allambee and Jax walked in front of us, Allambee in his shorts and Birks, Jax practically naked.

Our group followed, carefully weaving our way through piles of driftwood and rocks. As we moved away from the few artificial lights at the campground, it got darker. The glimmer of moon becoming our primary light. My son's pale silhouette almost glowing.

"He's gonna freeze to death," I whispered to Shayne.

"It's Malibu. He'll be okay."

Allambee and Jax stopped short of the water. Allambee kicked off his sandals and handed them to Rain. Then, he and Jax continued forward into the ocean until they were up to their knees. Allambee spoke to Jax and Jax moved further and further out in the water. The waves weren't huge but I could see that he was having trouble keeping his balance as the force of the sea pushed against his chest.

"This is crazy," I said to Shayne, trying to keep my voice down. "He could drown."

"If it's easy, it's meaningless," Shayne said. "He'll be okay."

I watched, not knowing what was coming next nor what to do. Everyone was just standing there. I didn't want to ruin the whole thing but I was panicking. Suddenly, Jax screamed loudly and dunked himself under the water. I grabbed Shayne's arm. A few seconds later, he popped back up a little further out. The paint on his head mixed with the sea, dripping down his face and body. He screamed again, then disappeared under the water. My heart raced. He surfaced a little further down the shore.

Jax went under two more times and each time, I gripped Shayne arm tightly barely able to stand it as we waited. Finally, Jax stopped going under. He swam toward the shore until it looked like he was standing, the water rising up to his neck with each swell. I relaxed and let go of Shayne's arm.

With the next wave, Jax walked toward the shore, his body clear of all the black and white paint. He was almost out, just up to his waist, when the wave receded, pulling his legs out from under him. He fell, smashing down into the sand then disappearing as the next wave covered him.

"He doesn't understand the undertow," I said. We all moved closer to the water. Allambee stepped out, looking for Jax. He resurfaced a little further out than he'd been before and swam toward the shore. He tried to walk in again but once again fell and disappeared.

"We've got to do something," I said to Shayne.

"One more time, and I swear I'll get him," Shayne said.

I didn't have time to respond because Jax resurfaced. He bobbed as though his toes were barely reaching the ground. He looked behind him as the next wave came in, then put his arms together and dove into it, using his body to ride in. He ground hard into the shore and instead of standing, crawled up and out of the sea until he was well clear of its grasp.

He rolled onto his back, panting. A tiny rivulet of blood trickled from one of his knees. Everyone gathered around him. I moved to go to him but Shayne gently put up an arm to stop me. Allambee moved in close and Jax sat up. The two embraced and Allambee stepped back so Jax could rise on his own.

"I did it," he said. "I did it."

Jax led the way back to the campground. He was probably freezing but he didn't seem to mind, proudly stamping across the sand in his soaked loincloth. I didn't know whether to be relieved or furious. He was okay but he might not have been. He could have gotten hurt. Or maybe not. We'd all been right there ready to help if he'd needed us.

The campfires were still burning when we arrived, their flames lower. Shayne put on a couple more logs and stoked them. Jax sat between them and we all resumed our places. The flames burned hot at my face and chest after the coolness by the sea. I heard the whistle of cheap fireworks in the distance, someone beginning their New Year's celebration early.

Allambee stood over Jax and began singing. When the song was over, Allambee patted Jax and smiled. Then, the shaman turned to us and said, "Thank you for helping our son find his way tonight," apparently indicating that the ceremony was over.

We sat a little longer around the fires but soon everyone began to pack gear into their respective vehicles. There was no need to stay until midnight. The pagan traditions of The Farm didn't observe the first day of the Gregorian calendar as New Year's. We'd always celebrated our new year at Ostara, the beginning of spring.

We drove down PCH back to The Farm, only a few headlights passing us. After helping unload the cars, I followed Shayne and Jax to the trailer. Shayne seemed wiped out. He was an early riser and we were well beyond his bedtime. He opened the door.

"Are you staying?" Shayne asked.

I looked into the dark space of the trailer. I wanted to stay. I was unsettled. I felt as though I'd been through my own ordeal. I wanted Shayne to hold me, to put his arms around me, and maybe more. The same thing I'd been doing for years, letting him be my safety net. He'd asked me back. He loved me. But he wanted something from me that I didn't seem able to give anymore.

"We should probably take a break, you know, from the..." I said, hesitating because Jax was standing right next to me. "I think the physical stuff is confusing things."

"Okay," Shayne said. He pecked me on the cheek—a kiss that couldn't be mistaken for anything intimate—and disappeared into the trailer.

Jax hugged me, squeezing hard and hanging on. I felt strength in him. He was growing bigger and stronger every minute. Soon a man's body would be behind every action he took.

"It was good, right?" he said, brightly. He was happy. It meant something to him and that was the point.

"It was good," I said, forcing myself to sound upbeat and reinforce what he was feeling. I had no idea what I was feeling. The evening had started as I suspected, something created for Westerners enamored with traditional peoples from other places, but it had gone somewhere unexpected and I'd found myself standing on that shore desperate to run to my son instead of away. Something I hadn't felt in a long time.

"Thanks, Mom," he said. "I'm gonna sleep in my hut." He hugged me again then wandered off to wherever his place was on the property.

I walked up the path to the gate. The smell of marijuana wafted toward me. Rain, Calvin, and the shaman were seated in the screened patio off the main house. Candles flickered around them. Rain stood up when she saw me, so I walked over instead of heading out.

"I feel change and promise on the horizon," she said as she opened the patio door for me. "Change and promise."

"One can hope," I said.

Calvin offered me the joint.

I shook my head. "Can't. Working later." He passed it to Allambee, who took a long slow drag. I studied the shaman's eyes, his almost black pupils. He was unreadable, nothing given away by his empty expression.

"Thanks for tonight," I said. "I appreciate everything you do for Jax. I really do. I know it's been different for a while, but you guys are great. I couldn't love you more." I meant every word of it. Calvin and Rain had never been anything but good to me, welcoming, loving, supportive. They expected nothing in return. Rain spread her arms for a hug. I leaned in and let her embrace me.

"Change and promise," she said again, as if it were a mantra.

I fished my keys out of my pocket. "I should go."

Allambee passed the nub of the joint back to Calvin who examined it for viability then took a final hit. I wondered if they'd been talking about me. My skepticism? My reluctance? In Allambee's mind was I part of the problem? The entire problem?

The shaman looked at me as if he knew I was thinking about him. "Mrs. Sky?" he said.

"Bernadette... um, Bee."

"Bee." He repeated it and bounced his head a little as if my nickname needed confirmation. "Your child? He speaks to a doctor...?" He pointed to his head. "A mental health doctor?"

"Yes," I answered hesitantly, wondering if I was about to get a lecture about the evils of Western medicine and psychiatry. He'd spent hours with my son in the last week preparing for the ceremony, more than any single doctor or therapist ever had.

"Good," Allambee said.

"Thank you," I said, liking him a whole lot more in that moment than I had the rest of the night.

"I'm too high to get up," Calvin said, suddenly grabbing my hand and pulling me down next to him for a hug. "Be careful out there. People are fucking stupid."

I nodded assuming he was talking about drunk drivers, but it was pretty good advice about the world.

THE HANDFASTING 1992

"So Jenn's not coming?" I said, trying not to freak out. I was sitting on the floor at the foot of the bed tucked between Pam's legs. I'd described a rather complicated hairstyle that she was trying to recreate for the handfasting, which was supposed to start in less than an hour. Rain was next to her, holding the baby's breath and every so often passing a piece over to be incorporated in the braid. Kara stood in the narrow space outside the bedroom door. She'd just announced that my other supposed best friend was not coming to the handfasting but hadn't bothered to tell me.

"How can she not be here? She's supposed to be tying one of the knots," I said. "Did she say anything else?"

Kara shifted from one side of the door to the other. "She seemed a little freaked by the whole pagan thing."

"What exactly did she say?"

"Dude, I don't remember. I might have been a little high at the time."

"It's important," I said. "My sister's not coming either. Half the people who were supposed to be tying knots are *not* here. It's just you and my dad now. And God, my mom's gonna hate all this."

The trailer door opened behind Kara. Shayne stepped in, wearing a new linen tunic and shorts. He squished in next to Kara, who glanced at him then back to me.

"She said she couldn't go to some witch thing," Kara said.

"Witches? Where?" Shayne said.

"Apparently, my friend Jenn isn't coming because we're pagans," I said.

"Doesn't sound like a friend worth keeping," he said.

"I thought the groom wasn't supposed to see the bride before —" Kara left the sentence incomplete.

"No patriarchal traditions here," Shayne said. Then, as if to prove the point, he pulled out a joint. "Anyone up for a toke?"

Everyone nodded. Shayne lit up, took a long drag, then passed it to Kara. She took a hit but then her face scrunched up as if she'd smelled something foul.

"That's some shitty weed," she said. She popped open the little, purple purse attached to the belt of her denim jumpsuit and pulled out a thick joint. She took a hit then passed it to Shayne.

Shayne grinned. "This one's worth keeping."

"How come no one else is concerned that my sister and someone who's supposed to be my best friend can't be bothered to come to my handfasting?" I said.

Shayne knelt in front of me, let me take a drag off the joint, then passed it back to Rain.

"*Bébé*, don't worry. I'll figure it out," he said. "The only thing that matters is that you and I are here."

"Colleen was sixteen and pregnant at her *Catholic* wedding, which I went to, and she can't come to this?"

"It'll be okay. I promise. We don't need anyone to make us whole," Shayne said. "We could do this alone in our underwear. It's about us spending our lives together." He kissed me and then took my hand. "I love you. You are my..." He put his face close to mine and we whispered the words together: "One, only, forever."

I kissed him. He always said that when I was feeling down and no matter how many times I heard it, it made me feel better. But in this case I wasn't sure he really understood. He never wanted to see his family again. Soon after we met, he'd legally changed his name and moved to The Farm, living in a tent on the spot that our trailer now sat. I wanted to live my own life, but didn't want to lose my parents and siblings in the process.

"Well spoken," Rain said. "Everyone needs a partner who can talk 'em off the ledge."

There was a knock on the door. The whole room went quiet. No one ever knocked at The Farm. Shayne went and opened the door.

"Hey, Ma and Pa," he said.

I tried to act nonchalant. The room reeked of pot and my parents were coming in. But this was my house. That was the point. My space, my life. Shayne pulled my parents into exuberant hugs.

"Let me give you the tour, Mrs. R," he said, grabbing my mom's hand as if she might get lost in the 27-foot trailer. Over the last four months, me, Shayne and my dad—but mostly Shayne and my dad—had transformed the 1975 Overlander from a beaten-up camping trailer into a livable, if tiny, home.

I'd been planning to move to The Farm as soon as I graduated, then discovered I was a whole term of required classes short of the degree requirements. I was so frustrated I wanted to drop out but my parents offered to buy the trailer and convinced me to finish my degree while it was getting fixed up.

"This is quite the transformation," my mother said.

"Shayne's a hard worker," my dad said. "He's got a real knack for carpentry."

The crazy thing was that my parents actually liked Shayne. Things were less tense when he was around. He was my buffer, an anomaly that left my parents baffled and defused. After we met, I was spending so much time with him that they insisted I bring him home for dinner. So I did. They listened politely as he lectured on the inherent exploitative nature of capitalism and the unfair concentration of wealth. After that he came over all the time.

They'd ask about his family, try to talk about careers, and he'd philosophize about egalitarian methods of compensation. Over time they warmed to him or at least got used to him. I suspected they just didn't know how to respond and I liked that. I liked how he unsettled people, threw the conversation in a whole new direction that left everyone speechless.

"You look very nice," my mother said but I saw a grimace underneath her smile. It was probably the dirt. She'd brought it up again and again. Wasn't living here going to be so dirty? And what happened if we had kids? What was the big deal? We'd figure it out if I got pregnant.

After the tour, my parents left with Shayne and Kara. The moment had been slightly uncomfortable but having my parents there was better than not. I couldn't believe that neither Jenn nor my sister were coming. My sister was pregnant again and supposedly having some gravitas morning sickness. I wanted to believe that that was indeed the reason she wasn't coming but I suspected that the paganism was an issue for her, too. Colleen wasn't exactly an open-minded sort.

I closed my eyes and tried to hear Shayne's words in my head. He'd fix it. He'd figure something out. He always did. He could always find the bright side, always gentle his way through even the roughest patches and come out unscathed. He'd make it all okay. At least, I hoped he would.

Pam finished my hair about ten minutes later. The baby's breath hovered all around my head like a halo. Rain had transformed an old set of antique curtains into a beautiful dress with long bohemian sleeves and a matching train. I felt like a fairy about to take flight as the two women helped me make my way to the sacred circle, a grass patch surrounded by rocks and shaded by giant oaks at the bottom part of the property.

Shayne was standing at the center of the circle. A table that was serving as the altar was behind him. Flowers, incense, stones and a wooden box that I hadn't seen before were arranged around a large mirror. Calvin was nearby talking to some of our friends. His thick ponytail of red dreadlocks swung like a giant tail across the smooth leather of his vest every time he moved. The crowd quieted when I arrived. Rain and Pam helped arrange the dress and train then stepped out.

Calvin lit a stick of incense, stood at the center of the circle, and faced the mountains. "Guardians of the North. Spirits of earth. I call upon thee." he said. "Bless this circle. Nourish our hopes to fruition."

"Hail and welcome," the pagans in the crowd called back.

He turned. "Guardians of the West. Spirits of water. I call upon thee. Bless this circle. Flood our roots with love."

"Hail and welcome."

"Guardians of the South. I call upon thee. Spirits of fire. Bless this circle. Light our passion."

"Hail and welcome."

"Guardians of the East. Spirits of air. I call upon three. Bless this circle. Breathe into us the joy of life."

"Hail and welcome."

Calvin set the burning incense on a tray on the table, then turned back to Shayne and me. He stood tall. His voice boomed.

"With this handfasting, you, Shayne and Bernadette, bring your lives together and join our special family. As certain as the sun rises and the seasons change, you will be challenged. Today you stand here to declare to the gods and goddesses and all those gathered that you will support each other through all life brings to you. You will equally share the unique burdens that land in your path."

Calvin leaned in and feigned a whisper. "Or to say it another way, there ain't no such thing as certainty. It's a wild ride. You hang on tight to each other and hope for the best."

The crowd laughed. I turned to Shayne and smiled. Calvin continued and as I listened, I gazed at the man I was about to be joined with. Rain was right. Shayne had talked me off many a ledge. I felt a kind of calm with him that I experienced with no one else. He was the antidote to every stress and fret inside of me. He saw and loved something in me that I couldn't see myself. With him, my guard fell. Our life wasn't going to be bound by the rules everyone kept telling me I needed to follow. We'd make our own rules. Follow our own path.

Our final project for theater had been a play, a one-man show I'd written specifically for him. He started as a child, then in each act took on a new age and set of circumstances until he was old and dying, finally understanding that every choice he thought he'd made was his destiny at play. The class gave us a standing ovation. It was the most amazing thing that had ever happened to me.

Calvin continued. "A handfasting, which is kind of obvious from the name, is a ceremony where the partners' hands are bound together as a sign of their commitment. To begin, Bernadette and Shayne are each going to speak."

Calvin nodded in my direction. I turned to Shayne. "I think about the first time we met a lot. *That* moment has everything in it that brought us here to *this* moment. I was confused and alone, and a little afraid. I didn't know what I was doing. And then you walked in. I couldn't take my eyes off you. You made me laugh. You made me feel special and I wasn't afraid anymore. I'd never met anyone like you. Someone so ready to run headlong into a new adventure without looking back. The world is so much more interesting with you. It's like you take everything bad in me and make it good. You listen to my dreams and, when everyone else is telling me I'm about to fall off a cliff, you tell me that you'll jump with me. I love you."

Shayne looked at me a little teary-eyed. "I totally want to kiss you right now," he said. "But we're not supposed to." The crowd laughed again. Calvin wagged a finger in mock enforcement of the no-kissing rule, then nodded in Shayne's direction.

"*Bébé*, I have no idea where to start. You've got so much inside of you just ready to burst out, like I touch you and we're immediately on fire. You're so smart and creative. I feel so lucky to be here with you at the beginning. Most people are so full of themselves and you're like the exact opposite, like you don't know how amazing you are and it's my job to tell you. I just want to be with you all the time. We're gonna do great things."

Calvin paused for a moment then said, "Please join hands."

He pulled a small satin bag out of his pocket, reached in and brought out the handfasting cords. He lay them over Shayne and my joined hands. I suddenly remembered that two of the people who were supposed to be there to tie the knots weren't. A hint of panic rushed through me, which Shayne must have felt because he squeezed my hand and smiled.

"Today there will be four knots to represent the four elements," he said. "And four people special to the couple will tie the knots." Kara, Rain and both my parents stepped forward.

"These tied cords are a physical representation of you binding your lives together," Calvin said. He picked up the first set of cords.

"Like water, be gentle enough to go with the flow but strong enough to support each other."

"We will," we said together and Rain came forward to tie the first knot.

"Like air, find joy in each other's passions," Calvin said.

"We will," we said and Kara secured the second one.

"Like fire, burn brightly with compassion for each other."

"We will."

My father tied the cords and kissed me on the cheek.

"Like earth, provide a fertile ground for your love to grow."

"We will," we said together.

My mother stepped forward and paused for a second as if not sure what to do. Our eyes met. She smiled and tied the final knot.

"Do you choose of your own free will each other as life partners?" Calvin asked.

"We do."

Calvin held the top of the now tied cords. "You may now release your hands."

We pulled our hands out and Calvin held the bundle of cords. Shayne walked over to the table and picked up the box, opening it as he got back to me.

"I know we said we didn't want rings," he said. "But I wanted something for when we're apart from each other."

"Right," someone shouted from the crowd. "You two never come up for air."

Shayne pulled out a silver bracelet that looked like woven rope. He slipped one onto my wrist. We'd agreed we didn't want something as traditional as rings. This was a surprise and exactly right. I pulled out the other one and slipped it on his. Calvin placed the handfasting cords in the box and closed it.

"Well, you might as well kiss her now," Calvin said. Shayne leaned in for a kiss and the crowd clapped.

MY PARENTS STAYED until the second round of mead was getting poured. It was turning into the typical hippie party that every event at The Farm eventually became—drinking, dancing, smoking. I walked with them to the gate. I was pretty high. I'd managed to get in a couple of surreptitious drags when my parents weren't looking, not quite ready to openly smoke in front of them though pretty much everyone else was.

"Thank you," I said, hugging and kissing each of them goodbye. "I'm really glad you came."

"Congratulations," my father said.

"You can bring me back my Pyrex the next time you come to the house," my mother said, referring to the lasagna dish she'd placed on the potluck table with a *Goodness, it's just such a mish-mash of things.*

I closed the gate behind them but the sleeve of my dress got caught in the latch. As I stood there working to free it, I heard my parents talking.

"I just don't understand," my mother said. "I never imagined this kind of life for her."

"At least she's not living in a tent," my father said.

"Or pregnant," my mother said.

This was how it was going to be, people moving away from me because of the life I was choosing to lead. A flicker of distress sparked in me. Then suddenly, Shayne came bounding up, a bottle of mead in his hand. He kissed me, then wrapped his arms around me. I grabbed the bottle and took a swig. Yes, this was my life. He was my man. I refused to care what anyone else thought.

The streets were deserted as I drove home after the coming-of-age ceremony, everyone but me apparently inside waiting—with bated breath no doubt—to welcome in the New Year. I got to my door just before midnight. The house was empty. Kara, still at the hospital. Jax, at The Farm. But it felt like something was lurking. It was probably just the let down from the drama of the day, my emotions wound taut repeatedly, then released in a surge. Or maybe it was the trip to Mexico looming. Still I went from room to room, checking for an intruder—the kitchen, the bathrooms, the bedrooms—all the time knowing it was foolish. I wandered into Jax's room and sat on his mattress.

Confirming that I was alone had not made me feel better. The more I told myself everything was okay, the more anxious I became. My mind raced, a frenetic animal running from hidden pursuers. It couldn't be okay. Something was wrong. Something was waiting for me.

I glanced around his room hunting for clues, hints of what the next disaster would be, knowing I wouldn't find them. I never did. No parent should fall for that whole respect-your-kid's-privacy thing. That's how you end up with a dead kid or worse. I physically searched Jax's room every month or so. But short of coming across a loaded gun, it wouldn't matter what I found.

Last year if I'd come across a pencil sharpener the size of a thimble, I wouldn't have thought anything of it. But a few months before the finger incident, Jax had pried the tiny blade out of one and sliced up his legs. Wordlessly, I'd helped him wash the seeping grooves, as he chanted, "I'm sorry. I'm sorry." Afterwards when he was finally asleep, I'd gone into my room and screamed into my pillow.

Now, I straightened out his blanket. The space smelled like him. That same scent I'd noticed when I held him close at the ceremony, his unique aroma. Outside, I heard staggered shouts of "Happy New Year!" and a random gunshot. People *are* fucking stupid, I thought.

I jumped when my phone vibrated in my pocket. It was a text from Kara: "Leave your bag by the door. I'll pack the car. It's starting." It was followed by a rain emoji, an indicator that the OR was getting bloody and Dr. Ivanov had traded out her usual expensive shoes for rain boots. I sent back a sad face.

It was way too early to go to sleep. If I went to bed at midnight, I'd be up at nine, which would leave me exhausted about halfway through my shift the next night. I packed my bag for Mexico, took a shower, then watched a bunch of old TV shows before finally drifting off in the middle of an episode of *Friends*.

WHEN I WOKE UP, it felt like I'd catnapped, a worst case scenario for day sleeping. I'd have to force myself to stay in bed desperately hoping for a second wave of slumber. I debated checking the time but quickly gave in. I turned the clock. The red digits glowed, pulsing with a subtle hostility: 6:25 pm. It took me awhile to process the information. I'd overslept not underslept. I must have forgotten to set the alarm. I only had thirty minutes to get to work.

I jumped out of bed and got dressed. I grabbed an instant coffee and a PBJ then tossed a container of indeterminate leftovers and a banana into my bag. I left my duffle for Mexico on Kara's bed, picked up my phone and headed out the door. It wasn't until I was stopped at the intersection of Wilshire and the 405 that I realized that Kara should have been in her bed. She certainly would have had a long night but there was no way she could still be in surgery.

I reached for my phone and switched it on. The white apple logo was just materializing on the screen when the light changed. I dropped the device back onto the seat. I'd have to wait to find out what was up.

Because I was so late, I had to drive all the way to the roof of the parking structure to find a spot. My phone buzzed in my bag as I grabbed my belongings. I ignored it. Even a momentary pause might be the difference between on time and not. As someone who frequently needed flexibility from management to handle situations with Jax, I tried to be a stellar employee otherwise. I'd never cut it so close before.

I hurried down the stairs and across the street into the main doors by the pharmacy, clocking in at exactly seven. Technically being in the building on time was adequate, but group report on the unit, the way we each got assigned our patients for the night, would start without me. I'd definitely get some unpleasant looks from my co-workers.

When I came through the unit doors, two of the day nurses stared at me a moment longer than felt normal. I was confused. I was late but I wasn't *that* late. Maybe because I'd switched shifts, they were worried I was going to be a no-show. I glanced at my phone just to be sure. There were a handful of missed calls from the hospital but nothing from Kara.

I hustled toward the break room for report. Once I got my

patient assignments, I'd call Kara. I was just about to open the door when I saw Gene, the charge nurse, coming toward me, wearing new glasses with a distinct 70s style.

"Is this your Smokey and the Bandit look?" I teased. The whole unit must be running late if Gene was out here.

"I need to speak to you," he said without responding to my joke.

"Okay," I said. I knew it. The whole thing with Margaret Ann had been too good to be true. Somehow she'd screwed me. I waited for him to tell me what was going on, but he didn't.

"In private," he said.

My stomach dropped. The only other time a charge nurse had pulled me aside to speak in private *before* my shift was when I'd made a medication error, hung a bag of antibiotics intended for my other patient. The nurse on the shift after me had caught it.

"Can I put my stuff in my locker?" I asked trying not to sound as concerned as I was. He nodded. I stepped into the break room surprised to find the rest of the staff getting report from the relief charge nurse. Something was wrong. Really wrong. People noticed me but didn't look at me. They were deliberately not turning in my direction or making eye contact.

I shoved my bag in my locker. My last few shifts were a blur: car wrecks, motorcycle accidents, strokes, transient ischemic attacks, resected tumors. The same kinds of patients I'd had for years. I couldn't remember anything unusual. But that's how accidents are. You aren't expecting them. They just happen.

Gene was so close to the door I almost walked into him as I came out. My stress level doubled. Whatever was going on was so serious he was keeping tabs on me. He gestured down the hall to the manager's office, which was usually locked during night shift. The door stood open, bright lights glaring.

My heart pounded in my ears as we walked past the patient rooms. What was going on? What horrible thing had I done? I wanted to ask in a calm voice, "What's this about, Gene?" so he could say, "You just need to sign some paperwork." But I knew any words that came out of my mouth would crackle and break before taking shape. He let me go into the office first.

The room was long and rectangular, with a length of desk running down one side. The opposite wall was windows looking out to the parking structure I'd just run in from. Three rolling chairs were evenly dispersed along the desk, tucked in neat and tidy. I took the furthest seat. Gene closed the door, muffling the familiar noises from the unit that I hadn't realized were a comfort until then. He took the middle chair and rolled too close. All I could do was keep quiet.

"Kara Fink's your friend, right?" he said.

The question caught me off-guard. He knew Kara and I were friends and why would he be asking about her? I panicked. Kara must have told someone about Mexico. But we hadn't done anything yet. How could we be in trouble? It had to be more nonsense with Margaret Ann, another bullshit rumor, the favor of switching shifts a red herring so she could set us up.

"Yes," I said, trying to keep the fear out of my voice.

"Kara was in a car accident this morning."

"What?" His words were wrong. They didn't make sense.

"She was t-boned at Wilshire. They think a guy coming off the freeway ran the light."

"Is she okay?" I asked but as soon as the words came out my mouth, I knew. She was *not* okay. That's why the door was closed. That's why everyone was acting so strangely. "Is she dead?"

Gene took off his glasses and wiped the back of his hand across his forehead as if the room were hot and he was sweating. "No... but..."

He didn't have to say more. I understood. If nature had its way, there would be no halfway, no in-between created by the "wonders" of modern medicine. Humans intervene because sometimes, only sometimes, they work miracles. Surgeons reach their hands into the abyss and pull back someone very much like the original. Someone bruised and scarred, never *exactly* the same, but close enough to make it worth the attempt. But sometimes, no matter how hard they try, one piece is so damaged it's a null, a black hole dense enough to suck in life itself.

"Here?" I said, suddenly sickened by the reality of what was happening. She was here. Of course she was here. It was the closest hospital. I might have just walked by her.

"Room seven."

"Eliot!" I blurted.

"We had trouble getting a hold of him. But he's on his way." He glanced at his watch. "He should be here pretty soon."

I stared at him. I was numb, more than numb, hollow.

"I took you off the schedule for the night," he added. I hadn't thought of that yet, hadn't gotten to the part where I might be working while my best friend died in the next room.

"Do you need a minute?" he asked.

I nodded. How many times had I said that exact line then handed someone a box of tissues or a glass of water, closed curtains so they could have privacy, shut doors so they could cry as loud and hard as needed? How stupid these things we said were. A minute? For what? I needed hours. A lifetime.

Gene got up. He put a hand on my shoulder and rested it there as if he wanted to say more but we both knew there was nothing more to say. Nothing would make it better or different. He gave my shoulder a squeeze.

"Take as much time as you need," he said, then closed the door behind him.

I sat there, staring out the window, searching for something that made sense: Street light. Stop sign. Tree. Everything in me wanted to run, not to her, but away. I knew this story and its ending too well. I didn't want to be in it. I was supposed to be on the sidelines, holding hands, offering comfort. I was not supposed to be onstage and neither was she.

When I came out of the manager's office, I stood there a second, not sure if I'd be able to move. I had to focus on breathing, on picking up one foot and putting it out in front of me so I might move closer to her. Angie and Fiona were at the computer station outside room seven giving shift report when I walked up. They both gave me the same sympathetic half-smile.

I took a few steps closer and saw what everyone else had already seen. A head lying on the white background of the sheet, as always, the bed at 45 degrees and facing the door. Words from Angie and Fiona's report drifted over to me: seven fractured ribs, punctured left lung, severe diffuse axonal injury, Glasgow Coma Scale three at scene. I didn't need a translator. I spoke that language.

Her head had been snapped back and forth during the accident, her brain scraping against the inside of her skull, severing large sections of axons, the communication pathways. She'd been in a coma at the scene, completely unresponsive, no reflexes. She wasn't going to wake up and even if by some "miracle"—if you want to call it that—she did wake up, she wouldn't be who she had been. Not just her personality but everything. She might not be able to walk, to speak, or to move her limbs. She might just lie there moderately aware of things around her, not conscious enough to even know she was human.

"Can I go in?" I asked. I didn't really need permission, but nurses are protective of their charges. Angie nodded.

I reached to slide the door open and automatically my mind started a task list: turn patient on the even hours, attach endotracheal tube securement device, change bloody pillow cover. I started every shift making mental notes of the care I would provide through the night but this person in front of me wasn't my patient but my friend.

I forced myself to breathe as I took in the full image of her. Her features were obliterated. Her eye sockets were giant saucers of crimson. Something had impacted the left side of her face. It was purple and swollen. She had multiple lacerations on her forehead, across her eye and down her cheek. A thick tube was in her mouth secured with tape. The ventilator stood like a sentry by the bed.

I took a step forward then stopped again. On one side her hair —the hair I'd braided just days ago—was long and matted with blood. On the other side, it was shaved. A row of staples lined her scalp like train tracks. There would be a soft spot where they'd cut out a chunk of skull to let her brain swell so it wouldn't be crushed by the house that was supposed to protect it. They'd probably done it when they were still hopeful or not certain what she'd want.

I felt oddly out of place, as if I didn't spend more time here than anywhere. But I had a routine at work: confirm medications, pumps and orders; trace lines, bag to pump to patient; zero the arterial line; get a square-wave; note the central venous pressure; check drains; assess eyes, heart, lungs, bowels; examine every inch of skin. I did the same thing every night with every patient. Without my routine I felt adrift—no beginning, no middle, no end—a drop of ink in the sea, losing its shape, diffusing, dissipating, disappearing.

The patient rooms had always seemed practical and organized. Everything in the same location: hospital bed, table, chairs. The drawers of supplies—syringes, boxes of gauze, saline flushes, needles—all in the same configuration. No time wasted searching. Now they felt impersonal. The drawers restocked by the health techs. The beds restocked by car accidents, gun shots, strokes.

I believe they can hear you. How many times had I said that? But standing in the room with Kara, I was mute. Everything was closing in, too many beeps and buzzes. The ECG machine got louder, mocking my silence. The high-tech bed shifted, hissing air at me like I was in its way. Numbers and lines flashed on the monitor, things I understood but at the same time were inconsequential.

My friend was only vaguely visible in the broken, beaten body in front of me. Maybe I didn't want to see her. Or maybe she wasn't really there at all. Maybe she was on a journey, safe in another universe, and she'd just forgotten to say goodbye. I stepped closer. I could smell her, Kara, above the hospital smells: the dried blood, disinfectants, medications, soap. I even thought I could smell her cherry Chapstick.

"Can you hear me?" I said, then scolded myself silently. *If you are going to talk, at least don't be an idiot.* But I didn't know what to say. I said the same thing to my unconscious patients every night: "Hi (patient name here). My name is Bernadette. I am a nurse. You are in the hospital. You had a (fill in tragedy here). I'm going to be taking care of you tonight."

I'd describe everything I was doing: "I'm listening to your heart." "I'm checking your pulses." I imagined it was terrifying lying there with bits and pieces of the world reaching you, unidentifiable sounds, sensations, and lights. People poking and prodding while they talked about the latest sports scores or gossiped.

But what was I supposed to say to my friend who was dying or was already dead, gone in every way that mattered. I finally understood the other side, how people could just stand there, how they could be brought to a standstill. Everything and nothing to say.

"It's Bernadette," I finally said. "I'm here."

I lifted the sheet. Amazingly, her right hand was unscathed. Every inch of her was damaged, bruised, and assaulted yet there was her perfectly beautiful hand. I held it. It occurred to me that she might be wondering why I was there, not Eliot. "Eliot's on his way," I said. "He was in Aspen. But he's coming."

After that I didn't know what to say. If anyone knew the direction things were headed, she did. She was a trauma surgeon. It was probably obvious to her in whatever brief moment of awareness she'd had of the accident, the twisted irony: This is how it will be, death by trauma.

I patted her hand, something I never would have done in real life, or was this real and that other world the fabrication, the alternate reality? I couldn't hug her. Couldn't bait her with snarky retorts. Patting her hand like a doting grandmother was all I had. The totality of our friendship reduced to a ridiculous pat, pat, pat. Fiona came in.

"Would you like some water?" she said.

I shook my head. She positioned a chair behind me and I fell into it. Still holding Kara's hand, I let my head rest against the bedrail. Fiona checked the monitor settings and the angle of the bed. She put her stethoscope in her ears and placed its diaphragm on Kara's chest. I glanced at the monitor showing her heart beating, promising something it couldn't deliver: life.

Fiona stopped on the opposite side of the bed and looked at me. Her head tipped to one side and the corners of her mouth turned up while the rest of her face seemed to fall. My ability to interpret human expression was gone. I saw the muscles and skin move but couldn't define the emotion.

The looks were killing me. I saw pieces I recognized. The masks we put on and take off without changing anything on the inside, without feeling anything. They were my faces, mastered in years of being too close to death. I hated them, reflections in a funhouse mirror, grotesque and distorted.

"She's an organ donor," Fiona said, then nodded as if I'd responded and walked out. Without Eliot's permission, they couldn't tell me if she was brain-dead. But from that little piece, that public information from her driver's license, I could make some guesses. They'd probably already tested her once. It was just a waiting game.

If she was brain-dead, Eliot would say his goodbyes, then they'd take her to an operating room, where a special team would procure her viable organs. He wouldn't wait. She wouldn't want him to. She'd save someone else's life yet again, some kid with idiopathic viral cardiomyopathy or some twenty-year old with cystic fibrosis. If she wasn't brain-dead, it would be a little different. They'd take her to the OR and do a terminal extubation, removing the tube and ventilator that were keeping her alive. Then, once she was declared dead, they'd proceed.

Suddenly as if my thoughts had manifested him, Eliot appeared on the other side of the door. His blond hair shone golden under the lights, but his face was grim and washed out like a ghost. He was stripped down to black ski pants and a pale blue, thermal undershirt. A lift ticket dangled from a loop on his pants. He must have literally been pulled from the slopes, sweater and parka left somewhere, a man coming to bid farewell to his wife.

Fiona was speaking to him. He nodded. One of the doctors would come now. That's what happens when the next of kin shows up. But this doctor would be someone Eliot knew, someone who had been to one of their notorious Halloween parties bearing expensive bottles of wine.

Some doctors are better at this moment than others, but the world is too used to TV resurrections, good-looking hero-types saving the day. A physician can describe all the damage and say, "There isn't anything else we can do." And then a spouse, bright-eyed and hopeful, asks, "But he's going to be okay, right?" People can hold on to the tiniest of threads, weave a tale in which time heals any and all wounds.

Standing there at Kara's bedside, I wished I was that kind of person. I wished I believed in healing hands, the power of prayer, anything that would give me just a second where I didn't under-stand. But it didn't matter what I believed. Every time I believed in something I found it wanting, gaping holes behind the curtain, the side stage where you weren't supposed to see.

Fiona patted Eliot on the back. That's all you have at a moment like this: heartfelt but hopelessly futile gestures. Eliot slid open the glass door and stepped in. His eyes were red and puffy. He hesitated as if he might not be in the right room, then walked toward the bed, not looking away from her face, even when her blood pressure alarm flashed red and beeped. I reached up and silenced it. I stepped back so he could have the spot on her right side where she looked at least a little like herself. He moved forward and took her hand.

"Oh, my love. Oh God." He sobbed, his shoulders shaking as he kissed her cheek. He brought her hand to his lips, then ran it along his face. I started to cry myself, shaking my head and letting my face fall into my palms. I turned to leave.

"Don't go. Please," he said. The sadness in his voice was like a living thing reaching out to drain me. I stopped. He wrapped his arms around me, and we sobbed together. We stood a long time, crying and crying, trying to find whatever speck of solace there might be in each other's arms.

"What do I do?" Eliot implored. I wasn't sure what he meant.

As far as I could tell there was nothing to do except what we were doing: crying. I noticed Dr. Ivanov outside the door. She must have gone home this morning like Kara and come back to this.

I loosened my embrace with Eliot and pointed. "I think she's here to talk to you."

Eliot let me go and turned as Dr. Ivanov came in, her heels clicking on the floor like tap shoes. She was an attractive woman with shoulder length black hair and a purple and white patterned dress. Her white coat was the only suggestion she was a doctor. The two of them, minus the lab coat, looked as if they belonged anywhere but here.

"Eliot," she said. She grasped both of his hands. "I'm so sorry."

Eliot's sobbing subsided for a moment.

"I know Paul talked to you earlier," she said, "but I want to be sure we've answered all your questions. We did everything we could. But..." She left the sentence unfinished, her eyes welling with tears.

Eliot nodded, then glanced back at Kara because the alarm went off again.

"It's just her blood pressure," I said. "It's a little low."

Eliot turned back to Dr. Ivanov.

"Take as much time as you need," Dr. Ivanov said. "She was a wonderful person and a great doctor."

She *was*. Past tense. Yet she was right there, almost there, like if I waited long enough, called to her hard enough, I might find her and pull her out. Dr. Ivanov hugged Eliot, then me. She left, her white coat flapping behind her like a cape, a powerless superhero.

"I need to go," I said, suddenly overcome by a desire to run. It wouldn't change anything. I couldn't actually get away, but I couldn't stand it anymore.

"Wait." Eliot's voice quivered. "How does this work? They said she's probably..."

"Brain-dead?" I said, when he didn't finish. "They have to test her twice, and then if she is, whenever you're ready you tell them. Are you going to wait for her parents?" Kara's aging parents had retired to Florida years ago and her father's health was in decline. It might be a day or two before they could get here.

"Should I?" he said.

"You have to do what you think she'd want."

"She wouldn't want to be like this," he said.

I shook my head. No, she wouldn't.

"I can't believe this is real," he said. "She called me before she left the hospital. I was at breakfast. She called to say good night." He looked back at Kara confused, unable to reconcile those two things, the flimsy divide between life and death, too much to comprehend. "She was heading to your place. It must have been minutes after that. By the time I ordered coffee she was…"

A crushing ache gripped my stomach. The tears came back. I walked over to her, kissed her cheek and whispered, "I love you. Goodbye."

I hugged Eliot one more time and made my way to the door. I wondered how long he would stay there. She was already gone but how long would it take for him to actually let her go?

THE PARTY 2011

I hadn't wanted to come to the party. Parking my 2009 Civic—which I was still paying for—amongst the luxury vehicles outside Kara's house didn't make me feel better about it. I was probably going to be the only guest not making a six-figure income and was certainly going to be the only one who'd spent seventeen years on what most people, after I explained The Farm to them, decided to call a commune.

I didn't fit in Kara and Eliot's world. I didn't fit anywhere. Sometimes it felt like my years on The Farm had been spent in a foreign country and I was experiencing reverse culture shock. Walking into Kara's living room only intensified that feeling.

Straight-laced, serious types in elaborate Halloween costumes mingled in her cavernous Mediterranean-style home. A full costume had seemed silly when I was getting ready but now I felt underdressed. Everyone had gone all out with their outfits, stage-level ensembles. My "costume" consisted of black and white cat ears. I made my way through the crowd and found Kara in the kitchen.

"Thank God, you're here," Kara said, giving me an exaggerated hug. "I'm drowning in psychiatrists."

Eliot was a fairly well-known research psychiatrist at the University of San Diego. Apparently, most of the people at the party were his colleagues. I only recognized a couple of doctors from my work.

"*Rocky Horror?*" I said, gesturing toward Kara's costume—rainbow shorts, a sequined jacket and a top hat.

Kara nodded.

"Cat?" she asked as she handed me a margarita.

"How'd you know?"

When she'd invited me, Kara had insisted it wasn't a "doctor" party but then hadn't been able to name a single person who was coming that wasn't one. She'd even tried to count two PhD researchers.

"PhDs aren't doctors?" I'd said.

"I thought you meant MDs."

"I said *doctor* party not MD party."

"Just shut up and come," she'd said. "You never do anything fun."

That was what had convinced me. Not only did I never do anything fun, in the two years I'd been away from The Farm I almost never did anything other than work. Every so often Kara dragged me to a yoga class or we went out for a drink, but months would pass between events without me coming up for air. A Halloween party with a bunch of doctors wasn't my first choice for fun, but it was better than nothing. Maybe only slightly.

"How was the guest house?" Kara asked. I'd just started looking at different apartments that might put Jax in a better district.

"Great. Walking distance from the school. Two bedrooms, cute little kitchen, and this weird extra room, like a half-bedroom or something. But it's not gonna work. It's a good $400 more than I can actually afford. I don't know what I'm going to do. Any minute now the other parents are going to set my place on fire to get us out of the district."

Eliot came into the kitchen in a green lab smock and oversized pearls. I suspected he was supposed to be Frankenfurter, the main character from *Rocky Horror*, a movie Kara had been obsessed with in high school and apparently still was, but he hadn't done any of the makeup or hair. He looked more like a lab tech from a 50s nuclear reactor than the "sweet transvestite" from the cult classic. He reached around Kara, grabbed some drinks off the kitchen island, and left without a word, which seemed unusual. They were always pretty lovey-dovey when they were together.

"Is something wrong?" I asked.

"I'm not going to Aspen this year," Kara said. "And I've decided to start staying in a hotel near the hospital when I'm on call. All this driving is killing me."

"And he's mad?"

"He doesn't like it. He'd be with me twenty-four hours a day if he could."

"Forgive me for loving my wife," Eliot said coming back into kitchen. He opened the fridge and pulled out a platter of appetizers.

"I don't even know why you want me to come," Kara said. "It's the same thing every year. I freeze my ass off. Everyone teases me about not skiing. Your parents hate me." She turned to me. "Cuban Catholic was not on their list of appropriate marriage partners."

"They'll come around," Eliot said.

"We've been married thirteen years. I think I've given it a fair shot," Kara said.

"You'd rather be alone in some hotel in LA than in Aspen?" Eliot said.

"Honey, I love you. *You* are great. But I'd rather be pretty much anywhere than with your parents."

Eliot stood there in the middle of the kitchen holding the platter as if he'd forgotten where he was supposed to be taking it. Then, he frowned.

"I know," he said. "They're such snobs. I just hate that you'll be alone over the holidays."

"It'll be okay," Kara said. "I'll be at the hospital. Benny will be there. She's always working."

Eliot shook his head slightly then left with the tray.

"I'm not *always* working," I said.

Kara looked at me flatly. "When was the last time you took a vacation?"

"I can't afford a vacation. I can't afford anything."

"Oh my God," Kara suddenly exclaimed, making everyone within earshot turn their heads toward us. "Tell me more about the guest house."

"The guest house I can't afford?" I said, confused.

"The extra room," Kara said.

"It's like a utility room or something. Why?"

"Is it big enough for a twin bed and a nightstand?"

"Yeah, but it's tiny. There's no closet or anything. And who could I live with with Jax and night shift?"

"Someone who only needs to stay there a couple times a month when they've been on call."

It took a second for me to figure out what she was talking about.

"You?" I asked.

"It's perfect. A hotel is going to cost at least $150 a night. And I can't leave any of my stuff there or cook," Kara said. "Eliot will feel much better if I'm with you."

I sat there thinking through what Kara had suggested. It could work. I'd been planning on changing to a weekend schedule to better accommodate Shayne's lack of a vehicle and Kara was usually on call on the weekends. When she was staying at the house, Jax wouldn't even be there. The thought of Kara being around during the holidays gave me an idea.

"Maybe Shayne could keep Jax for the whole week and we could do something while you are at my place," I said.

"It will be like a vacation," she said.

THE PARTY ENDED a little after midnight. Eliot and a friend were making sure a few people who drank too much got home safely and I was helping Kara clean up. Just like Kara had expected, Eliot was happier with her spending the holidays with me than alone and the more I thought about the arrangement, the better it seemed. A move would put Jax in a new district, one with more resources. He could change schools right after the holidays. Only one thing bothered me and as Kara and I moved around the house picking up bottles and glasses, it kept nagging at me.

"Am I your slumming?" I asked.

"What?" Kara said. "What does that even mean?"

"Am I your charity case? You're swooping in to save me because I can't figure it out for myself? I'm really happy actually but I feel bad. I should be able to figure this out myself."

"First off, no. You are *not* my charity case. I need a place and this, honestly, is ideal," Kara said. "And secondly, why would it even matter? It's okay to let me help you. You don't have to overthink it. Sometimes you just take the help from wherever it comes and you just say thank you. You're my best friend. Why wouldn't I help you?"

"I don't know. I guess all these rich doctors made me feel poor and stupid."

"Did you talk to any of them?" Kara said. "Most of them are boring or fake or both. You're real. You're neurotic as hell sometimes but you might be the only real person I know."

*A*s I put on my black slacks and blouse, it occurred to me that the purpose of a funeral might be to force those in mourning out into the daylight. For almost three days all I'd done was lie in bed—years of stolen hours demanding to be repaid. The solitude and silence of the house called to me. Its shadows invited me to burrow in, hide, find a place in darkness. If it hadn't been for the service, I might have never come out.

I was fixing my makeup, when the doorbell rang. I found Shayne on my front step, in black jeans and a white dress shirt that was at least a size too large for him. I hadn't seen him in anything but shorts, t-shirts and his work boots for years even in winter. It was like he was playing dress up.

"What are you doing here?" I said. "I'm about to leave."

"I didn't think you should go alone," he said, smiling then looking down, both our gazes falling on his work boots.

"How'd you get here?" I asked. I wanted to be upset. He shouldn't have just shown up. He should've called. But I was glad to see him.

"Calvin." He tipped his head in the direction of the white pick-up idling a few houses down.

194

"Come in," I said and waved at Calvin who was apparently waiting to see if I'd send Shayne packing.

"You would've said no if I asked," Shayne said as he stepped into the house. "So, I didn't ask."

We stood for a second in the hall, me still stunned by his unexpected presence, him tentative in my home, a space he was rarely in. The last time he was here was when Jax broke Leo's fingers, disasters drawing us together. He handed me a brown envelope.

"Jax made this," he said.

The front of the handmade card was a wild mix of colors, abstract flowers and trees. The note made me cry: *Dear Mom, I'm really sorry this happened. I liked Dr. Fink. She was nice.*

I took a breath then wiped away my tears.

"Thank you," I said.

WE WERE MOSTLY quiet on the drive to the funeral home in Costa Mesa. I told a few stories about Kara and Shayne listened. Whenever tears came to my eyes, he patted my leg.

The funeral home was packed, mostly with people who didn't know Kara that well: Doctors I'd met at the Finks' infamous Halloween parties. Colleagues from the hospital. A couple of nurses from the unit. Eliot stood near the closed white coffin at the front of the hall. Kara's parents, who I hadn't seen since high school, were beside him. Like mine, they seemed older than they should be, life passing too quickly.

Eliot raised a hand in my direction as Shayne and I walked up the aisle. I nodded my acknowledgment. He'd asked me if I wanted to speak but I couldn't fathom standing in front of a crowd of mostly strangers, trying to use words to make sense of things. I had no idea how he was going to manage. She was my best friend. She was his wife.

The service seemed to be starting so Shayne and I took a place in the second row. One by one her peers spoke about what a great doctor she was, how kind she was, how special. Their words burned like embers. Shayne put his arm around me, and I sank into his shoulder. Kara and I were supposed to be in Mexico. How were we here? What a fool I'd been to think that I'd ever been in control of anything, that I'd ever been anything but powerless.

Eliot took a place at the podium. He turned, his eyes fixing on her coffin.

"This was not how we planned it," he said. "This is not how anyone plans it. We were going to get old together. Retire somewhere warm. You all know Kara didn't do snow." A few cautious laughs came from the mourners. "But here we are."

"There are a lot of cliches about living in the moment and appreciating everything you have and, oh my God, they're true. I like to think I did. But I don't know. I took for granted that we'd have more time and all I keep thinking about is that last phone call. Did I say I love you? I think I did. I hope I did."

He wiped his tears with a tissue, then went on. "I remember the first time I saw her across the room at Jeffrey Gold's party. She was… God, she was beautiful. Radiant. She was so out of my league. You know I asked her out on a dare? A stupid dare. Seriously, the greatest thing that ever happened in my life was because some jackass, whose name I don't even remember, thought it would be hilarious to watch me go up to the hottest girl in the room and get annihilated. But she was nothing like what people expected. She was gorgeous, but she was funny and smart, totally unique."

Eliot talked for a while longer making me and everyone else cry a few more times. But the rest of the service was a blur. Shayne and I stayed at the reception long enough to talk to Eliot and Kara's parents, but I didn't want to talk to anyone else. We left and I drove Shayne back to The Farm.

The muted greens of the canyon enveloped us as we took the

winding road up into the canyon, the earth embracing me. I parked by the fence and we sat quietly for a minute. Shayne was perfect sometimes. Sometimes he did exactly the thing I needed even when I didn't know I needed it.

"I'm glad you came," I said, without looking at him. "Thank you."

He leaned over and hugged me.

"No problem," he said. Then, he got out of the car and disappeared behind the huge wooden gate of the world we used to inhabit together.

JANUARY 5TH 1:00 PM

*A*fter dropping Shayne off, I decided to go to my parents'. An hour visiting with my mom might settle me enough to find the resolve to go back home. The last place I wanted to be was alone at the guest house but I was supposed to be returning to work that night. I'd need a nap to get through the shift.

My father was in the driveway working on his little black Toyota truck when I arrived. The door was propped open, his torso hidden inside the cab. I stood back trying to figure out what he was doing. His head was under the dash like he was hot-wiring it, a skill that I *wasn't* sure he *didn't* have. Tools were strewn on the cement near the vehicle: hacksaw, hammer, screwdrivers, pliers.

The Club was on the steering wheel. If he did get it started, he wouldn't be able to turn the car. He'd either crash into the garage door or roll back into the neighbors' car—not ideal but better than careening around the neighborhood streets or getting lost. He climbed out when he realized I was there, a bulky wrench in his hand, one he'd use to tighten the piping under a sink. I was relieved. Even I knew you couldn't hot-wire a car with a wrench.

"Whatcha doing, Dad?" I asked.

"Fixing my truck," he said. "Something's wrong with it."

He sounded so determined. If I hadn't been so utterly depressed, I might have laughed. He would fix the truck like he'd fixed the cactus and my mom's statues.

"Do you have the right tools?" I asked. He couldn't meet me in my world, so I might as well meet him in his. He picked up the wrench and stared at it.

"This thing doesn't seem right," he said.

He set the wrench down next to the other rejects and then stomped into the ivy on the left side of the house, presumably heading to the backyard and his workshop. The entire time my parents had lived there, we'd used the right side of the house to go to the yard. That's where the stepping stones were.

Before the dementia Dad would have gone that way too. With the dementia, he typically walked through the house to the workshop making hundreds of trips, as if determined to risk the death stairs as many times as possible. This was the first time I'd seen him or anyone trample through the thick field of ivy, but he'd obviously been doing it all afternoon. A well-worn path of crushed and broken leaves was visible through the dark green, the newest victims of his illness.

I walked in the house. "Mom?" I called.

"Kitchen," she said. She was at the window looking at the front yard, her shoulders pulled up tight, mouth pinched into a straight line.

"Why is he going through the ivy?" I asked.

"How would I know?" she said sharply. She wrung the dish towel that was in her hands, twisting it tighter as she stared out at his path. She turned. Something about my face or clothes must have reminded her about Kara and where I'd just come from.

"Oh, sweetheart," she said. "I am so sorry."

She spread her arms wide, the towel swinging from her hand like a flag guiding me. I fell into her. The damp rag cool against my neck. I cried, strangely reassured. In her arms it felt like everything was okay, even when I knew it wasn't. When I finally let her go, we each took a seat at the kitchen table. We could see a side view of the driveway. The truck's door sat open awaiting my father's return.

"Was it a nice service?" my mother asked, staring out the window.

"As funerals go, it was peachy."

"I sent a card to her parents. I signed for you."

I heard my father coming up the stairs into the living room.

"Do you know what he's doing?" I said quietly to my mom but then Dad came into the kitchen, a sharp metal tool that looked suspiciously like an ice pick in his hand.

"Howdy, stranger," he said to me. "When did you get here?"

"A few minutes ago," I said, wondering how one of us might lure the pick from him without irritating him.

"Something's wrong with the truck," he said. He spun the pick inside his closed fist as if winding it up.

"Would you like some tea and cookies?" Mom asked.

As often as not, you could get Dad to change directions with an out-of-the-blue offer like this one. It was like waving a red muleta in front of a bull. You'd see the shift in his face, a switch flipping. Suddenly, he'd be in the new moment with you and the beer or cookies or dinner you'd distracted him with and everything else would be left behind in the vortex. Dad glanced around the kitchen, then at me, then at Mom.

"Something's wrong with the truck," he repeated.

My mother's forced smile barely masked her grimace. "Okay, dear. We'll have tea later," she said. Dad headed back out the front, closing the door hard behind him.

"He's probably going to damage it with that thing. Was that an ice pick?" I asked.

"I don't know."

"What's he doing?"

My mom's brow furrowed, then she snapped. "Didn't you

hear? He's fixing the truck. Something's wrong with it." The sarcasm was concerning, not typical for my mother at all. She got up and stood by the window again, her jaw clinched so tightly I heard her teeth grind.

"He's been at this all morning. It's like a magnet. He won't stop," she said.

"Maybe now's the time to donate it."

She nodded, which didn't mean she was going to do it. Colleen and I had talked to her as much about the truck as we had the workshop, to no avail. Mom was convinced Dad would notice the truck was gone and its absence would be a source of tension. But I suspected there was more to it. Each thing was a concession, an admission that another line had been crossed, that he'd plunged further into the abyss of his dementia.

I looked at her, standing in the exact spot where she'd waited for me so many times after curfew. She'd loomed then, the largest power in my life, now she hovered desperate and ghostly, the shadow of the person she'd been. She was being pulled into the void along with my father. Tethered to him, she was unable to break free.

I walked over to her and put my arm around her shoulder. We stared out the window at my dad. His head, once again buried under the steering wheel of his truck attempting to fix whatever he thought was wrong with it. He stood up, the ice pick in his hand. I was relieved to see there was no blood; he hadn't hurt himself. He dropped it on the ground and started down through the ivy again. My mother faced me.

"Do *you* want a cup of tea?" she asked.

"Sure," I said. She put on the kettle and set out two cups. I kept watching my dad.

I wanted to tell my mother about Mexico, that I'd been trying to help her. For the first time, I could see myself doing it, mixing the pills with a drink, giving it to him. I'd lead him to their bedroom, help him lie down. We'd hold his hands and watch as he drifted off to sleep, his breathing slowing further and further until he exited this world.

But now, the humane thing was out of reach. The one person who could help me was gone. We were left with things I couldn't imagine myself or my mother doing: suffocating him with a bag of helium, leaving paper trails as we tried to get prescriptions for medications we didn't need, figuring out a carbon monoxide system that didn't kill us in the process. I'd failed. All that was left was the nursing home.

Dad came through the house again, this time walking out the front door without stopping at the kitchen. I got up and took my mom's spot at the curtains. He was throwing all his physical strength into whatever he was doing now, his body rocking back and forth just inside the door of his truck. With that intensity, he was going to break something for sure. The kettle whistled and Mom poured the tea. She set our cups on the table and we both sat.

"Do you want me to try to get him again?" I asked.

"Later. I need a minute." She looked weary, dark, puffy bags under her eyes. "I had to go pick him up three times last night. Either I sleep so light I wake up whenever he moves, or I am so exhausted he's halfway to the shop before I realize he's gone."

I wondered if we could put padlocks on the doors or dead-bolts that needed keys from the inside. Was that even legal? Was it some kind of imprisonment? It probably wouldn't work anyway. He'd just wake her up or start pounding on the doors. A memory care unit was the only solution.

"Colleen came by yesterday," my mother said.

"With the kids?"

"No, just her. We talked a long time."

The thought of my sister encouraging my mother to do the same thing, not actually resolve the issue, angered me. She was just making things harder.

"We need to start looking for a place," I said, expecting my mother to contradict me quickly like she always did. But she didn't. "You can't do this much longer, Mom. I understand how hard this is going to be. I know you don't want to put him in a home but taking care of him is too much. He wouldn't want you to suffer and he'd definitely not want to be the cause of your suffering."

I saw a slight shift in her expression. I'd finally done it, found the right words. We were going to talk about putting him in a home. Something we'd never been able to do before.

The front door slammed. I dropped my head. Dad was going to ruin it. In a second, we'd be dancing around his confused words and ideas, our chance for a real conversation gone. My father stepped into the kitchen.

"I fixed it," he announced, proudly brandishing the two halves of the severed Club in his hands. My mouth dropped open. My mother gasped. Somehow, he'd managed to saw, pry, and force the thing off the steering wheel of the truck.

"Good job," I said, without thinking. Part of me was impressed. My mother glared but also looked like she might pass out. I stood up and went over to the stove to pour my dad a cup of tea.

"William?" My mom's voice was suddenly filled with concern. I turned just in time to see my father crumple to the floor. We both rushed over to him.

"Dad? Dad?" I shook him and checked his breathing and pulse. Both were fine. "I think he fainted."

"This happened a couple of days ago," Mom said.

"Why didn't you call me?" I asked before I remembered what I'd been occupied with. "Did you take him to the doctor?"

"No, I thought it was just a spell."

"Grab a pillow from the couch," I said.

I wet a washcloth with cool water. He moaned softly as we tucked the throw pillow under his head and I wiped his forehead with the cloth. After a while, he opened his eyes and blinked.

"Dad? Are you okay?"

"Wrr... her.... kth..." His words were slurred.

My heart sank. I turned to my mother. "He's having a stroke."

Our eyes stayed fixed on each other. I think both of us considered leaving him, seeing if this new attack in his brain could somehow release him from the other tortures it imposed. But it was too risky, totally unpredictable. He was more likely to end up physically debilitated than dead, which would only make it more difficult to care for him. The faster we got him to the hospital the better.

"Call 911," I said.

In less than fifteen minutes, the kitchen was filled with firefighters and paramedics. There were six of them altogether. Each one bigger and more muscular than the next. There was barely enough room for all of them. They circled around my dad who sat up, one half of the club amazingly still gripped in his right hand like a prized trophy he needed everyone to see.

One of the paramedics knelt on the floor next to him. "What's your name, sir?"

Another came up to me and my mom and asked, "When was the last time someone saw him normal?"

"He's got dementia," I blurted, realizing it sort of answered both of their questions.

"Wi... ll... iam. Ro... g... ers," my dad said, his words broken and slow but clear. His slurred speech had disappeared with the appearance of the paramedics. It was classic. This kind of thing happened all the time at the hospital. I'd insist a doctor come to see a patient and the second they showed up whatever I'd called about resolved.

"He was fine about twenty minutes ago," my mother said. "He was standing there telling us he fixed his truck. Then, he collapsed."

"What are you doing?" my dad said as one paramedic put a stethoscope to his chest and another wrapped a cuff around his arm. They were being too brusque, touching and poking. Confusion turned to frustration in my father's eyes. One of them pricked Dad's finger for a blood sugar without explaining what his was doing.

"Ouch," Dad said loudly and took a swing with the hand that was still holding the club. One of the firemen forced it from my dad's grasp.

"Don't hit!" the fireman said sternly.

"He has dementia," I said again. I moved in between them and got close to my dad. "It's okay," I said. "They're like doctors. You fell and they're going to take care of you."

Dad looked around as if judging whether or not I was telling the truth. "I didn't fall," he said. "That's something I would remember."

"But you're on the floor," the paramedic who'd pricked my dad's finger offered. "How'd you get on the floor?"

Dad appeared to realize for the first time that he was indeed on the ground. "Why am I on the floor?" he asked.

I looked into his eyes, trying to convey enough earnestness to break through the fog. "You probably fainted but you were talking funny so you might be having a stroke," I said. Dad frowned and shook his head. The firemen rolled a stretcher next to him.

"What's that?" Dad said. He was getting panicky. I didn't know what to do. If he was having a stroke or some kind of blockage, it was better if he went by ambulance, but I didn't think I'd be able to get him to cooperate.

"It's a bed. You get on there and they put you in the ambulance and take you to the hospital," I said.

"Why do I need to go to the hospital?"

"Get on the stretcher," the fireman who'd grabbed the club said.

"Have I mentioned that he has dementia?" I said. I was furious with myself. We would have already been at the ER if we'd just put him in the car and driven him ourselves.

"I don't have that," my dad said.

I rolled my eyes and sighed. My mom came over. She patted his head and kissed him on the cheek. "You're going to get on the stretcher and you and I are going to go for a ride with these nice men." My mom put on her best smile. Dad relaxed. She patted the stretcher. The gesture seemed intimate, like she was inviting him to bed rather than trying to get him to do as he was told. My dad scooted on to the stretcher and the paramedics strapped him in.

"Stop that," my dad shouted.

My mom took his hand. "It's okay. I'm here. I'm going with you," she said.

JANUARY 5TH 3:00 PM

*T*he hospital was a mile from my parents' house. In the emergency room, a woman with a singsong Caribbean lilt in her voice let me into the treatment area. "Bay five. Right back that way, honey," she said kindly, in contrast to the harsh metal buzz of the security door.

A square island of long, grey counters lined with computers sat in the center of the space, each station with a nurse charting at it. ERs aren't as noisy as you might think. Sounds are contained, brief: footsteps rushing down the hall, bustling at the crash bed, terse directions to a team. It's the dread-filled silence that haunts, encapsulating too much. The mother leaving her drowned child. The friend and his OD'ing buddy. The ninety-year-old whose wife of seventy years has succumbed to the heart attack she insisted was a sore shoulder.

For a second I thought I wasn't going to be able to handle it so close after Kara's death, but this ER had a suburban calm that didn't touch me. I couldn't see any numbers on the treatment rooms and was about to ask someone where my dad was when I heard him bellow from the far corner, "Don't do that."

I hurried around the nurses' station to the room. My mom

was whispering, trying to calm him. One of techs was holding his arm, while another started an IV. I shook my head. We shouldn't have bothered with the ER. His speech was completely normal now, not slurred, not even slow. I hadn't seen him walk but I was pretty sure if they let him, he'd stand up and head straight for the exit, no deficits in sight.

It was probably a trans-ischemic attack that wouldn't leave any sign that it had been there. We were going to spend hours waiting, having doctors and nurses tell us obvious stuff that no one could change: there's been a progression of ischemic changes in his brain. As soon as the techs left, my father began fiddling with the IV. The nurse came in, a young Asian woman with smooth shoulder-length hair framing a makeup free face. She looked like a teenager.

"He's gotta go to CT," she announced without introducing herself. "One of the techs will take him." Her Valley girl accent was so strong I felt like I was back in high school.

"I don't think he'll be able to stay still for a CT," I said.

"Well, he has to," she said harshly, ready to shoot down any argument I might make.

"He has dementia."

"He's being worked up for a stroke." If she'd added a "duh" at the end I wouldn't have been surprised.

"I know he's being worked up for a stroke," I said. "But he has dementia. He doesn't understand. He won't stay still for a scan."

"I don't have that," my dad interjected helpfully.

The nurse raised her eyebrows as if vindicated by my demented father's announcement that he didn't have dementia. Part of me was tempted to see what happened. He'd rip out the IV in no time if my mother didn't keep moving his hands away from it. I doubted they'd get him out the door before he got upset. They wouldn't be able to put him in the tube for the CT scan without him completely losing it. But letting all that happen wouldn't help anything.

"Can I talk to the doctor?" I said.

"The doctor ordered the CT," the nurse said.

"I understand that but the odds of him sitting still are next to none."

"A CT is short. He seems like he'll be fine."

I gritted my teeth. I wanted to call her something totally unhelpful. But I looked at her name tag and said, "Mindy, you just met my dad. You have no idea whether or not he'll be fine. I'd like to speak to the doctor."

Her eyes rolled ever so subtly, and it took everything I had not to lash out. I wasn't about to tell her I was a nurse and give her a chance to redeem herself. I wanted the full Mindy experience so my complaint to her charge nurse would be that much better.

A few minutes after Mindy left, an older woman, tall and lanky, came in. Neon green Dr. Martens peeked out from beneath her blue scrub pants. Her stride was awkward like one leg was shorter than the other. But her smile was broad and warm.

"Mr. and Mrs. Rogers?" she said as she stretched out a hand for my mother and father to shake. "I'm Doctor Kuznetsov. The nurse mentioned that you don't want to do the CT scan."

My dad looked at Dr. Kuznetsov then turned to my mom. "It's time to go home. We're wearing out our welcome."

I explained my father's dementia.

"That's a slightly different story than the one I heard," the doctor said.

I nodded instead of saying, "Mindy sucks."

"You have a couple of options," she said. "We could give him something to help him be still for the scan or we could take our chances and not do the scan. He's not having symptoms now but that doesn't mean there isn't something going on."

"Whatever you think, doctor," my mother said.

"I'd like you to consider what is best for you and your

husband. CT scans for suspected strokes should be done as soon as possible. Do you have any questions I can answer?"

My mom shook her head. Dad's left hand was twitching. Whatever minuscule patience he had was rapidly being used up. We could probably leave, and everything would be fine. But we were already in the emergency room. Why not get the scan and at least be sure he wasn't having a stroke?

"What would you give him?" I asked.

"A small dose of a medication called Ativan."

"Is that okay, Mom? It will make him super relaxed and maybe a little happy."

My mom nodded.

"I'll write the order," Dr. Kuznetsov said. "Perhaps you could go with him, Mrs. Rogers. We don't normally let family in the scanning room but in this case, we'll have you stay with him right up until they start. The technicians can show you a safe place to stand."

My mom nodded again, her face drooping with exhaustion. Her weariness had disappeared briefly with the rush of energy from the crisis. But now she looked worse than she had at the kitchen table, as if she might fall asleep standing up. I hoped they'd find some reason to admit him just so she could get a good night's sleep. I knew all about being sleep deprived.

Dr. Kuznetsov walked over to my dad. "Mr. Rogers, I'm a doctor. I'm concerned you are having a stroke. I want to run a special test. We are going to give you medicine to help you feel calm. Your wife will go with you."

Dad nodded as if he understood but I knew he had no idea where he was or what was going on. Without Mom, none of us would be able to manage him. Dr. Kuznetsov left and Mindy came back to give my dad what I assumed was the Ativan without bothering to say anything to us or him as she did it. A second later, a Hispanic man, at least six feet tall with broad shoulders and a muscular chest and biceps that pushed against his scrubs, pulled aside the curtain. "Hello, Mr. Rogers and familia," he said. "I'm Hector. I'm going to take you to CT."

My father's body stiffened as Hector undid the brakes and the stretcher lurched forward. My dad looked from side to side as if unsure under what power he was moving. My mom and I followed Hector down the hall that led out of the ER. I noticed my mom's purse slung over her shoulder. In the midst of the crisis she'd remembered her bag. I had nothing. No driver's license. No credit cards. I'd left everything in the kitchen, grabbing just my keys and heading out.

We turned right, then left, down beige nondescript hallways. My dad kept looking from side to side. His head bobbed over the edges of the stretcher staring at the ground and the wheels, then turning back to look at Hector, who must have smiled because my dad returned a cautious grin before turning to face forward again. He seemed to be getting more rather than less anxious. I hoped the Ativan would kick in soon.

"Helen!" my father suddenly shouted. "Helen!!"

Hector stopped the stretcher so my mom could get alongside.

"I'm right here," my mom said.

"Where are we going?" my dad asked, raw panic in his voice.

"You might be having a stroke, so they are going to take a picture of your brain."

"I don't know how to take pictures with my brain," my dad said convincingly. "It's time to go home. We're wearing out our welcome."

Hector started slowly moving the stretcher again. My mom rushed to keep up still talking to my dad, "It's going to be very fast, Bill. It doesn't hurt. It's just a picture."

My dad leaned his body away from my mom and looked over the other side of the stretcher. He was leaning so far, I thought he might fall off.

"Sit up straight for me," Hector said. "It's safer that way."

Surprisingly, my dad complied but he turned his head around

to look at Hector and watched him for the rest of the trip down the hall. Hector parked the stretcher right outside a door with two red letters on it: CT. My mom took my dad's hand.

"I'll see if they're ready for us," Hector said, then disappeared behind the door. My dad pulled his hand loose from my mom and started fiddling with the belt around his lap.

"What's this thing?" he said. He tugged at the strap, which made it tighter. "It's choking me."

"Let me get it for you," I said, reaching down and working the long end loose. My dad's forehead was beaded with sweat and his whole body rather than just his hand seemed to be twitching now. His IV was displaced and a small pool of blood welled up under its clear dressing.

"Helen! Helen! Helen!" he shouted.

"Dad," I said. "Calm down. Everything is cool. We're going to be here for just a few minutes and then we'll go."

My mom got closer and spoke quietly to him.

"HELEN!" he screamed even though she was right next to him.

I knew right then where things were going. Everything was moving in a particular direction that none of us could stop. Every second took an eternity. It was like I was inside and outside the moment, part of it but also watching from a distance.

Hector leaned his head out of the door to see what was going on. My father grabbed the belt that was strapping him to the stretcher with both hands and tugged and pulled with the intensity of a wild animal that has just discovered it's caught in a trap.

"Dad, it's okay. Everything is okay," I said and even my own voice seemed far away, as if I wasn't right there with everyone.

"THIS IS AGAINST THE GENEVA CONVENTION!" my father screamed at the top of his lungs. His arms flapped up as he pulled against the belt. His torso swung wildly trying to get free. Finally, the strap gave way and my father's arm shot to the side.

His elbow smashed into my mother's face. She staggered back a few steps, then dropped to the ground.

It was an accident. My dad didn't even realize my mom was standing there. He couldn't see her, didn't know her. But I am sure it didn't look that way to anyone else.

"Call a crisis team!" Hector shouted back into the CT room and within a few seconds there was an overhead page: "Crisis Team to CT scan. Crisis team to CT scan."

My dad jumped off the stretcher. "HELEN!" he screamed oblivious to my mother on the floor a few steps away from him. He'd become blind to the world around him, drifted even further away. Hector went for my dad, placing his huge arms around him from behind as my father flailed and fought. Two security guards came running down the hall.

"He has dementia," I shouted but no one heard or noticed over my father's howls and screams.

I went to my mom, who was awake but stunned. Blood trickled from an inch-long spilt at the top of her lip, dark against her pale skin. She shook her head watching the spectacle of my elderly father valiantly struggling for what he probably thought was his life, caught in the embrace of a man twice his size. The security officers tried to rationalize with him.

"You need to calm down," one of the officers said.

My father wrestled against Hector's hold, his head and shoulders bucking. A security guard put a hand on his shoulder and my father opened his mouth and sunk his teeth into the guard's flesh.

"Oh, shit," I said under my breath.

"Let go. You need to let go," the security guard said as he pried my dad's jaw open with a plastic stick he apparently carried for this exact purpose. I huddled with my mother, waiting for something to change, hoping that my dad would give up and calm down.

Dr. Kuznetsov showed up. She tried for a second to talk to my father. But quickly gave up and injected something into his deltoid. After about five more minutes of flailing, Dad quieted, melting into Hector's arms. Hector helped him back on to the stretcher with the aid of the security officers. Tears streamed down my mother's face, but she was quiet.

Dr. Kuznetsov came over to us. "I am going to admit him for an evaluation. I suspect that was a bad reaction to the medication, but I want to be sure." She looked at my mom's lip, which was swelling and turning red. "Do you live alone with him?"

My mother nodded. She raised a hand to cover her lip, suddenly self-conscious, then pulled it away staring at the long smear of blood across her palm.

"I think you might need stitches," Dr. Kuznetsov said.

"He didn't do it on purpose," my mother said.

"I know," Dr. Kuznetsov said. She grasped my mother's other hand. "But that doesn't mean you couldn't get hurt. He's a strong man."

We all looked over to my father who was almost asleep on the stretcher. He seemed smaller now, incapable of the explosive rage we had all witnessed. They rolled him into the CT scan without any problem. Dr. Kuznetsov went back down the hall to the ER.

My mom and I waited in the hall until the scan was finished. Hector rolled my father out. He paused so we could say our goodbyes. I leaned over my dad and touched his cheek. He was totally out.

"Try to get some rest," I said, knowing my words were meaningless. Even without the meds he couldn't have heeded them.

"I'll come and get you in the morning," my mother said, giving my father a kiss. I did a double-take. Was she saying it just to keep him calm or did she actually believe that after that display she was coming back tomorrow to pick him up?

We watched them shrink in the distance as they moved down the hall. At the end, they turned left and disappeared from view. My mother and I stared at the empty hall uncertain that this was it. I was strangely expectant, as though someone might pop back around the corner and say, "Just kidding" and my dad would return, not my dad with dementia but my dad without dementia, as if this was the end of a terrible joke and we'd finally reached the punchline.

*B*ack in the ER, Dr. Kuznetsov sewed up my mother's lip. I watched, all the time wondering if my mother could really be thinking about taking my dad back home after that.

"If you end up with a scar, it will be a small one," the doctor said, tying off the last stitch. My mother winced. "Ice tonight. It will reduce the swelling."

"How long will they keep him?" my mother asked.

Her busted lip made it difficult to judge whether she was hoping for a long stay or a short one. I wanted to scream. We'd been so close to discussing the nursing home and now we were back at the beginning.

"A couple of days I imagine," the doctor said as she tossed used supplies in the trash and removed her gloves. "The nurse will go over the discharge instructions with you." For a second, I thought she was talking about me but then I realized she was referring to Mindy, now the least of my problems.

Once they were done with her, my mother and I left, walking past the drop-off circle in front of the ER and heading to the parking structures. People, young and old, healthy and infirm, bustled around, going to appointments, visiting loved ones, picking up prescriptions. How were they not staring at us? Nothing was right in our world anymore. Wasn't it written all over our faces? Didn't we look crushed, broken?

I held the car door open for my mother. We both got in and then started for home. Sitting at a red light at Canoga and Burbank, I studied the lush landscaping and bold colors of the apartment building on the opposite corner. When I was a kid, the area was a field. All the way from Canoga to Topanga Canyon, it was grass, Eucalyptus trees, and horses. It didn't seem that long ago. You could still find orange orchards throughout the Valley then, all replaced with something newer and gaudier, something void of an element I couldn't name. No more ice cream parlor. No more Victory Drive-in. No more Busch Gardens.

"That's where Farrell's was, right?" I said to my mother as we passed the Burger King, as if confirming it would change something, make life less transient. She nodded. These new places had supplanted the locations of my youth. Some person in the future would wax nostalgic about the Whole Foods where he got organic, gluten-free pizza like I was remembering pastel sugar dots on long strips of paper from Farrell's. I felt trampled, like they'd dropped these buildings on me.

The tools of my father's afternoon project were still strewn around the driveway when we got home, just where he'd left them. My mom got out. She walked past them without a glance and went into the house. I began picking them up, wondering why I was bothering. Let them lie there. Let them rust. Let them be stolen. None of it would make any difference.

With his tools in my arms, I traced my father's path through the ivy down the right side of the house, following in his footsteps, searching for whatever understanding might be found by placing my feet in his prints in the dirt, a sliver of insight maybe hiding behind a bush along the path.

The door to the workshop was wide open, the lights still on. I stepped in. As I sorted his tools putting them back in the labeled boxes, my eyes kept drifting to the Bermuda Triangle, that shadowy spot under the house. The darkness unified there, light never reaching it. You couldn't see where it ended.

I stared. Then, with my father's wrench in hand, I got down on my hands and knees and crept up into that space, crouching lower and lower as the wedge got smaller and smaller, until I was right next to the spot that I used to imagine disappearing into as a child, the place where I expected the darkness to break at the touch of my hand like the glassy surface of a pond. My heart raced. I'd never been able to reach into there, always too afraid, always waiting for something to pull me in. I pushed the wrench forward tentatively, poking around until the wrench hit something solid. I reached in with my hand, my fingers finding cool earth and wooden beams.

"Stupid hole," I muttered, then slowly climbed out. Back at the shelves, I stood staring at the darkness, its lure, its promise, its lie.

"Fuuuck!!" I screamed and threw the wrench toward the space. "Stupid fucking nothing hole!" I grabbed tools from the boxes and hurled them at the space with all my might, screaming and shouting, each crash and thud relieving something within me until I was spent. I fell to the ground and cried.

MY MOTHER WAS SITTING at the table when I finally came back into the house. Our cold cups of half-finished tea languished in front of her. My dad's empty cup sat on the counter where I'd left it. We'd stumbled back into a half-lived moment and didn't know what to do next.

I started to clean. I washed cups, returned pillows to the couch, scrubbed furiously at a black half-moon scuff from one of the fireman's shoes. I should have done something sooner. Never let it get to this.

Normally my mother would have been the one fluttering, a hummingbird in constant motion, wiping already clean counters, washing cups just after they were used. Can I make you something? Tea? Cookies? A sandwich? But my tiny overburdened mother sat slumped over the table, her short, grey hair messy, her face tired. Her lip was morphing from a bright red line to a swollen purple lump. Her eyes stared vacantly forward. Three blotches of blood stained the front of her grey t-shirt.

I expected her to speak at any moment, to capitulate, admit defeat. It wasn't safe for my father to be at home. She couldn't care for him by herself. She had to get it now. Something else was going to happen. But she did get it. That's why she'd asked me to help. I just couldn't give her the help she actually wanted.

"I'm going to bed," she announced.

I glanced at the clock. It was six-thirty. She stood up and hugged me, then gave me an extra squeeze as if we might not see each other for a while.

"I'll call Colleen and Adam," I said.

"Okay, honey," she answered without a hint of emotion. I might as well have been calling my siblings about something incidental, not to tell them that Dad had lost it and was in the hospital.

I pulled out my phone, then realized that I wasn't even sure what ward he was on. We hadn't checked. It seemed odd. We didn't even know exactly where my father was. They'd whisked him away, and more than anything, I'd felt overwhelming relief. He was safe. The drama had been paused for a moment and we could breathe. But it was a guilty relief: getting the thing you need most at a terrible cost.

A reminder for work populated to my screen. Damn! After the funeral I was supposed to have gone home for a nap and then, right about now, I should have been getting ready for work. Even before my dad's meltdown, it felt impossible—how could I ever walk those halls, sit in those chairs, occupy that space? It felt like an affront to Kara's life. Now, it was out of the question. I called in sick. I had no hours to cover me but I didn't care.

I sat at the kitchen table. It had taken all my will to escape the gravitational pull of my house. I didn't want to go back to isolation. But it felt strange to stay at my parents' while my mother slept. I only had one place to go.

It was dark as I entered The Farm. I walked toward the main house but stopped at the bottom of the path. Light glowed in the windows. Everyone was seated around the long, kitchen counter and the various sofas and chairs for a family dinner, one of the pleasures of communal living. What was so wrong with this life? From this vantage point it was perfect. I was the problem.

I watched as Jax got up from his chair and set his bowl on the counter. He said something then went over to Shayne and playfully punched him in the arm. Shayne grabbed him and they wrestled. It was like a snapshot, a radiant moment captured in the wooden window frame just for me to see. All other incarnations of my son seemed unreal, figments of my imagination.

I walked down to the Airstream. In the bedroom, I let myself fall back onto the bed. If I'd kept falling, plunging through air and never finding anything solid beneath me, I would have been happy. That's what I'd wanted at the Bermuda Triangle, escape. I longed for it.

My world was losing its form. The molecules of solid objects slowed down so that I might slip between them and be absorbed. When my body thudded against the mattress, tears came. I cried until I was too exhausted for more. Drained and beaten, I drifted. Not asleep. Not awake. Swimming in a half world that I wanted never to leave.

The squeaky hinges of the Airstream door and then Shayne

and Jax's voices brought me back. I was relieved when Jax said he was spending the night in his hut. Shayne seemed unsurprised to find me in his bed. He sat at the edge of the mattress.

"Is it your dad?" he asked. I told him what had happened at the hospital. "You thought something like this was coming," he said.

"I guess you're never ready for it," I said. "This changes everything. I don't know if they're going to let him go home with her."

"That would be great, right? If they made her find a place for him? Can they do that?"

The eagerness in his voice surprised me. He was right for asking. Of course, they couldn't do that. They couldn't force my mother to put my father in a facility if she didn't agree. Even after that display, they'd have to let her take him home if she wanted to.

I sighed. "Probably not. I can't see how they'd just let him go home with her after that. It was insane. But I don't know. I don't think they can make her do it."

I sat up and scooted to the edge of the bed, just a foot or so between us. He seemed to be doing his best to keep his physical distance, to do what I'd asked. But I needed him. I wanted him to make love to me, to fuck me, whatever option was offered. I longed for his warm, sweaty skin against mine. I needed to feel his heart pounding in his chest as he pressed against me and for a brief moment to feel like I had power, like I could rage against everything and it would matter. I put my hand on his thigh.

"I thought we weren't going to do that anymore," he said.

"I know that's what I said but I was wrong."

"Wrong forever or just tonight."

I didn't want to answer. Not now. He was all I had, flawed, not more than me, just different. But I wasn't ready to jump back in.

"*Bébé*, I've told you what I want. You were right. This is the problem. This means something to me. I thought it meant something to you."

"Fine," I said, standing up, ready to storm off only I didn't have anywhere to storm off to except my lonely, empty guest house. I stepped out into the trailer's narrow hall. "Thanks for adding one more shitty thing to my shitty day."

"That's not fair," he said.

"Life's not fair. Nothing's fair," I said. "I just need…" I didn't know how to finish the sentence. "Something," I said. "I've never needed it more."

"It's me you keep coming back to," Shayne said. "Me. How do you separate me from the sex?"

"I don't know."

"You keep building up these walls and pretty soon you'll be the only one behind them."

"Everything's broken."

"Yeah, it always has been and it always will be," he said, then stood up and came over to me. "Whatever you keep looking for out there, it's not there. Stop looking out there." He pressed a palm flat against my chest. "Look in here. Stop pushing everything away. Let someone in." Shayne reached out and twirled a piece of my hair. "*You* are the girl who wrote all those plays, who joined with me at the handfasting. You are the strawberry in the Green Machine. Let yourself be that girl."

I leaned in and nuzzled his neck. He didn't respond but didn't pull away either. Inside I was screaming for him. He took my face in his hands and stared into my eyes, as if trying to read the cloudy mess behind them. He leaned in and kissed me. Tears ran down my cheeks.

He gently reached under my blouse as if I were breakable. I grabbed at my shirt and tore it open. I would not be fragile or tender. I would not take what the universe delivered without a response. Once I was naked, I undressed him with urgency.

He lay back on the bed, offering his muscular body up for my use. I climbed on top of him and we moved into a familiar dance, only the tears were different. I couldn't remember a time when we had made love through tears. But I couldn't think of a time I needed this act more. Our rhythmic movement, the sensations of our bodies uniting, the feelings running through my body. My howls against the cruelty of life.

THANKSGIVING 2013

I'd just dropped Jax off at my parents' house and was on my way to pick Shayne up from The Farm to take him to our family's Thanksgiving dinner. The drive gave me time to process what my mother had told me. My father had been acting strangely for about a year. He angered easily, cried with little reason, and sometimes answered questions with nonsensical information. We'd hoped it was a side effect of one of the many medications he was taking to control his blood pressure, cholesterol, and diabetes. A drug switch would be an easy remedy. We were terrified it was Alzheimer's.

Mom had finally taken him to a geriatric specialist and the verdict was bad: Vascular dementia. Small vessel disease, a relative of the heart disease that had left his mother a widow with three children in her thirties, was narrowing the arteries feeding my father's brain. Tiny sections were starving to death. The quadruple bypass he'd had at fifty-five had saved his life. Now the same perpetrator was climbing in a different window.

I parked at the gate and walked toward the main house, Champ bounding alongside me. The earthy scent of pot wafted in the air. I found Shayne on the patio. The dog curled up at his feet.

"Hiya, *Bébé*," Shayne said, patting the place next to him on the wicker love seat. I sat. Shayne took a long drag on his joint then tentatively offered it to me. I hadn't been high in a while. I took a hit, knowing I shouldn't but also not caring.

Shayne and I were in a good phase. I was spending a lot of my free time at The Farm. The respiratory therapist a few years earlier had lasted only three months, then I'd dated some other guys. But nothing was ever quite right. Shayne was easy. We'd been cruising along happily for almost six months and Jax had finished the first quarter of second grade with what we now viewed as only minor incidents. No suspensions. No trips to the emergency room.

"Something's wrong," Shayne said, reading me as usual with telepathic accuracy.

I nodded.

"Alzheimer's?" he asked.

I shook my head. "Vascular dementia. Not that it makes any difference. It's awful either way." I started to cry. Shayne set the joint in his makeshift ashtray—a pickle jar lid—and hugged me.

"I'm sorry," he said, squeezing me, then gently releasing the hug.

"It's basically exactly what he was afraid of," I said. "Life sucks." I picked up the joint and took another long drag. We passed it back and forth a few more times then Shayne crushed it out.

"You should probably slow down. This weed's powerful. I'm seeing rainbow halos," he said. "Stare at the lights."

The patio ceiling was lined with strings of tiny Christmas lights, only two-thirds of which worked. We leaned back in the love seat together. I scooted closer and snuggled into him as he put his arm around me. Shayne was right; the pot was strong and mildly hallucinogenic. My stress about my Dad was slowly anesthetized and replaced with irrational joy coming from the lights, which seemed to pulse rhythmically, like tiny colored hearts.

"You know, I've always thought that things like dementia and Alzheimer's weren't really diseases," Shayne said after a long while. "I think the person or their soul or whatever is ready to go somewhere else and they leave. They go on a journey."

My eyes felt heavy from the high, so I closed them. The darkness behind my eyelids was in motion, alive with colors. I stared into it. A small black circle opened in the center and, as if Shayne's words were coming to life in my mind, I saw my father in his workshop. He turned and waved, then climbed into the space we called the Bermuda Triangle and disappeared.

Shayne continued, "I think they're off in this parallel world where, you know, everything is cool and they're fine. They've just left this piece of themselves here."

I stared into the darkness behind my closed eyes for a moment and basked in that notion, my father somewhere else, safe and intact. Believing it felt good. It was so much nicer than little dead spots multiplying in his mind. As soon as I opened my eyes, however, the dream or hallucination stopped. The momentary comfort was shattered.

"That's ridiculous," I said. "You don't think his dementia is real?"

"Nothing's real," he said.

What else should I have expected from Shayne? "It'll be real enough when we're wiping his butt because he can't remember how," I said, shifting away from him toward the front of the seat.

"The whole thing is a cosmic illusion, the force of Maya persuading us it's real."

"Well, it's pretty fucking convincing," I said and stood up. I left him on the patio and walked up the hill to the barn. I hated him for telling me his stupid story and I hated myself for being lulled by it.

As I neared the stalls, the horses put their heads out. I patted each of them, staring into the quiet of their liquid brown eyes. I wished I could stay, but I had to get back to my parents' house. I had no idea how long I'd been sitting with Shayne. My mom had said it would be about an hour before the meal was ready, and I didn't want Jax alone there too long.

I turned from the barn to head back down to the house when something dropped to the ground in front of me. I looked down. A small house sparrow lay on its side. I waited for it to move, to pull itself together to fly away but it didn't. It just lay there, still, not twitching, not breathing.

"What you got there?" Calvin's deep voice said from behind me.

I turned and met his gaze, then pointed to the bird. "This bird literally just fell dead right in front of me. It dropped from the sky."

Calvin came closer and inspected the little creature. Then, he scooped it up with a scrap of bark and tossed it on the manure pile next to the barn. I cringed. They used the manure pile to fertilize crops.

"Everything dies, honey," he said. "Ashes to ashes."

"My dad has dementia," I said. The pot was making my mind and my mouth loose. "Shayne thinks he's off in some parallel universe where he's fine."

"That man's got himself some unique points of view," Calvin said.

"It's stupid," I said.

"Everyone is making this shit up as they go along. There ain't no right answers."

"You know I was thinking about getting back together with him. Like today, I was actually thinking I was going to move back in with him and now I don't know how I was even thinking about that at all."

"You think about things a lot. I don't know if that's always a good thing."

"If you figure out how I can stop, by all means let me know," I said, then walked back toward the patio. Shayne was still reclined on the wicker seat. I banged on the frame of the screen door.

"If you're coming, we need to go," I said.

He got up and walked over, looking at me from the other side of the screen. I thought he was about to apologize. I debated whether or not I would forgive him.

"*If* I'm coming?" he said.

"You don't have to if you don't want to."

"What do you want me to do?"

"I think too much," I said. "I go back and forth and back and forth like at some point it's all going to become clear, like there is an answer there and I can't find it but if I just look hard enough, think hard enough I'll see it. But you know what? There are no answers. It's all bullshit, like you said."

Shayne smiled. "That's not quite what I said."

"Well, that's what I heard," I said. "I'm leaving. For real this time. I don't want to do this anymore. I don't want to be this halfway thing because that's all there is." It felt good to say it even though I immediately began wondering how long it would be before I fell into his arms again.

"Okay," he said quietly, as if my words had no impact, which was more infuriating than if he begged me to stay. I wanted him to fight, to scream and throw things but he never would. He had this preternatural ability to never take the bait. I turned and started walking away. When I was about halfway to the gate, he called after me.

"*Bébé?*"

I turned.

"I am really sorry about your dad," he said.

"Me, too," I said and left.

. . .

I PARKED up the street from my parents' house, close enough so I could see it but far enough away that my sister, who was doing something at her car, might not see me. I was fairly high. Indulging in heavy-duty weed may not have been the smartest move before a family event. I hadn't been high in a long time, let alone at my parents' house. Shayne and I used come to my parents' house high all the time, running off to the bathroom together, cracking up at something that was only funny because we were loaded. But now I was in it alone and the grim reality of my dad's condition was turning the high into a low.

My sister was spending forever at her car. She was hunched over like she'd dropped something and was holding it in her shirt. I watched, wishing she'd go inside so I could make my way into the house as unobserved as possible. Finally, she walked back across the street, a casserole dish in her arms.

My mind drifted. My parents had lived in the same house my whole life, a reassuring piece of the world standing still. I felt safer there than anywhere, as if I were a child again and believed that they would always be able to protect me. But one way or another, Shayne was right. It was all an illusion. I got out of the car and walked to the house.

Dinner wasn't on the table yet. My sister and my mom were in the kitchen. Most of the kids were in the living room. I wandered downstairs. Jax and his cousin Logan were in my old room. Logan was a few months younger than Jax and was showing him something on a handheld Nintendo game. They should have been friends, being so close in age, but they weren't. Logan treated Jax like he was mentally challenged, talking slowly, giving him directions like he was a toddler. I was surprised Jax had never hit him.

Standing at the door watching them, I got sadder and sadder. My mom had set the space up with bunk beds for grandkids to stay but that had been happening less with Dad's ever-increasing emotionality. It was only going to get worse. I hurried into my parents' room as emotions bubbled up in my chest.

My parents' room was tidy, as always. Bed made. Nothing on the floor. No clutter on the surfaces. I walked over to my mother's dresser. Necklaces, years of gifts from Dad, dangled from a jewelry stand he'd made for her, a varnished tree branch set in a marble base. He'd gotten the idea from a magazine and brought it to life. I reached out and touched the closest necklace, a horseshoe lined with tiny diamonds.

Technically, it had been a gift from me and my dad but it had mostly been his gift. He'd taken me and my $23.72 to the jewelry store to buy a Mother's Day present only to have me burst into tears when I realized how little my hard-earned chore money could purchase. I delightfully accepted when he offered to do a joint gift.

I touched the bumblebee necklace around my own neck, also a gift from Dad, then started to cry. I wandered into my parents' bathroom, crawled into the bathtub and pulled the curtain closed. It was something that only made sense because Shayne and I used to do it all the time when we were high and couldn't stop laughing or keep our hands off each other. I lay there awhile, my mind drifting.

Someone came into the bathroom. The door locked. I stayed still, unsure what to do. How could I have forgotten to lock the door? I heard faint moaning. It was Colleen, crying. I listened until I knew I couldn't keep quiet through whatever was going on.

"Are you okay?" I asked through the curtain.

"Holy crud!" Colleen exclaimed.

I pulled back the curtain. My sister was sitting on the closed toilet. "Holy crud? Is that a thing?" I asked.

"What are you doing?"

"Hiding. I'm high. Really, really high." As I said it, the sensations seemed to increase, the power of suggestion.

"Typical," Colleen said.

"Actually, I haven't been high in like two years but it seemed like a genius idea after Mom told me about Dad's dementia. Now, not so much. Is that what you're crying about?"

"No," Colleen said but didn't offer any more information.

"Are you going to tell me what you're crying about?"

"I came in here to be alone. I didn't know I was going to get ambushed."

"Fine, I'll leave." I climbed out of the tub but had to hold onto the sink to keep from falling.

"I'm having a miscarriage," Colleen said. "Or I had a miscarriage. It's the end now."

"You're forty-five. How are you even pregnant?"

"It was a shock for me too," Colleen said. "I definitely thought Lance was the last one."

I sat on edge of the bath.

"Liam's really mad," Colleen said.

"Liam's mad at you for having a miscarriage?"

Colleen sighed. I'd said something wrong but I couldn't figure out what. My sister was staring down at her hands, fiddling with a rosary, wrapping it around her fingers, rubbing it, twisting and untwisting it.

"There was some trouble with the baby's heart," Colleen finally offered. "The doctor said it wasn't going to live even if I made it to term."

"That's terrible," I said. "But that's not your fault."

"I was going to have an abortion," Colleen whispered.

Holy shit! I thought but managed to stop myself from blurting it out.

"It's okay," I said instead. "I can't imagine anything harder than having a baby only to watch it die."

Colleen gave me a disappointed look and a little shake of her head. "I wasn't worried about me. It was the baby. I didn't want it to suffer. It was wrong. There was no way it was right to bring a baby into the world knowing that it would hurt every second of its existence."

It didn't seem like I should say anything so I nodded and hoped she would go on.

"I made the appointment," Colleen said. "It was tomorrow. I was going to lie to my husband and have an abortion against his wishes." She sat there clearly devastated by what had almost happened. "And now here I am. I don't know if God is punishing me or if he saved me from myself."

My issues with Shayne suddenly seemed foolish. I was mad at him for words, for the way he saw the world, not real things. Colleen and I talked a little longer and hugged. Then, one of the children knocked on the door to tell us it was time to eat.

J awoke alone in the trailer, Shayne already off working somewhere on The Farm. I'd used him, taken something without giving anything in return. I felt guilty but not guilty enough to wish that I hadn't done it. And I hadn't gotten away scot-free. His palm against my chest had seared me. His words left a smoldering mark I couldn't ignore. But I also couldn't do anything about it right now. My father's hospitalization was only a temporary reprieve.

I left without finding Shayne and drove back to my parents' house. It was still early. If my mother had actually fallen asleep at six-thirty, she would have to be up by now. But I sat in the car staring at the house. It always felt like the safest place in the world, me running home to safety, now it was more like running into a house on fire.

Instead of going inside, I grabbed my extra set of scrubs from the back of the car and went down the side of the house to Adam's old bachelor pad. The single large room where my brother had lived until he was twenty-five and where I'd spend much of my final term of nursing school looked about the same as it had ten years ago: Tan comforter with a cheesy, fake Native

American print; navy, blue corduroy love seat; card table cum dining area. It had been my halfway house between The Farm and the real world. Now it was the one place I could get away from everyone and everything in my life.

The bulbs in the bathroom were out. I left the door ajar. Beams of light shone through the crack from the living room. I pulled an old towel from the bottom of the mismatched stack in the cupboard, then climbed in the shower. I turned the water as hot as I could stand, trying to melt something away, uncover that girl Shayne had been talking about.

I hoped sleep had rejuvenated my mother. Maybe she'd finally see that the only viable option was a home. But she hadn't seemed to the night before. I didn't really know where things stood. We had to make progress. The hospital wouldn't keep him forever. We had to get a plan that Colleen and Mom could follow while I worked the next three nights. I'd jammed four shifts together to have more time off for the mini-vacation, not knowing that my world was going to disintegrate during that time.

I put my dirty clothes in my car and let myself into the main house. My mother was at the kitchen table wrapped in my father's bathrobe, sipping tea through a flexible pink straw, cookies on a plate in front of her. Her lip was puffy and purplish red. She'd resumed yesterday's show with slightly different cast members. She looked at me, smiled weakly and took another sip. The swollen skin pulled against the stitches creating an awkward sneer.

I sat at the table. "Did you sleep okay?"

"I slept like the dead," she said flatly as if there was nothing odd about her choice of words.

Suddenly, I realized I hadn't called my siblings. "I didn't call Colleen or Adam," I said. "I completely forgot. I went over to The Farm and..." I'd only had one thing to do and I'd messed it up.

"It's okay, sweetheart." Her voice was calm in contrast to my sudden panic. "There was nothing to be done."

I'd totally, but unintentionally, blown it. I'd been so self-absorbed, like it was all happening only to me, it had completely slipped my mind. I pulled out my phone and texted my brother and sister. Within seconds, the house phone was ringing.

I guessed it was Colleen even though at this time on a Sunday they'd be in church. Church was about the only time Colleen didn't instantaneously answer texts but I'm sure this one got her attention. Who knew when Adam would respond?

"I'm okay," my mother said. "We'll go over soon but I'm not sure where he is in the hospital."

I couldn't hear the other side of the conversation. But if it was my sister, she was probably having difficulty, like me, processing that Mom—usually fixated on my father to the degree that she didn't hear you when you were sitting right next to her—didn't know the specifics of his location. She knew he was at the hospital but seemed surprisingly unconcerned about the details. This was not the slightly frantic, hyper-vigilant mother we'd grown accustomed to over the last few years. She was calm.

After a long time of just listening, my mother offered, "Once we get over there, I'll let you know where he is and then you can come." I desperately wanted to know what my sister was saying. Was she helping my mother prepare for the inevitable moment where we'd have to send Dad to a home or was she fueling the crazy idea that somehow it would all work out even though it wouldn't?

"I don't know," my mother said. "I just don't know."

Finally, the call ended, and my mom sat down next to me. She didn't say anything. She sipped her tea through the straw, then broke a cookie in half and nibbled at it on the side of her mouth without the split.

"Was that Colleen?" I finally asked. "What did she say?"

"She's just worried about Bill," she said not calling him Dad like she usually did when speaking to us.

"You didn't tell her about your lip," I said.

"I didn't want to upset her."

"She's going to notice as soon as she sees you at the hospital." The moment felt unbalanced. Everything was off. "You can't bring him back here," I said.

Her eyes met mine. She smiled, something resigned, not happy. The gash and stitches distorted her expression but I understood. This had never once been about a nursing home.

Distant memories of my grandmother flooded my mind. At the end, she just sat there when we visited, a scaffolding of bones for skin and hair and cotton sweat clothes with elastic waistbands. Her eyes were vacant. No one and nothing meant anything to her. She shat herself. Pissed herself. Food dripped down her face in globs when they fed her. Even the most basic of human drives, sustenance, had faded from her mind.

My father only wanted the good stuff. He wanted one of us to end it before he got like his mother. He'd meant exactly what he'd said so many times—*take me out in the backyard*—but how had he ever expected us to do that?

My mother finished her tea. She washed, dried and put away her single cup and plate, then cleared the pack of cookies from the table. She left the kitchen and a few minutes later I heard the creaking of pipes and the rushing of water for a shower.

My mother and I took separate cars to the hospital, me following right behind her the short distance. I would spend a couple of hours visiting with Dad, try to talk sense with my mother and sister, then head home for a nap before work. The scene from outside the CT scan replayed in my head. My mother's face had to be enough to get my sister to understand how serious this had become.

I parked next to my mom in the concrete structure and we walked in together. Like every hospital there were too many halls and turns and doors that looked the same. We ended up at geriatrics but needed geriatric mental health, which was on a different floor. We went back to the elevator. Mom's hand tapped against her thigh.

"That sign isn't very clear," she said pointing at the words that had steered us wrong.

By the time we found the right unit, Mom's hand was nervously flapping against her leg like fluttering wings. I buzzed the intercom.

"We're here to visit William Rogers. Daughter and wife," I said.

A moment later, a round-faced woman with a helmet of tightly permed hair inspected us through the small square of glass in the door. She glanced behind, her then let us in. She looked to be in her early sixties. Her blue jeans were a little too snug, causing a fold of skin from her plump frame to pop out around her waist and push against her pink cat t-shirt. No uniforms in psych, which felt weird since I was wearing scrubs.

"Welcome, I'm Donna. I'm the charge nurse. Mr. Rogers is in the activities room." She secured the door behind us. The lock engaged with a harsh, metallic click. In the less than twenty-four hours he'd been there, my dad had likely tested the robustness of that lock in a million escape attempts. I imagined him pacing the halls, coming to the door, twisting that knob in frustration, then doing the exact same thing again a few minutes later. How many times had he asked about my mom, told them he needed to go home, insisted that he didn't have dementia, that they had the wrong guy, a case of mistaken identity? If only that were true.

"I'll take you to him in a second, but what questions can I answer first?" Donna asked.

My mom and I searched through the uncertainty to find the right questions. Neither of us came up with anything.

"Is this the first time Mr. Rogers has been in the hospital for this?" Donna asked.

"Yes," we said in unison.

"They gave him a medication called Versed yesterday, which made him sleepy. He was out for a couple of hours. But it sounds like he was pretty active through the night. I don't think he slept much. And he's kept us pretty busy this morning. He's got a lot of energy. We haven't given any medications except what is listed in his medical record. We'll want to double-check all those with you today after your visit."

I wondered if the meaning of the word "visit" was clear to my mom. He was not going to leave with us, that option was off the table.

"How long has he had dementia?" Donna asked.

My mom didn't seem inclined to answer so I did. "Five or six years. It took us a while to realize what was happening."

Donna nodded. "Being a caregiver is challenging. This type of episode, a break, is very common. I know that might not be comforting but just know it isn't unusual."

A female patient walked toward us then stopped. She wore two hospital gowns, one in the front and one draped around her like a robe. Her face was pale and wrinkled and her long white hair flowed behind her, a cape of grey and silver. She stared, suspicion in her eyes.

"Are you ready?" Donna asked us. We followed her a short way down the hall and turned into the activities room. My dad was seated at a molded plastic table with rounded corners along with ten other patients of various advanced ages. They all looked older and more subdued than my father.

"Helen!" my dad shouted as soon as he saw Mom in the doorway. "Where have you been?" His voice was sharp and accusing. "These people won't let me leave." He pointed at Donna. "This one is…" The word he was going to use seemed to leave him as he was about to utter it.

He looked around the room as if hunting for what he'd been about to say. His gaze landed on me for just a moment and then passed by as if I wasn't even there. I was invisible to him, less significant than the nurses and other patients. I wondered if it was the Versed or the new environment. Or was this it? A fleeting moment that no one else noticed or understood, the moment my father forgot me.

He turned back to my mother. "Where have you been?" he said. "I've been looking all over for you." He noticed the gash on her lip. "What happened to your face?"

"I bumped into a door."

"You should be careful," he offered helpfully.

Mom took a seat next to Dad. Donna and I moved back outside the doorway, close enough to hear but outside his focal area. Mom took Dad's hand and started patting it, just like I'd patted Kara's hand. When everything else has been stripped away, all that's left are futile gestures.

I turned to Donna. "Do you think I can talk to the doctor? We've got a lot to figure out. Do you know the results of the CT?"

"No stroke. Maybe a trans-ischemic attack, that's a—"

"I know what a TIA is," I said, too abruptly. "Sorry, I didn't mean to snap. This whole thing, we're all under a lot of stress."

Donna was unflustered by my rudeness. "She lives alone with him?" she asked.

"Until yesterday. She's... she doesn't want to put him in a memory care place. He kind of made us all promise we'd never put him in a home." The statement seemed ridiculous spoken out loud to a complete stranger, flimsy and foolish, like I was a kid trying to lie my way out of a situation where I'd been caught red-handed.

"My grandmother had Alzheimer's," I added as if that would made it all logical. I expected her to come at me like Adam had, how we were so stupid to overdramatize things.

"It's not unusual. Most people don't want to put their loved one in a care facility," Donna said. "They tend to feel guilty about it."

"So, we're not special?" I joked.

"Of course, you're special," she said, kindly ignoring my deflection. "You're a unique family in a unique situation. No one else can truly understand what you as individuals are going through. But many people with dementia become too difficult for a single person to care for. It's sad that people feel that getting help is something to be ashamed of."

"I think it's my mom you need to be having this conversation with," I said. "I got so close to convincing her yesterday and then all this happened and somehow it's made her go back not forward."

"We need to get going," my father announced, his voice loud as if he wanted to be certain the whole room could hear. "Don't want to wear out our welcome." He put both hands on the table and pushed himself up. He moved around the unfamiliar room, unsettled. He opened and closed two cabinet doors searching but not finding whatever he thought he would. He couldn't place himself. As he went to the doorway on the other side of the activities room and looked out, his expression showed more and more confusion. His forehead wrinkled. His mouth hung open. His eyes darted from face to face. He was lost and he knew it.

"They will recommend placement," Donna said as we watched my father pace. He seemed to have lost the intent to vacate the room and was examining a sparsely filled bookshelf with a look of bewilderment on his face. He wasn't paying attention to Mom or me or any of the other patients. "Given the little time I've spent with your dad, it seems like the safest call."

I looked at my mother as Dad wandered the activities room. Her swollen lip and purple bruise was undeniable evidence that placement was, indeed, the safest call. My father turned and noticed my mother again. "Helen! Where have you been? I've been trapped here for years." He sat down next to her. "What happened to your face?"

He seemed worse. Maybe he was more confused because of

the different surroundings but his intensity was higher, more desperate. There was nothing he could hang on to except my mom. I turned away and started to cry. Donna and I stepped out of view of my parents. She put an arm around me.

"This is really hard," she said.

"No, it's not that," I said. "Well, yes, it is but also my best friend just died."

"I'm so sorry," Donna said.

"What do I do?" I said trying to pull myself together. "Even after this, I think she's going to try to take him home with her again. Can they make her put him in a home?"

"No, they can't."

"Is there someone we can talk to? Like a counselor or something?"

"Tomorrow. There's no social worker on Sunday. Don't worry. They're not going to discharge him for a few days."

"But she could just take him home right now, if she decided to, right? AMA?"

"Yes, if she insisted. It would definitely be against medical advice."

Donna took me to the nurses' station. She checked the social worker's calendar and gave us the latest appointment time in the book, so I'd be able to get some sleep after work. I had to keep my mom focused on the practical, the possible. This was our moment. There were no easy answers. Actually, there were no answers at all, just the next step on the never-ending path of my father's slow drawn-out demise. I couldn't get us off that path. All I could do was try to keep my mother safe.

"Thanks," I said to Donna once we had the time set. "Can you believe we never really talked about a memory care place until last week? Not seriously. Mom never let us."

Donna smiled and it didn't feel fake or rote. "It doesn't surprise me at all."

"Still not special?" I said.

"Very special," she said.

I walked over to my mom. "I'm going to go downstairs and find a cup of coffee," I said. "I'll call Colleen and let her know where we are." My dad looked at me as I spoke, no recognition in his eyes. I put a hand on Mom's shoulder and tried to sound as casual as possible as I said, "We have an appointment with the social worker tomorrow at three."

By the time my sister texted to say she was at the door, I felt like I was going to spontaneously implode if my father said, "Helen! Where have you been?" one more time. There'd been no change in his awareness of me. The more I tried to engage with him, the more intensely he focused on my mother, which agitated both of them. So, I stayed back watching the same ten minutes on repeat. Donna walked with me to buzz Colleen into the unit then left us in the hallway.

"How's Mom?" Colleen asked after giving me a perfunctory hug.

"Emotionally, your guess is as good as mine. She's certainly a little off but who wouldn't be? Physically, I think she'll be fine."

"What?"

"Dad hit her," I said. I studied my sister's face, gauging her reaction as I explained what had happened outside the CT scan. She frowned the whole time I was speaking, occasionally punctuating the end of my sentences with a sigh. I was deliberately circumventing my mother. I wanted Colleen to get the gory details, not the watered-down version my mother would deliver. Alone I probably couldn't keep Mom from doing something rash like taking Dad home AMA. But if my sister and I presented a unified front, we might be able to buy a few days and, with a social worker on my side, I hoped we'd be able to figure something out in that time.

"I'm worried she's going to try to take him home and pretend like none of this ever happened," I said. "After what I saw, I know she's not safe."

"How long do the doctors want to keep him?" Colleen asked.

"I'm not sure. A couple more days? We have a meeting with a social worker tomorrow. They think he needs to be placed."

"That's not what he wanted," Colleen said.

"You think I forgot?" I said. "In case you haven't noticed, life isn't in the business of giving people what they want. Or maybe that's just me."

"There's no need to get snippy. I'm just trying to honor Dad's wishes."

"I know what Dad said. I was there, too. But Mom's not safe. That makes it a different story. I think that would have been the line for him too, don't you? Do you really think he'd be okay with the idea that he might hurt Mom?"

"No, but…"

I cut her off. "It can't keep going like this. People who don't even know us can see it. This is the end."

"She's not going to agree to something he didn't want."

"He wanted one of us to take him in the backyard and blow his brains out like a fucking lame horse. Who's going to do that? You? Mom?"

"Stop swearing."

"Oh my God, Colleen. Really? You can't leave me alone in this. There's no way to do what Dad wanted. I know. I tried. He has dementia and it's going to get worse and worse. He never wanted to be like this and never wanted to be in a nursing home. I get it. But there is no other answer. I'm begging you. I'm at the end of my rope. You're the only one who can help me. If you don't, then the next time he's lost or hits her, it's on you, really."

The white-haired woman wearing the two gowns came out of the activities room and walked over to us. The noise attracting her. She stared, then began singing in German or Dutch. We waited until she gave up. I turned back to my sister and tried to calm myself a little.

"Look, we don't need to resolve this right now. All I need is for you to say that you won't let her take him home today. That's it. We can talk about everything else tomorrow with the social worker. Please just tell me you won't let her take him home."

Colleen's lip trembled. For a second I thought she was going to cry. "Okay," she finally said softly, then walked toward the activities room, apparently instinctively knowing where to find our parents. I followed. Dad's face brightened as she came through the door. He stood up and walked over to her.

"Hey, you!" he said, waggling a finger in her face. "*You* can get us out of here." It was clear he recognized her but he didn't say her name, my pathetic consolation prize for having been completely forgotten. Colleen placed her two hands around his pointing finger, brought it to her lips and kissed it. Her face warmed with a wide smile.

"Sure, Dad. Why don't you show me around first?"

My sister's gaze seemed to rest on Mom's face before she guided Dad out of the activities room, their hands hanging between them like a child and parent, Colleen in the parent role. Mom deflated in exhaustion as soon as Dad was out of sight. I'd been no help at all. I was invisible to my own father and worse, I wanted to get out of there as much as he did. The last two hours felt like two days.

"I have to leave soon," I said to my mom in spite of my guilt. "I have to get some sleep before work tonight." I told her about the appointment with the social worker again, focusing on the plan-ning-discharge part rather than the planning-discharge-to-a-place-other-than-home part. I'd bargained some time out of my sister and that would have to do.

The freeway was more crowded than it should have been on a Sunday afternoon. The car in front of me was a haphazard puzzle of bumper stickers. Every time the traffic stopped, I rolled close enough to read another one. Amongst the generic bands and radio stations stickers—Stones, Kinks, KMET, KROQ—were snarky lines: "I'm Pro-Sasquatch and I vote." "I'm not driving slow. You're speeding." "I take one day at a time, unless they all attack at once."

"One day at a time," I said to myself. In spite of everything, I felt better than I had at the hospital. I'd been going stir-crazy in the locked unit, unable to do anything useful. Getting out felt like an achievement. Tomorrow we'd talk to the social worker. We needed an outsider. Someone not beholden to our family nonsense. Just like Donna, they'd tell it like they saw it, practical and unsentimental. Colleen would have hours to absorb the reality of our mother's injuries. She'd come around. She'd see that our choices weren't harmless. Every day we left them together could end like yesterday.

The highway came to a standstill again. I tried to decipher a final, cracked and faded bumper sticker on the puzzle car. I inched closer: "The universe doesn't give a *fuck* about you." I laughed out loud. Exactly. Life was just a luck of the draw. My father's dementia and Kara's accident just different manifestations of our infinite unimportance in the big picture.

THAT NIGHT when I got to work I took a seat around the large break room table, waiting to get my patient assignment like always. Gene's sympathetic look made it clear he recognized I was back for the first time since Kara's death. No one else gave me a second glance. Gene read off the patients and their statuses. Nurses scribbled notes on their report sheets. We were all here to do a job. Kara's story was one more unfortunate reality that would end up in a long list of unfortunate realities we would witness in our careers.

Returning nurses began reclaiming their patients from the previous night. Fiona stood at the white board writing names next to the paired rooms. I could see what was happening long before it became the truth: Twenty-three/twenty-four reclaimed. Fifteen/sixteen reclaimed. Two with one open for the first admit, claimed. Room seven taunted me in blue ink from the white board. It wasn't intentional. The goal is always to have the same nurses with the same patients over a series of days. It's good for everyone. But what were the odds? No, the universe does *not* give a fuck about me and it was going to prove it.

The room bustled. Nurses who had their assignments headed out as I progressed closer to the reality of taking care of a patient in the room in which my best friend had just died. Gene grimaced as Fiona crossed the taken assignments off the board, apparently just noticing what was happening, only thirteen/fourteen and seven/eight left. Me and Margaret Ann at the table.

"You had thirteen and fourteen last night, right?" Fiona said to Margaret Ann, starting to write her name next to the pair.

"I'll take seven and eight," she said. Fiona looked puzzled, not understanding why Margaret Ann wouldn't want her pair back.

"I need a change," Margaret Ann announced firmly. She stood up abruptly and headed out for report without a word about what she'd done. Fiona scrawled her name next to seven/eight and mine next to thirteen/fourteen then picked up her own notes and left. Gene and I were alone.

"You okay?" he asked.

"No, but I have to come back some time. Not sure it makes a difference if it's today or another day."

He hugged me. "Let me know if you need anything," he said. "I've got your back."

"Thanks," I said. I lingered a few moments after he headed

247

out, trying to pull myself together. Gene *would* have my back. He would give me an extra break or two, set up a line, help me turn a patient. But he couldn't help with the real issue, which was whether or not I could do this again. Could I look at a patient and not see her face? Could I put that memory of her out of my mind and do my job? Or was I crippled beyond repair on the inside where no one could see it?

Halfway down the hall, I came to room seven. Margaret Ann stood by the door getting report. I glanced at the person in the bed. I knew it wasn't Kara, but my mind raced with crazy thoughts. Was it the same bed? It was possible. It could be the exact same bed in the exact same room. Suddenly it seemed like the most important thing in the world to figure out whether or not that was the same bed she'd died in. And if it wasn't, where was the one that she *did* die in.

I forced myself to pass, focus on the night ahead. Jalynne, the day nurse, was scrambling through papers and hurriedly typing things into the computer as I came up. She was relatively new, and I could tell she'd had a rough day. Her workstation was scattered with random supplies. She looked back and forth between her notes and the screen, a slightly distressed expression on her face. I sat.

"Thank God for night shift," she said. "I'm *so* done."

"It's nice to feel appreciated," I said pulling out my folding clip board and getting ready to take notes.

"I'm leaving you a train wreck. I'm sorry. I'm going to be here at least an hour charting."

"It's okay," I said. "It happens."

She pointed at room thirteen. "Sixteen-year-old male. Admitted around four. Gunshot to the abdomen. The bullet hit his spine. L5."

"Paralyzed?" I asked.

"Yeah, but he doesn't know yet. He's still out and they aren't letting his parents in."

"Why?"

She shrugged and pointed at the two officers in the room. "Police."

As she continued through all the important information, I jotted notes on my report sheet trying to conceal the fact that I was happy, or at least relieved to have a patient like this. I'd be busy all night either with his care or family drama. There would be no time for wallowing in my own problems. We got through the rest of report and I stood up to glance at the young man in room thirteen. Jalynne seemed to think I was inspecting her work.

"I'm really sorry," she said again. "I was drowning all day."

"Don't worry. It's a twenty-four/seven job," I said. "Why don't you go to the back station to do your charting? It's quiet."

She took her papers but left the supplies. Everything she needed for great nursing care was strewn across the workstation. She just hadn't had the time to take care of it all. I picked up the padded securement device for the endotracheal tube and suddenly my hand began to tremble. My heart pounded so hard in my chest, it felt like it was trying to break out of my body. A vice clamped down on my throat. I couldn't breathe. Tears rose in my eyes. I ran to the bathroom.

I couldn't get through the first three minutes back at work let alone the next three nights. I splashed cold water on my face hoping it would wash away the tears rushing down my cheeks as well as the ones still bubbling up inside me. I was done being a nurse. I was going to have to tell Gene. I wasn't going to be able to tend to wounds, take care of intubated patients, do anything that reminded me of her. I'd have to think of something else.

When I finally decided I'd been in the bathroom far too long, I splashed my face one more time and wiped it with the rough and scratchy paper towel. Margaret Ann was standing in front of the door when I opened it.

"Sorry," I said. "I didn't mean to take so long."

"You surviving?' she said, in a manner that suggested that we'd been nothing but friends.

I shook my head.

She put a hand on my shoulder. "It's going to suck. But you can do it. It'll get better if you do. If you don't, it'll never get better." She patted my shoulder, then turned back down the hall to the patients who should have been mine.

It was bizarre. The one person I could barely stand at work was the only one who seemed to notice what was going on. Either my perceptions of people were way off or sometimes the wrong person could do the right thing. Her advice was good. It was the proverbial getting back up on the horse. If I could get through tonight, I'd probably be okay. If I ran, the next time would be that much harder.

I ended up in the bathroom crying two more times before midnight but then things shifted. I got too busy and my hands and mind fell into their normal routines and habits. At around four in the morning, Gene covered my patients while I took a break. I went downstairs and out to the front of the hospital. I stood on the narrow campus street that led from parking lot to parking lot. It was lined with trees, the same trees I'd viewed from above the night Kara died.

A cool breeze blew, and the leaves rustled. The trees shimmered in the moonlight, an energy coming from them to me. I took a deep breath, letting it fill me. Everything felt alive: the air, the ground, the night. And I thought for just a moment that I understood something. I was always trying to find answers but there would never be one. There were only questions.

JANUARY 7TH 2:24 PM

I arrived at the hospital just in time for the appointment with the social worker. I'd had to cut my sleep time significantly shorter than usual to get there but I'd made it. Nothing I hadn't done before. Donna smiled at me through the glass and buzzed me in. Dad and Colleen were in the activities room seated on an otherwise unoccupied blue sofa. An old western played on the large flat-screen TV in front of them. Colleen stared at the show as if absorbed. Dad's eyes veered away every few seconds but then, following Colleen's gaze, came back to the TV. I watched from the doorway. John Wayne rode up dressed as Genghis Khan. Dementia or no dementia I couldn't see how Dad would ever buy his favorite actor as the Mongol ruler. I walked over to them.

"Where's Mom?" I asked Colleen.

"Downstairs dealing with paperwork," she said.

"How's it going?" I asked. I didn't want any surprises in front of the social worker.

"About the same as always," Colleen said, and I wondered when exactly this had become our always. I sat on Dad's other side. He glared at my leg next to his, so I scooted an inch or so further away. That seemed to satisfy him, and he turned back to the TV.

Donna came up to us. "Are you having a nice visit with your family?" she asked Dad.

He looked back and forth between me and my sister. "They aren't my family," he said, "but they're nice enough." I wanted to correct him, embarrassed that he didn't know who we were, like him forgetting us was a reflection of how much we'd been good daughters. Donna just smiled.

"The social worker said she'd be with you in a minute. You can wait in the conference room if you'd like." Donna gestured toward the thick glass windows of the nurses' station.

I stood up then felt foolish as Colleen started explaining things to our father. "Bernadette, Mom and I are going to go to talk to some people. We'll be back in a little bit." Sometimes he was as invisible to me as I was to him. Colleen patted Dad's shoulder and stood up.

"Where's Helen?" Dad asked.

"She'll be back soon," I offered before my sister could.

Donna led us through the nurses' station to a small conference room. Colleen and I sat. A few minutes later, Mom arrived, a folder of papers tucked under her arm. She set it down on the table and took a seat. The three of us sat in a strained silence broken by occasional unidentifiable noises from out on the unit, some of which I suspected were my father mounting his escape. My mother ran her tongue along the stitches on her face.

"Does it hurt?" I asked, the uncomfortable quietness compelling me to fill it.

"A little. The stitches pull," she said.

"I don't mean to be Captain Obvious here, but this is a game-changer," I said. "We have to find a place for him. He needs assisted living." Neither of them responded. Either I was indeed stating the obvious or they disagreed but weren't willing to engage. "This kind of thing could happen again. You aren't safe. He isn't safe."

Mom nodded slightly, like a rocking horse slowing to a standstill.

"Are we sure we've exhausted all the options?" Colleen said.

"He doesn't tolerate people in the house," I said. "They won't take him at the daycare places. He completely lost it at the CT. I don't even think we…" The door opened and a woman, presumably the social worker, came in before I could finish. The presence of an unbiased witness would change the tone of things, add some much-needed good sense, or at least I hoped it would before I lost it again. The woman deposited a disorderly stack of papers on the table and offered a hand to Mom.

"Good morning," she said but then glanced at her watch. "Or actually afternoon. I'm Betty. Social work."

Betty was African American, in her early 30s with thick braids cascading down her back, a few embedded with gold thread and shiny rings. The black flowers on her white dress were summery but at the same time sinister, like if you stared long enough, they would morph into ravens and fly at you.

"I'm sorry to meet under these circumstances. I'm going to ask some questions to get a better understanding of your situation. They're part of an official assessment so they might seem a little formal. Is that okay?" She was talking to Mom, who nodded.

"Do you feel safe at home?"

"Me? Or for him?"

"Either."

Mom waxed and waned between defending my dad—"He would never hurt me." "This was an accident."—and sharing her tribulations—"He wanders off day and night." "He grabbed the steering wheel." Her two conflicting missions—get help and remind the world of who my father had been—vying for prominence. Betty probably sat in this very room day in and day out listening to families sharing specifics like these, all slightly different yet fundamentally the same.

"Do you have caregiver stress?" Betty asked.

"Yes?" My mother's response was a question of its own as if she were incredulous that someone could not already know the answer to that.

"How do you feel you're coping with that stress?"

"Coping? I just am. That's all I can do. What else can I do?"

Betty scribbled notes on her form but offered nothing else. The stack of papers underneath her pad became more haphazard with each scrawl, a house of cards inching toward collapse, the precariousness of our situation manifested in the space with us.

"The team recommends that Mr. Rogers be placed in a facility that provides specialized care for dementia patients," she said. I wondered if Donna had told her anything. Were most families ready when it came to this point and acquiesced without resistance or discussion?

"Do you have a location in mind?" Betty asked.

All three of us shook our heads.

"Can you recommend any places?" I asked, trying to keep the conversation going in the direction of placement. Betty hunted through her stack and pushed a sheet across the table toward Colleen even though I was the one who'd asked the question. Did she just give off the air of being in charge?

"We don't endorse or even recommend these facilities," Betty said. "You'll have to call around and visit. But the sooner you pick the better. Ideally, Mr. Rogers will go straight there from here. It's less disruptive that way. Easier for everyone."

"Will Medicare cover any of this?" my mother asked.

I couldn't believe it. I glanced at Colleen. Had she been working on our mom, helping her get here? Had my sister actually listened to what I'd said and was helping?

"No, not Medicare," Betty said. "Do you have long-term care insurance?"

"I don't know what that is, so I don't imagine so," Mom said.

"It's insurance you purchase specifically to cover extended care at home or assisted living," Betty answered.

"No," my mom said.

"Are there any programs that might help?" Colleen asked.

I wanted to jump for joy. For the first time in this awful two weeks, we were moving in the right direction.

"They all depend on income and assets," Betty said.

"We get about two thousand from social security," Mom said. "We have some savings, but these places are so expensive."

"Unfortunately, you won't qualify for any assistance programs until you've spent off most of your assets except your primary home," Betty said, scribbling on her form again. "We can talk again then, if Mr. Rogers is still in the facility."

There was something about how she said it that sounded so final. My father would die in whatever place we found. He wasn't ever going home again, a reality that hadn't occurred to me until this moment. Without warning Mom started crying. Betty handed her a packet of tissues. I wondered if she came into every meeting with a new one, a cellophane wrapped stack of tear catchers. Mom wrestled with the plastic, the three of us staring but not offering help like helping would insult her somehow. After she dabbed her tears, Colleen put an arm around her.

"We'll figure something out," Colleen said. Mom leaned into her and then reached across the table, grabbing one of my hands and squeezing, emphasizing that "we" wasn't just Colleen and her.

I wanted to be happy. Mom was finally acquiescing but I was at a loss. She would go broke covering these costs and have nothing left for herself if she needed it. I wanted to be in a position to grandly say, "I'll pay for it." But I wasn't. Without the additional money from Kara, I wasn't even sure I was going to be able to stay in the guest house. It was impossible to tell how long my father might be in assisted living. Dementia didn't come with the same downward spiral as Alzheimer's. He was in good physical health. He could last a long time.

Suddenly Betty's paper tower collapsed, sheets spilling across the table and down to the floor. "I'm sorry," she said, catching what she could. We all helped gather the scattered documents then resettled at the table.

"Maybe we could each throw in some money," I said. "I could work extra hours at an agency. I could probably manage five hundred a month." I grabbed the number out of nowhere. It seemed doable. "What do you think, Colleen? Could you guys manage the same? Maybe you could tutor?" I offered.

Here and there between babies, Colleen picked up extra money working in after school programs to cover some unexpected expense. My sister didn't say anything. She seemed to be considering the possibility. I'd been prepared for a drawn-out argument in front of the social worker but I'd been completely unprepared for the concrete details of how we'd go forward.

"We'll figure something out," Colleen finally said. "We'll do what needs to be done."

Betty began discussing the details of discharge and transportation to whatever facility we ended up selecting. We agreed that Mom and Colleen would look at different homes in the next two days and I'd contact Adam to see what he might be able to contribute. The day before they moved Dad, the three of us would go to the assisted living place and get it set up. They'd move him on Friday. Betty told us we weren't supposed to visit for a while after he transferred.

The whole thing was anticlimactic, straightforward and businesslike. That promise had hung over us for so long and then it was just gone. I'd been right, with a stranger in the room, it all changed. The obvious had come into a different focus when others were watching. Colleen and Mom had finally seen beyond the bubble of Dad's impossible request and accepted reality.

I MARCHED through that night of work in a daze, forcing myself forward. One foot in front of the other. Nap. Commute. Work. Shower. Sleep. When I awoke Tuesday afternoon, I hoped to find the name of a place for my dad in my text messages but I only had a couple of updates on his unchanged condition. I tried to call both my sister and mom but neither of them answered. They only had one more day to find a place and get everything arranged. We might be able to still look at places on Thursday. It would be tight getting it all arranged before Friday but it might be possible.

I was just about to leave for my shift, when my phone buzzed. I opened my phone and read my sister's text: "Dad discharged. At home with Mom."

My jaw dropped. What the hell had happened? Had something drastic changed or had my mother and sister deliberately lied to me for some inexplicable reason? I didn't have time to call. It was 6:30 pm. I needed to leave for work.

I texted my sister: "What happened to assisted living?"

She responded with an infuriating thumbs up. What did *that* mean? I started to text back but stopped myself. The last thing I needed was to be getting angry with my sister via text while I drove to the hospital to take care of accident victims. I turned the buzzer off and left it in my bag until I was in the hospital on the elevator going up to the unit. I pulled the phone out and checked for texts. Nothing new.

I quickly fired off: "This isn't going to work. Something bad is going to happen. This was the right moment and now it's gone."

Then, I typed, "This is bullshit. You shouldn't have lied to me," but deleted it. I didn't know what had actually happened but the first thought that came to mind was that my sister and mother had never intended to put him in a home. They'd played along to appease me. But it was probably more likely that my mother had simply changed her mind and my sister wasn't fighting her.

After I got report on my patients and was starting into my nightly routine my sister finally replied: "Trust me. Everything is okay."

I shook my head. Was it? I'd have to wait to find out.

JANUARY 9TH 8:15 AM

*T*he next morning after my shift, I let myself into the empty guest house. The city was awakening around me. After a hot shower, I double-checked my messages — nothing from Colleen. I thought about calling her to figure out what was going on. But I was exhausted. Bone-weary, brain-weary exhausted. The situation would be exactly the same whether I spoke with her now or after I rested. And my chances of staying level-headed were better after sleep. But still a tinge of guilt swept through me as I turned off my phone and set it in the basket on the kitchen table like always.

Part of me hoped my mother or sister would need me for something and wouldn't be able to reach me. A passive-aggressive desire to prove a point. Let them deal with the mess they'd made. I would sleep until I woke up, no matter how late it was. No phone. No alarms. I'd let my body dictate its needs. It had been a rough few weeks. I tucked myself into my day-sleep cocoon of white noise, blackout shades, mask and earplugs, then climbed into bed, relishing how my body sank into the mattress and my muscles slackened and relaxed.

When I awoke, I knew it was late. The heaviness of afternoon lingered in the air. I took out my earplugs and removed my mask. The hum of the city crept in: sirens in the distance, screeching tires, random voices. I got up and lifted the shades. It was still light but not the height of the day, maybe three or four. I wandered into the living room, grabbed my phone and dropped down onto the sofa.

A string of notifications came up on my phone screen. My sister had called multiple times throughout the day but hadn't left any messages. I let myself feel smug for a second, enjoying an I-told-you-so sense of satisfaction. She'd sent only a single text: "Call me as soon as you wake up."

I left the phone on the couch and started a pot of coffee, debating how long I could justifiably wait before calling her. Maybe he'd gotten lost. Maybe he'd had another violent episode or didn't recognize anything and was more difficult to handle. I didn't want something bad to happen, but if it did it was on them not me. They'd have to bear the brunt of whatever came of their decision. When I finally had a fresh cup of coffee in hand, I settled down on the couch and returned my sister's call.

"What's up?" I said.

"Dad," she said, then paused. "Dad's dead."

"Really?" I asked with genuine incredulity as if it my sister might double-check and say, "No, sorry. My mistake," and we'd start the whole conversation over again.

"He didn't wake up this morning," she said. "I guess he had a heart attack or something."

I sat for a moment processing what she was saying then the emotions overcame me. I felt horrible. I'd deliberately delayed calling her back as long as possible. My father was dead and I was playing games.

"Where is he now?" I asked.

"The cremation company picked him up from the hospital this morning. It all happened pretty fast." She was calmer than I thought I would have been. But it was getting close to evening.

She'd had a whole day to get used to my father's death. It was only new to me.

"Cremation?" I asked.

"That's what Mom wanted. I think it's what they both wanted, you know, nothing fancy."

"I can't believe this," I said, suddenly realizing it was over. "This is... I don't know what to do. Is Mom okay?"

"She is now. It's been a rough day."

"Should I come over?"

"That would be great. I've been here forever and I need to get going. Liam's home alone with the kids. They probably haven't eaten anything except PBJs and Capri-Suns."

Our roles were reversed. My sister was unruffled and pragmatic in regard to death, as if she'd done this a million times before and was relaying someone else's story rather than our own. My mind raced. When did Mom realize Dad was not sleeping but dead? Had she called 911? Who took him to the hospital? How had they found a cremation company so fast?

I got ready quickly and jumped in my car, taking Bundy to Wilshire. It wasn't until I rounded the corner just before the VA hospital that I realized that this route, the quickest to the freeway, would take me through the intersection where Kara's life had ended. I'd managed to avoid it up until now. In my rush, I'd forgotten. There was no way around it now.

The light turned red. I was forced to stop at the spot where the crash had happened. I looked around, the grey pavement, the dirty white curb. Nothing marked the site and that seemed wrong. I wanted the unseen to be seen, for everyone to stop in this place and understand. This wasn't some generic death, this was my friend. But how many places were there like this, where someone's wife, or mother, or friend had died and the world just kept spinning?

I sat there until the light changed, then I held my breath and rolled through the intersection with the other cars. When I reached my parents' house ninety minutes later, it looked the same as always. It seemed like there should be some indication that someone had just died but there wasn't. Like Kara and the intersection, nothing was different. The plates had shifted under our entire world, but no one could see it from the outside.

I parked in front of the cactus tree that a week ago my father had been trying to put back together with his bare hands. The flat top where the piece had snapped off was covered in a gooey white substance, the cactus's self-generated healing potion. The traffic had given me time to get used to the fact that my father was gone. But I couldn't make peace with how I felt. I wasn't sad. I felt nothing but tremendous relief. My father and his dementia had been hanging over us, weighing us down. That was all gone, a long torture finally over.

"It's me," I announced as I walked in the front door.

"In here," my mother said from the kitchen.

Colleen and Mom were sitting at the table, wine glasses and a half-finished bottle of Merlot between them. They looked like they'd been up for days. Colleen, like me, was dressed in jeans and a loose black t-shirt. Her long, dark hair was tied in a simple ponytail with scattered strands hanging out around her face, as if a few had been dislodged every time she wiped sweat from her brow. Mom looked drained. Her face seemed more wrinkled, like she'd shriveled a little since I'd last seen her. Her lip was no longer swollen but the row of stitches was still there, a small section of train tracks leading nowhere.

We hugged. I expected my tears to come but they didn't. We'd all cried so many times about my father. We'd been mourning his loss for years. Death couldn't compete with dementia. Or maybe I was still too shocked, awash in the guilty relief of this tidy bow wrapped around our new reality. No more frantic searches. No more talks of nursing homes. No more impossible conundrums.

"I'm going to head out," Colleen said. "I've had enough for one day."

She walked over to the counter and picked up her giant black handbag. I took Colleen's place at the table, sipping her last bit of wine, then refilling the glass. No one was going to begrudge me Merlot for breakfast the day my father died.

As Colleen pursued jingling keys in the depths of her purse, I wondered what my mother and I were going to do after she left. Mom didn't actually need me. In a couple of hours, she'd be winding down for sleep. I'd be left wide awake and probably a little tipsy in a quiet house. My presence was pointless. Everything was taken care of.

"Got 'em," Colleen said triumphantly pulling out her cluster of keys.

I looked at her for a moment then noticed a paper on the fridge behind her. It was an official-looking, full-sized form with logos and signatures secured to the refrigerator door with four matching magnets. It hadn't been there before. I walked over to it: *Emergency Medical Services Prehospital Do Not Resuscitate (DNR) Form.* It was signed by Mom and some MD yesterday.

"What's this?" I asked my sister, who'd stopped in the kitchen doorway.

"The hospital gave it to us when we left," Colleen said. "Dad was DNR while he was there. The nurse who discharged him asked us if we wanted it." The acronym, D-N-R, rolled off her tongue as if she said it almost every day like I did.

"You got it signed and everything before you left?" I asked.

"Yeah," she said in the same calm tone she'd used when she told me our father was dead. Mom poured herself another glass of wine and gingerly sipped at it. I studied them both.

"I'm so glad they had us do it," Colleen said. "Today might have been terrible without it."

"You called 911?" I asked, not sure what was bothering me about the form.

"Mom did," Colleen said.

If my mother had called 911 and not had the form, the EMTs

would have had to have started CPR. There was almost no chance they'd have been able to revive him, not unless my mom had called within seconds of his heart stopping and even then, the odds were minuscule. But that's what they had to do without that form in place.

Maybe it was as straightforward as my sister had said, some kind of hospital policy I was unfamiliar with. It was a great idea. Most people want to die in their own home but instead meet their ends tangled in tubes and lines in an ICU. But it was another tidy bow on the convenient package of our father's death, a smooth spot where things could have been rough, and I couldn't reconcile it with my own experience. I'd discharged tons of patients over the years and never talked to them about a DNR at home.

"What happened to finding an assisted living place?" I asked.

"It was a lot more complicated than that social worker made out," Colleen answered. "They wanted to discharge him and there just wasn't enough time."

"Why'd they discharge him earlier than they agreed to?"

Colleen shrugged.

"Did you check at all?" I said, making no attempt to hide my suspicion that they hadn't. "Did you go to a single place and look?"

"Yes, we *did*," she said, clearly offended. "None of them felt right. We didn't want to get forced into some borderline situation and have to move him later. If we brought him home, there was no rush."

"That doesn't make any sense. It was easier while he was in the hospital. He was safe. You could have gone to a bunch of places."

"Look, I really need to go." Colleen adjusted the bag on her shoulder as if its weight was the thing she was trying to get away from not our conversation. "You can get on my case if you want, but you didn't see those places. Mom and I did. It didn't seem like taking one or two more weeks to get it right was going to hurt anything and it doesn't matter anymore."

It wasn't mean exactly, more matter-of-fact. I couldn't know what I would have done because I wasn't there. I didn't know what had transpired. I didn't know how easy or hard it was to find a place. *I* didn't know anything. Colleen knew everything. My sister stepped back into the room and gave my mother a peck on the cheek.

She turned to me and said, "Think what you want but we did what needed to be done."

My mother hadn't said a single word through our conversation and didn't offer input once Colleen was gone. She and I sat in silence as the engine of my sister's minivan shuddered and stalled twice before finally starting. They'd needed a new car for years, but they made it work. They got by on what they had. They did what needed to be done. I listened as she drove away, then my eyes drifted back over to the sign on the fridge. The clanging of the wall phone startled us both. My mother got up and answered it.

"Hi, sweetheart," she said.

I guessed it was Adam. After a few lines of conversation, it became clear that he'd been notified earlier and was checking on her. I got up and walked over to the sign on the fridge and reread it: "I understand DNR means that if my heart stops beating or if I stop breathing, no medical procedure to restart breathing or heart functioning will be instituted."

My father certainly could have had a stroke or a heart attack. Obviously, something had been wrong the day he collapsed on the kitchen floor. He'd probably finally succumbed to whatever it was. But the convenient timing of it all didn't feel right and I couldn't stop another thought from creeping into my head. My mother had done it. She'd managed to do it without me just like Shayne thought. I didn't know how but she had.

I looked at the form again, my head swirling with questions.

Why call 911 at all? But who else would you call? What would you actually do if you woke up and found your husband dead? And if you'd killed him, wouldn't you have to do exactly that, call 911, act surprised, avoid suspicion?

I left my mother, still on the telephone, and went downstairs to the master bedroom at the far end of the hall. I gently pushed open my parents' door. Everything was just as it had always been. My mother's dresser to the left, my father's to the right. Nothing odd. Nothing out of place.

I opened my mother's top drawer and sifted through her underclothes, hunting for clues. If she did it, there had to be some evidence. I went from drawer to drawer, rifling through t-shirts, pajamas, sweatpants. I checked the nightstands and under the bed. I went into the bathroom and examined every label of every bottle in the medicine cabinet. Then, I poked through the tiny trash bin and scoured the cabinet under the sink.

I returned to the bedroom and pulled down the comforter, leaning over to press my face against the pillow and sheets, searching for a chemical smell, a trace of anything abnormal. But the sheets were fresh and clean. I opened the closet, grabbed the old sheets out of the hamper and brought them to my nose. My father's familiar scent suddenly filled my nostrils and all the energy driving my frantic search dissipated. I dropped to the floor and sat, pressed the sheet to my face, inhaled again, and cried.

I'd been pursuing a toxic smell, something deadly. The distinct smell of my father overwhelmed me. The hazy filter of dementia lifted and he came back to me in a wholeness I hadn't experienced in years. His absence swelled into a profound emptiness that would never be filled.

Tears burst out of me. I sobbed. My panicked search for evidence was stupid. Nothing would change if I found some proof that my mother had done it, that somehow she'd ended my father's life and made it look like an old man dying in his bed, not for hate or revenge, but for compassion, to let him be whole again on some other plane instead of disintegrating here, fragment by fragment.

I heard my mother's footsteps in the hall. She stopped in the doorway, unfazed to find me on the floor in front of her closet crying, a dirty sheet in my lap. I wanted to care about whether she'd done it or not. But I didn't anymore. I was just glad that my father was free, and sad that I hadn't been able to help her, that she'd had to do it alone.

She came in and sat at the end of the bed. I brought the sheet to my nose again and sniffed, then passed it to her. She smelled it too. She smiled, pained and tight. We held each other's gaze, tears rolling down our faces.

DECEMBER 25TH (ONE YEAR LATER)

"*D*o you have the presents?" I said to Jax as he stepped out of Shayne's truck empty handed. His close-shaved head, khaki pants and white t-shirt gave him the appearance of a military recruit, but his new tidier appearance was not something I was going to complain about. He leaned over into the flatbed and pulled out the hand-decorated holiday bags that we'd filled with homemade soaps, peppermint bark, and scarves he'd knitted himself. Not particularly practical in Southern California but a straightforward project that had made him proud.

He and his occupational therapist had identified different hands-on skills that he wanted to perfect and he'd been steadily moving down the list. He and Shayne were building him his own tiny house. His goal was to be as self-sufficient as possible by the time he was sixteen.

I kissed him on the cheek. "Did you take your meds?" I asked.

"You don't have to ask me every day," he said, sounding like a typical irritated teenager. "I have an alarm and a calendar. I can handle it."

"Just checking. It's Christmas. It might have slipped your mind."

He rolled his eyes. "I'll put these under the tree," he said and went into my mother's house. I walked over to the idling truck.

"There's no parking," Shayne said. "I'm going to have to go around again."

"The joys of vehicle ownership," I said. "I'll ride with you."

I opened the door and hopped in. It seemed like a good moment for a break from the kitchen heat I'd been sweltering in with my mom and sister all morning. After driving around the block, we found a space a quarter mile up the street.

"I'm glad you're coming again," I said as we got out of the car. Shayne took my hand and we started back toward the house. Our relationship was strangely similar to what it had been for years, but it was different too. Or maybe I was different. I'd stopped fighting what it was.

At the beginning of the year, I'd let the Santa Monica house go and moved back to The Farm. It only took a few months before we both agreed that I needed my own space too, which came in the shape of Adam's old studio apartment. Most weeks I only stayed there a night or two, but it was just enough for me to breathe, just enough so I could let us be what we were without having to name it, or run away from it.

Jax was doing better too, not perfect but better. A few weeks after the coming-of-age ceremony he'd requested a family meeting with me and Shayne and his therapist and announced that he wanted to try medications. The first combination had left him constantly nauseated but they'd changed things up and save for a little weight gain, he seemed to be adjusting okay.

He was trying online school. It had been a struggle to find the right balance between Shayne and my work schedules but between my mother and sister, we were figuring it out. He spent the mornings with my mom, doing lessons and learning to cook. Then, he went to tutoring in the afternoon. Colleen picked him up from there. He was building a coop for his younger cousins and would bring them chicks in the spring for their own flock.

As Shayne and I entered the house, the savory smell of Christmas dinner engulfed us. I'd been so immersed in it that it had become undetectable. Stepping outside of it and coming back made me experience it more fully. My mother was alone in the kitchen. She turned and smiled, her eyes twinkling with a happiness that was good to see.

"Colleen has news," she singsonged but didn't say anything more. I had a pretty good guess though.

"Where is she?" I asked.

"Telling the children," Mom said.

Colleen's pack had been moving between the TV room and the living room all morning, alternating turns on the PlayStation with desperately eyeing presents they weren't allowed to open yet. Shayne and I headed to the living room but only Jax and Logan were there, casually talking about something that I guessed was a video game but otherwise didn't understand. I was about to head downstairs but my sister came back up.

"Can I gather from the glint in Mom's eyes that you are now officially a grandmother?" I said.

"I just got off the phone with Lincoln. A little girl. They named her Aya. Mother and baby are doing great." Lincoln was thirty-five now, an officer stationed at Yokosuka. He'd married a Japanese woman last year and here it was, life in motion.

"I can't believe it," I said. "You're old."

"I started too young to be old with this one. I'll be old when Luca has kids. And so will you, I might add."

My sister and I returned to the kitchen. My mother was standing at the table, wiping her hands on her apron.

"I've decided something," she said. "I want all the girls in this family to have a piece of my jewelry. That's my Christmas present this year. There's no point in waiting until I die for you to get it."

"Geez, Mom. That's a little morbid," I said.

"No, it's not. It will make me happy to see them on you girls and it would make Bill happy too. Pick one for Yuki. And baby Aya," she said. "I know she can't wear it yet, but we'll send it."

A few minutes later Colleen, Laura, and I were standing in my mother's bedroom in front of her jewelry tree.

"This is weird," I said.

"A little," Colleen said. "But maybe not. I mean she's right. If we're going to end up with them anyway, why not give them to us now when she'll see us wearing them?"

Laura began inspecting the various necklaces, not as familiar with them as Colleen and I. We'd seen them our whole lives. She picked up a heart necklace with three tiny diamonds in it and showed it to her mother.

"Would this be okay for baby Aya?" Laura asked.

"That one's perfect," Colleen said. She picked up a string of black pearls. "How about this for Yuki?"

We both nodded.

"Which one do you like?" Colleen asked her daughter.

Laura lingered over the different necklaces on the tree, coming back a couple of times to the horseshoe necklace. I wanted not to care but did. If I was going to come around to wearing any of my mother's jewelry that was probably the one. But I didn't have it in me to fight my niece over it. I'd have to let it go. Colleen picked up a solitary blue topaz.

"This would look beautiful with your eyes," she said holding it up to her daughter's neck as Laura gazed at herself in the mirror. Laura nodded and Colleen secured the chain.

"Go show your grandmother," Colleen said, and Laura dutifully followed her mother's instruction. I felt suddenly uncomfortable, alone with my sister in the room our father had died in. I'd forced last Christmas and the chaos of those few mad weeks out of my mind many times over the last year. There was so much else to focus on, but this room was laden with that moment. There was no way to avoid it.

"How are things going at work?" Colleen said.

"Good," I said, grateful for the small talk. "It's the polar opposite of what I used to do. It's slower, much slower, but I think that's what I need."

I'd been at a home hospice agency for six months. It was significantly less money but between Shayne working part-time as a handyman and me not paying rent in Santa Monica, we were getting by as well as we ever had. I liked helping people have a good and peaceful death. It was penance for all the times I'd had to do the opposite.

"I still can't believe I did night shift for so long. Day shift is a miracle," I added. "I feel like a different person. I think I was depressed. I've only just begun to feel normal again."

My sister pulled some necklaces and bracelets from the two jewelry boxes next to the tree and laid them out on the dresser. Looking at all the adornments our father had bought for our mother over the years made it impossible not to think about the two of them.

In the last few months, I'd watched families deal with the final moments of life in different ways and each time I came back to my father's death. I'd come to a kind of peace with it, convinced myself that it was most likely that he'd just died. They'd missed something at the hospital. Whatever had made him pass out had progressed, then mercifully killed him. That thought was easier than torturing myself wondering whether my mother had killed him. And if she had, how? I just didn't believe she could have done it. Standing there with my sister, a question crept toward my lips like it had so many times in the last year, never finding its way out. Did my sister know the truth?

"She's got stuff I don't even remember seeing," I said.

"He bought her jewelry for everything. It was kind of his thing."

I touched my mother's horseshoe necklace and looked at Colleen. Streaks of grey peppered her long, dark hair. Wrinkles spidered from the corners of her eyes. She looked like our mother. They were so much alike. Practical and organized. Planners and doers. Everything I wasn't. It was strange how different we were. Suddenly, my stomach twisted and my mouth fell open.

"What?" Colleen said.

"Did *you* do it?" I asked, as if my sister would know exactly what I was talking about.

"Do what?" she said.

The thoughts tumbling through my mind made me dizzy. "Did you help Mom kill Dad?" I said.

Her gaze stayed fixed on the necklaces in front of her. "You know how I feel about that kind of thing," she said.

"I know how you *say* you feel."

My sister turned to me. Her expression flat, not giving a hint one way or another. "What if I did?" she said. "What difference does it make now?"

"Did you?" I pressed.

"You were going to do it, weren't you? Why would it be wrong if I did it and not wrong if you did it?"

"I don't know, because Mom asked me, because I was trying, because you did it to..." I stopped.

"I did it to?" Colleen said.

I didn't answer. Everything I was thinking about saying was wrong. Colleen shook her head and smiled, a pitying grin.

"You know, Bernadette, I swear, you're the worst enemy you'll ever have." She paused, then said, "Life isn't in the business of giving people what they want."

"What?"

"You don't remember?"

I shook my head.

273

"You said that to me at the hospital," she said.

I nodded, vaguely recollecting a tense conversation with her in the hallway of the locked unit my father had stayed on.

"I can't imagine things being much worse for you than at that moment. Life dealt you a pretty crappy hand," she said.

I didn't say anything. I knew if I spoke, I was going to cry. Colleen picked up the horseshoe necklace and held it out in front of her. It dangled from her fingertips, swaying gently with her motion.

"*If* I did anything," she said, "I did it to save her." The sentence hung between us, unfinished, as my sister fussed with the clasp of the necklace. She stepped behind me to fasten it around my neck. "And you."

We looked at ourselves together in the mirror for a moment, me and my unkempt red-brown waves, my sister and her unperturbed calm. I wished I'd left it alone. I didn't want to know more. I wanted to be back in the story where my father had miraculously died a natural death at precisely the right moment. But now I had this one, my sister stepping in where I'd failed, overcoming obstacles I couldn't. I wasn't sure what to feel. Even if I'd been saved by the person I least expected, I was still saved. I just didn't get to be the hero of my own story.

My sister's brow furrowed a little. She stepped out from behind me and reached to adjust the necklace, her face so close to mine, I could smell the faint sweetness of her breath.

"Look at that," she said, "It's raining luck on your bumblebee."

I touched my fingers to the two pendants on my neck and said the only thing I could think of. "Thank you."

ABOUT THE AUTHOR

D. Liebhart writes (and sometimes lives) stories about ordinary people in extraordinary circumstances.

Curious about how much is fact and how much is fiction in House of Fire? Join the conversation: subscribepage.io/InsideHOF

Learn more about the author at: www.dliebhart.com

Post a memory to honor a loved one with dementia at: www.remember-for-me.com

ACKNOWLEDGMENTS

A huge thank you to:

Arielle Eckstut, Jami Attenberg and the Humber School for Writers for their help shaping this book.

The Women of the Gym Lofts (Ellen Dworsky, Lisa Knighton, Keena Neal, Jennifer Ruden, Alan Parker, James McGrath Morris, David Dunaway, Catherine Dowling & Neal Singer) for asking all the right questions. A special thanks to Neal for helping me see the ending I didn't know was there and Alan for being the best cheerleader anyone could have.

Liz Alterman for mentoring me through rejection.

Camilla Monk for making everything look beautiful.

Rebecca Klinger for being there for the long haul.

And last, but not least, my husband and daughter. Without your constant interruptions and complete disregard for a closed door, I probably would've finished this project a whole lot faster but likely would've been a whole lot less happy.

Made in the USA
Middletown, DE
10 February 2024

49443221R00159